P9-DCC-733

PRAISE FOR JOAN HESS AND HER WONDERFUL MAGGODY MYSTERIES

"Joan Hess is one of the few mystery writers whose books I devour as I do chocolate. I love Maggody and everybody in it."

—Barbara Michaels

"Delectable and continually surprising."
—*The New York Times Book Review*

"A rollicking tour de force."

—*Boston Magazine*

"Joan Hess is the patron saint of comic mystery."

—Sharyn McCrumb

"Bawdy entertainment."

—*Kirkus Reviews*

murder@maggody.com

"The latest in a very funny series. . . . Don't miss any of it."
—*Booklist* (starred review)

"Full of local color and colorful locals; the mystery is merely the container for this Southern-fried ramble through lovingly described and defiantly redneck country."
—Amazon.com

Misery Loves Maggody

"*Misery Loves Maggody* is one of the best in the series."
—*Tulsa World* (OK)

"It's treats all around in *Misery Loves Maggody*. . . . An uproarious cast of characters."
—*The New York Times*

"A riotous send-up . . . fast-paced and entertaining."
—*The Dallas Morning News*

"It's a rare treat to enter the world of Maggody and her citizens. . . . Hess has a wonderful sense of the ridiculous and a deft touch for creating endearingly wacky characters. And she is as good as anyone in crafting a classic whodunit plot with plenty of humorous ruffles and flourishes."
—*Flint Journal* (MI)

"Hess has another keeper. . . . Put in a little irony (or a lot), stir in outrageous but colorful and believable characters, mix them in absurd situations and you have *Misery Loves Maggody.*"
—*The Knoxville News-Sentinel* (TN)

"Entertaining . . . [with] corny, cavorting characters. . . . Hess is adept at creating plots and subplots that muddy the waters until everything is hilariously confused."
—*Colorado Springs Gazette*

"The real mystery is how Joan Hess could write twenty-two books before a mystery series fan like myself discovered her. But once I stumbled into Maggody, Arkansas, and met Police Chief Arly Hanks and the crazy cast of characters who live there, I soon felt like we were old friends. Plenty of murder and mayhem. . . . I laughed all the way to the end."
—*Grand Rapids Press* (MI)

"The fast-paced and funny volume will please mystery fans everywhere."
—*The Pilot* (Southern Pines, NC)

"Another hilarious romp with the folks of the small, back-woods town [of Maggody, Arkansas]. . . . It's not long until Arly is busy with her unique and entertaining style of crime-solving."
—*Abilene Reporter-News* (TX)

"Hess gives us the usual hoot of a good time."
—*Mystery News*

"If you've read any of the previous Maggody mysteries, you know what to expect. If not, you're in for a treat."
—*The Advocate* magazine

"Fans of the Maggody series will revel in this entry. . . . Hess does again here what she has done so expertly before: keep a firm hand on outrageous characters whose peccadilloes are worthy of a French farce."
—*Publishers Weekly*

Also by Joan Hess

The Maggody Series
Malice in Maggody
Mischief in Maggody
Much Ado in Maggody
Madness in Maggody
Mortal Remains in Maggody
Maggody in Manhattan
O Little Town of Maggody
Martians in Maggody
Miracles in Maggody
The Maggody Militia
Misery Loves Maggody

The Claire Malloy Series
Strangled Prose
Murder at the Murder at the Mimosa Inn
Dear Miss Demeanor
A Really Cute Corpse
A Diet to Die For
Roll Over and Play Dead
Death by the Light of the Moon
Poisoned Pins
Tickled to Death
Busy Bodies
Closely Akin to Murder
A Holly, Jolly Murder

For orders other than by individual consumers, Pocket Books grants a discount on the purchase of **10 or more** copies of single titles for special markets or premium use. For further details, please write to the Vice President of Special Markets, Pocket Books, 1230 Avenue of the Americas, 9th Floor, New York, NY 10020-1586.

For information on how individual consumers can place orders, please write to Mail Order Department, Simon & Schuster, Inc., 100 Front Street, Riverside, NJ 08075.

Joan Hess

murder@ maggody.com

AN ARLY HANKS MYSTERY

POCKET STAR BOOKS
New York London Toronto Sydney Singapore

The sale of this book without its cover is unauthorized. If you purchased this book without a cover, you should be aware that it was reported to the publisher as "unsold and destroyed." Neither the author nor the publisher has received payment for the sale of this "stripped book."

This book is a work of fiction. Names, characters, places and incidents are products of the author's imagination or are used fictitiously. Any resemblance to actual events or locales or persons, living or dead, is entirely coincidental.

 A Pocket Star Book published by
POCKET BOOKS, a division of Simon & Schuster, Inc.
1230 Avenue of the Americas, New York, NY 10020

Copyright © 2000 by Joan Hess

Originally published in hardcover in 2000 by Simon & Schuster, Inc.

All rights reserved, including the right to reproduce this book or portions thereof in any form whatsoever. For information address Simon & Schuster, Inc., 1230 Avenue of the Americas, New York, NY 10020

ISBN: 0-671-01685-7

First Pocket Books printing January 2001

10 9 8 7 6 5 4 3 2 1

POCKET STAR BOOKS and colophon are registered trademarks of Simon & Schuster, Inc.

Front cover illustration by Ben Perini

Printed in the U.S.A.

For Margaret Maron,
who helped me move the body that dark and stormy night.

murder@
maggody.com

1

We were not rockin' and rollin' in Maggody, or even reelin' just a bit. There was so little action, to be frank, that I was reduced to wandering down a dim hallway in the high school, trying to remember where the cafeteria was, so that I, Arly Hanks, chief of police of a staunchly stagnant community, currently unarmed but the possessor of a handgun, four bullets, and a really scary radar gun, could snooze through a school-board meeting.

If I'd had cable, I wouldn't have been there. And, well, maybe if I hadn't heard rumors that the meeting might turn lively. The rumors came from a most reliable source, aka my mother, who keeps a firm finger on the pulse of Maggody, Arkansas (population circa 755, not taking into account pets, farm animals, or the infrequent transient trolls living under the bridge north of town). Ruby Bee Hanks, proprietor of the bar and grill of the same name, as well as the Flamingo Motel out behind it, does not spend her days hunkered on the roof of the building, binoculars poised, but she might as well. What she doesn't learn while dishing up chicken-fried steaks and pitchers of beer is gleaned by her best friend, Estelle Oppers, who operates Estelle's Hair Fantasies in the front room of her house out on County 102. Between the two of them, they hear it all. And I mean *all.*

In contrast, I don't hear diddly-squat in my two-room police department, except for the infrequent complaint about a stolen dog or vandalized lawn ornaments. Every now and then I get a request from the sheriff to handle a car wreck on a county road. Not having much else to do, I usually comply, although I'd been known to clutch my throat and feign laryngitis. Sheriff Harve Dorfer, a good ol' boy with the silhouette of a Sumo wrestler and the instincts of a polecat, rarely falls for it.

I hadn't expected much more stimulation than that when I'd crawled back home after a nasty divorce in the equally dim halls of justice in Manhattan. All I wanted, I told my mother when I knocked on her door at midnight, was time to restore my spirits. Maggody had seemed the perfect haven, in that nothing had ever happened of note in my twenty-odd years of growing up here. Oh, Hiram's barn had burned, and a cheerleader was spotted dashing for the woods with smoldering panties in hand. The ownership of the Pot O' Gold Mobile Home Park had changed hands more than once, and the Dairee Dee-Lishus was currently run by a surly Hispanic whose tamales were noticeably better than his social skills. A New Age hardware store had come and gone, as had a veritable parade of wackos including porn moviemakers, tabloid reporters, feminist rabble-rousers, and militants. The Esso station had finally collapsed into an untidy pile of charred beams. Mayor Jim Bob Buchanon, who was still running the town as though he fancied himself to be Caesar Ozarkus, had put in a convenience store known by locals as the Quik Screw. Now it was gone, replaced by a good-sized store called Jim Bob's SuperSaver Buy 4 Less.

Not that we did.

But there I was, discomfited by a sense that I should be (but most certainly wasn't) dressed in a navy blue skirt and white blouse complete with a Peter Pan collar. What I was doing was eyeing the obscenities scratched on the lockers while I tried to remember the location of the cafeteria. I'd come in the right door, but had taken a wrong turn. The story of my life, perhaps. I strained to hear voices other than the ghostly echoes of Mr. Woolsey stressing the significance of cosines, which he'd pronounced "cousins," and Lottie Estes explaining the role of potholders in a well-organized kitchen. The band room was down here, I thought, and the shop. The cafeteria was at the end of a different corridor.

Seconds before panic sank in, I saw a light and headed toward it. Latecomers were not streaming into the cafeteria like lemmings, but quite a few citizens were doing their civic duty. I nodded at Larry Joe and Joyce Lambertino, who, for the first time in years, had no children clinging to their legs. Elsie McMay toted a knitting bag only slightly smaller than a subcompact car. Kevin and Dahlia Buchanon struggled with a double-stroller and two sleepy cherubs. Why they were there was bewildering, in that Buchanons in general have a poor track record in educational endeavors (and think a Ph.D. is a brand of motor-oil additive). Kevin has been spotted puzzling over a soda can with a poptop.

Members of the Buchanon clan, scattered across Stump County like chickweed, are renown for beetlish brows, yellow eyes, and thick-lipped sneers. They do not patronize the Brains "R" Us outlet at the mall.

One of the wilier members of the clan was seated at a table on a podium. Jim Bob Buchanon had his hand over the microphone as he hissed at his wife beside him. At one end of the table, Peteet Buchanon appeared to be in the midst of a near-death, or perhaps near-life, experience. At the other end, Roy Stiver gazed at the ceiling, either composing poetry or doing his level best to transport himself elsewhere. Roy's the closest I have to a kindred soul in Maggody, although the company he keeps (Jim Bob and Larry Joe, for example) is suspect. I rent what we both laughingly refer to as an efficiency apartment above his antiques ("New & Used") store. There have been nights we've sat in the dark and drowned our sorrows in bourbon and silence. And there was the night he started reciting Kipling, but we swore never to discuss it. Some episodes in one's life are best left on the ethereal plane.

So be it, Gunga Din.

Ruby Bee and Estelle had saved a chair for me in the front row. I smiled and nodded at various folks, most of whom eyed me with some suspicion, since my involvement with the community stopped with handing out warnings for moving violations and shaking my finger at miscreants for such crimes as forgetting to pay at the self-service pumps. In my defense, I am always polite to co-launderers at the Suds of Fun Launderette, even offering to make change, and downright deferential in matters of prime produce at the supermarket. However, the consensus in Maggody is although I have every right to be there, I shouldn't. It has crossed my mind.

Nightly.

I slipped in between Ruby Bee and Estelle. "Did I miss anything?" I whispered.

"You missed the first ten minutes of complaining about the cafeteria budget," Ruby Bee said with a sigh. "Jim Bob thinks serving moldy bread is like giving the students a free dose of penicillin, which he said most of 'em could use, considering the prevalence of sexually transmitted diseases. Peteet said those students with objections could just scrape off the mold. Mrs. Jim Bob reeled off some Bible verse about bread being the staff of life, although she did stop short of describing it as manna from heaven."

"Sorry I missed it," I said.

Estelle drove her elbow into my rib cage. "I'd like to hope you'll support Lottie Estes. She's worked so hard for this that I don't want to think what she'll do if it doesn't get approved. We have to make it clear we're behind her one hundred and ten percent."

I managed a weak nod as I sank back to determine if I had any cracked or, more likely, splintered, ribs. Estelle and I see eye to eye at perhaps five feet ten, and neither of us carries any excess weight. On the other hand, she has the advantage with her blazing red beehive of hair and heavy-handed makeup, giving her a few extra pounds, courtesy of Mary Kay. Ruby Bee appears more ingenuous, despite her unnaturally blond hair and conspicuous pink eyeshadow, but should it deteriorate into mud wrasslin', I'd take bets either way.

After a certain amount of dithering about locker searches, teacher retirement pensions, and handicapped parking spaces at the football stadium, Hiz Moron the Mayor Jim Bob introduced Lottie Estes. He did so with a curled lip and a squint, both traits of the clan. Unlike most Buchanons, Jim Bob can outwit a possum. A rabid possum, anyway—and I'd prefer the company of the latter.

"Lottie here," he began grandly, "has some foolish ideas about bringing computers to Maggody. Now she insists on dragging out the meeting with her proposal, even though most of us would rather be on our way home to put on our pajamas and watch television. Mrs. Jim Bob has let me know that there's a slice of lemon meringue pie just waiting for me, and I guess everybody here knows who makes the best lemon meringue pie in Stump County."

Ruby Bee rumbled, but held her peace. Mrs. Jim Bob (aka Barbara Ann Buchanon Buchanon) produced a frigid smile, in that she—and everyone else—knew what Jim Bob would rather be doing at the moment. Lace nighties rather than flannel pajamas may have been in more than one individual's thoughts, and no one was including Mrs. Jim Bob in the scene.

"Lottie," he went on, "has, without so much as consulting the very school board that pays her salary and retirement benefits, applied for and received a grant in the sum of fifty thousand dollars to put in a computer lab at the high school. Sounds good, don't it? Free money to buy all kinds of equipment and give our kids a chance to get their butts kicked into the new millennium."

Mrs. Jim Bob stood up and snatched the microphone out of his hand. "I feel sure Mayor Buchanon could have phrased that better. Nobody in Maggody wants our youth to be at a disadvantage when they go out to find gainful employment, marry, and start families. We want them to have a solid education based on decency and a healthy fear of eternal damnation should they stray into wickedness."

She sat down and crossed her arms, daring anyone to contradict her.

"Amen!" boomed a voice from the back of the room. None of us bothered to turn around, since we'd all recognized the resonating timbre of Brother Verber, guardian of the flock at the Voice of the Almighty Lord Assembly Hall. Despite its name, Mrs. Jim Bob pretty much ran the show.

It was time for Lottie to seize the floor, if not the moment. She rose, flapping her hands as if she might stir up enough agitation to send all of us swirling into each other like autumn leaves. "This is ridiculous!" she said. "We have the grant. The money is available. Why would we not want to accept it? Our youth need to become computer literate. Where does wickedness come into this?"

Mrs. Jim Bob cocked her head like a greedy robin. "I have been told that pornography is easily available on the Internet."

Before Estelle could prompt me with her elbow, I stood up. "I've been told pornography is easily available—period. Should I shut down the post office?"

"We don't have a post office, missy," Mrs. Jim Bob said, then realized she'd been baited and shot me a beady glare before resuming the pulpit. "But I do think we have to share a concern that our youth might find themselves staring at pictures of naked people. We cannot allow such a thing."

Lottie flapped harder. "We have the funds to hire a teacher to oversee the program, and I've found the perfect candidate. He has assured me that he'll be able to block access to pornography. Our students will be reading government studies and downloading images from museums."

Mrs. Jim Bob turned up her nose as if she'd caught a

whiff of sour milk. "There are graven images to be found in many a museum, Lottie. There are portrayals of bare-breasted women engaged in licentious behavior, condoned by the secular humanists but potentially destructive to the innocent children stumbling across them."

"Hey," I said, "buy me another box of bullets and I can shoot all the curates."

"We are not discussing health care," Mrs. Jim Bob countered coldly. "Unless we can feel confident that our teenagers will not—"

"May I speak?" said a young man who was obviously going to do so with or without her blessing. "My name is Justin Bailey. I have a degree in computer sciences from Farber College, and I'm currently doing research in preparation to begin a graduate degree. Miss Estes has tentatively offered me a position as lab supervisor and systems administrator. In that capacity, I can assure you that filtering software will ensure no one can access—"

"Speak English!" Jim Bob snarled.

We all turned around to stare at the alien from cyberspace. He had thin brown hair that allowed a mild glimmer on his scalp, and eyeballs that seemed a tad too conspicuous behind wire-rimmed glasses. His short-sleeved white polyester shirt and clip-on bow tie did not make a compelling fashion statement. Had I encountered him on a Manhattan sidewalk, my instinct would have been to cross the street. Then again, his fingernails were clean and the corners of his mouth free of saliva.

Rare traits in Maggody.

"Inappropriate web sites will be blocked," he said. "Some students will attempt to circumvent my restrictions, but I'll monitor their activities and cut them off within a day. Those who persevere will be kicked out of the lab."

"He has excellent credentials," gushed Lottie. "I see no reason why our youth should go out into the world without the best possible—"

Jim Bob banged his fist on the table. "It's a matter of money! You may have this goddamn-fool grant, but we have to provide the facilities and the utilities and all kinds of expensive things. We can't afford a crossing guard at the intersection by the Pot O' Gold. The football team's playing in last year's uniforms. The table saw in the shop is duller than a widow's ax. Now why should we use this windfall so's our students get to stare at buck-naked ladies when we could be buying a real nice van to transport the basketball team to out-of-town games?"

Justin grimaced. "You could use the money for cases of canned corn in the cafeteria, for that matter. The Internet is here and now, however, and those who don't have a clue are going to be sucking up exhaust fumes as the rest of the world drives by."

"It's clear nobody is stopping around here," Ruby Bee contributed. She may have expected some show of support, but the silence was on the profound side. "Lottie's right. We can't be sending out our youngsters without what they need to succeed. I don't see why utility bills should be more important than being able to compete in college. You ask Arly here how she fared when she—"

"I fared," I said hastily. "I agree that this computer lab is a good idea. As alarming as the concept may be, it's reality. We can't ignore it."

Lottie beamed at me. "What's more, we can all venture onto this mysterious Internet. Justin will teach classes during the school day, and then share his expertise with adults in the evening. All of us can learn to"—she giggled in what struck me as a vaguely unbalanced way—"surf the net. Our little community can have its very own web site, where we can share the particular delights of Maggody. Merchants like Jim Bob and Ruby Bee can advertise their specials. Estelle can let everyone know when she's having a sale on cosmetics and perms. Brother Verber can put up photos of activities at the Voice of the Almighty Lord Assembly Hall and cite Bible verses for daily meditations. Tourists will come swarming in to appreciate our uniqueness."

"Or to stare at Raz," someone muttered from the back of the room. "Him and that sow make a better sideshow than anything in a museum, buck-naked or not."

"Hush your mouth, Idalupino," said Mrs. Jim Bob. "Just how much would these adult classes cost, Lottie?"

"Not a penny, since I included Justin's overtime in the budget. The students will put together this web site as a class project."

"I say we ought to do it," said Estelle, no doubt imagining dozens of cars parked in front of her house and credit cards in every hand. She caught my smirk and snorted. "For the sake of the youngsters, that is. All the rest of it is nothing more than gravy on the biscuit, though there ain't one thing wrong with putting Maggody on the map. Let's have a vote."

Jim Bob sucked on his lip for a moment. "The decision is up to the school board. We'll discuss it among ourselves. This meeting's adjourned."

"I don't see why we can't discuss it here and now," said Roy. "The only time we're supposed to have private sessions is when it's a personnel matter and somebody's feelings might get hurt, like Garbanzo Buchanon's when we heard he was prying open lockers to steal peanut-butter sandwiches out of lunch boxes while he was supposed to be sweeping—"

"I said the meeting's adjourned, Roy. That means it's over. The rest of you might as well leave, 'cause nothing more's gonna happen tonight."

Some of the citizens may not have understood the word "adjourned," but everybody got the message and began to shuffle. Ruby Bee, Estelle, and I had reached the door when Lottie rushed over to us.

"I want to thank you all for your support," she said. "I don't know why Jim Bob's in such a snit over the idea. I had to submit a budget as part of the proposal, and I don't think the bureaucrats at the agency would take it kindly if the money went for a van for the basketball team."

"How'd you ever put together this budget?" asked Estelle. "I wouldn't have the foggiest idea where to start."

Lottie smiled modestly. "My cousin Lulu Ferncliff, who's a librarian over in Paragould, took a computer class at Farber College last summer. Justin was the teacher, and he told them how they could apply for grants for their schools. She passed the information on to me, and I tracked him down. He didn't charge so much as a dime to help me wade through the paperwork. He even showed me what all there is on the Internet and how the students can use it to enrich their homework. Why, we can all be gazing at the ceiling of the Vatican. It's going to be wonderful!"

My eyebrows wanted to rise to the ceiling of the cafeteria, but I managed to keep them under control. "Is Justin going to live here in Maggody?"

The topic of discussion moved into our circle. "It'll be

interesting," he said, twinkling at me in an effort that fell flatter than any of Brother Verber's homilies. "I've leased a trailer at the Pot O' Gold. My wife is hoping to make some kind of contact in the community. Her degree's in sociology."

"She's going to analyze the denizens of the trailer park?" I said. "I'm afraid she'll find a rather sorry group of people. Most of them are scraping by, saving their money, and hoping to move along. There's not much drama in the Pot O' Gold."

Estelle clutched my arm. "You bet your booties there is! You heard about that fellow that calls himself Lazarus? Just last week he rented the double-wide across from Eula Lemoy. She said hello to him in a right friendly fashion and he just stared back at her like she had a hunk of spinach caught in her teeth. He drives a big ol' motorcycle and—"

"An odd name," I said, "but none of our business, or Eula's, for that matter."

"What's more," Estelle went on in a voice well suited to a death scene in a Wagnerian opera, "I encountered him in the supermarket only yesterday. His hair hangs to his shoulders, and might as well be slicked down with lard. I was real surprised not to see a swarm of flies around him. He reminded me of one of those fellows you see on those shows about escaped criminals. As sure as I'm standing here, he's up to no good."

I took a breath. "So I should go out and shoot him because you don't like his hair? If that was my criterion, the population of Maggody would plummet."

"Do you and your wife have any children?" Ruby Bee asked Justin, her eyes glittering with interest.

"Not yet," he said. "We've agreed to wait until I finish grad school. I can't see myself writing a dissertation with a screaming baby in the next room. Chapel understands."

She moved in like a famished mosquito. "Her name is Chapel? I disremember ever hearing that name before. Where are her people from?"

I grabbed her elbow and began to drag her out the door. "Your stint as Lois Lane is over, so give this man a break. Should Lottie's proposal be approved, you'll have plenty of time to get the details."

Lottie's eyes welled with tears. "I'll feel like such a dithery old fool if Jim Bob turns it down. The elementary school has a portable classroom that we can use. It needs a good cleaning and some cubicles and chairs, but it'll work out just fine. Mr. Darker, the principal, says we can put it out behind the gym. That way, in the evenings we can park thirty feet away and not have to go traipsing through the school while the floors are being waxed."

"And just where was Mr. Darker tonight?" asked Estelle. "It seems to me he should have been here to add his support."

"He has a touch of stomach flu."

Ruby Bee yanked off my hand. "Or more likely a yellow streak up his backside. Is he scared of Jim Bob?"

"There's no call to go into that." Lottie's lips began to tremble. "It may be that Jim Bob was in his office this afternoon, but Mr. Darker's been having difficulty with his bowels all week. Every time he went into the faculty restroom, the teachers deserted the lounge like fleas on a drowning dog. On Tuesday, Miz Pitman dawdled. She was still feeling so faint after seventh period that I was obliged to supervise pom-pom practice."

I glanced at Justin, who was blinking nervously. "Don't worry about local politics," I said to him. "In a town this size, issues take on a certain intensity. You should have been here when Ruby Bee switched from popcorn to pretzels for happy hour. I arrested three good ol' boys, and she threw twice that many out on their butts. Now, if you'll excuse us, we all need to be on our way. That includes you, Estelle."

Lottie was trying to explain realities to Justin as I managed to herd Ruby Bee and Estelle out into the hall. I was about to ask about the easiest route out of the building when Daniel and Leona Holliflecker cut us off.

They were a bland couple in their mid-fifties, definitely not the sort to drink a few beers on a Friday afternoon or come dancing on a Saturday night. He had some kind of middle-management job at the poultry-processing plant in Starley City; she was a minor force in the Missionary Society at the Assembly Hall and a tireless champion of conservative dogma, such as school prayer and creation science. Our paths rarely crossed, which was okay with me.

"Ruby Bee, Estelle," Leona said, ignoring yours truly, "I want you to meet my niece. She's staying with us for the time being." She pushed forward a gaunt girl with oversized, panicky eyes and black hair that hung past the middle of her back. "This is Gwynnie Patchwood, my brother's eldest. She's hoping to find a part-time job. Gwynnie, say hello to Miz Hanks and Miz Oppers."

Gwynnie gave us a brittle smile. "Pleased to meet you. I sure am happy to be here in Maggody. If you ever need somebody to do some cleaning or run errands, I don't have anything else to do. Whatever you want to pay me is all right."

"I believe, Gwynnie," said Daniel, "that the law dictates minimum wage. Please do not act as if you're being forced into servitude simply because Leona and I expect you to contribute to the household expenses."

"Shouldn't you be in school?" asked Estelle.

"You don't look a day over fifteen," added Ruby Bee. "Daniel here was on the school board a few years back. I'd like to think he understands the importance of education."

Leona stepped in front of Gwynnie. "She's seventeen, not fifteen. She had to drop out of school, so we agreed to take her in until things get settled. If you find it in your hearts to offer her an hour or two of work every now and then, she'll be grateful. She is not, however, looking for charity." She looked at Daniel. "I'd like to get on home. No matter what you and Gwynnie say, Jessie Traylor is not my idea of a reliable person."

"I agree with you, Ruby Bee," said Daniel, "but it's too complicated to explain. Gwynnie's working on her GED. I'm hoping these evening computer classes will motivate her to take classes at the community college in Starley City."

Ruby Bee smiled at the girl. "I'll sure keep you in mind, honey. I've been thinking about cleaning out the pantry. It's a big job."

Gwynnie nodded, then trudged off between Daniel and Leona, her shoulders hunched as though a guillotine was awaiting her at the end of the hallway.

"Kinda sickly, ain't she?" said Estelle as we followed at a polite distance. "What she needs is a dusting of blusher and a delicate touch of mascara. She'd look like one of those cover girls on *Seventeen* magazine. Big eyes, wide mouth. Maybe I'll just call her to help me reorganize my cosmetics shelf, then offer to fix her up. It's real sad to think of her spending all her days and nights at the Hollifleckers' place."

Ruby Bee shook her head. "I've seen her a time or two with some of the girls, but I'll bet she hasn't been going to the dances and parties."

Both of them looked at me.

"Wait just a minute," I said, holding up my hands. "I am not going to get Cinderella a date to the prom. This may be hard to swallow, but I am not dearly beloved by the local teenagers. My car is egged on a monthly basis. Last week some clown put a very dead squirrel under the hood and I came damn near throwing up when I turned on the engine. Either of you is free to assume the role of her social secretary; heaven knows you've had enough practice on me."

On that high-minded note, I went out into the crisp, cool spring night and drove to Farberville in hopes of an adequately entertaining movie, a box of oily popcorn, a watery soda, and an evening's respite from the two busiest bodies in Maggody.

2

Y ou were out late last night," Ruby Bee said as I walked into the barroom the following afternoon. It was not a mild observation, but something more akin to the opening statement of a prosecuting attorney bent on obtaining the death penalty. "What's more, I called the PD three times this morning—that's three times, in case you aren't listening—and you weren't there. Is there something going on that I should know about? You seeing a man on the sly? Is he married and you're ashamed to admit it? Is he getting a divorce from his wife? Are there children involved? How old are they?"

Estelle was perched on her favorite stool at the end of the bar, situated conveniently near the ladies room and allowing her a panoramic view of the dance floor and booths along the wall. "Ruby Bee was so worried that she wanted to call Sheriff Dorfer, but I talked her out of it—this time, anyway. You have no business causing your own mother to stew like a mess of turnip greens. She's liable to get ulcers like poor Collera Buchanon. You remember what happened to him, doncha?"

"I'm already feeling twinges," said Ruby Bee, squeezing out a tear for optimum impact. "The next thing you know, I'll be in intensive care with a tube in my nose.

Maybe I'd better get to work on my obituary while I still have the strength. Once they put needles in me, I won't be able to lift my hand."

There'd been an incident in which such a thing had happened, but I doubted we were in danger of a relapse brought on by my failure to keep them supplied with my itinerary. "What did happen to Collera?" I asked as I chose a stool at the opposite end of the bar.

Estelle gave me a haughty look. "He's in the graveyard out behind the Assembly Hall. Some say when the moon's lost in the clouds, you can hear him moanin' something awful."

"Hit by a Greyhound bus, wasn't he?" I said, checking the glass domes for pie. I knew precisely who made the best lemon meringue pie in Stump County, although I was going to have to come up with a slick alibi to get a piece of anything more than my mother's mind.

"He wouldn't have been lying in the middle of the highway if it weren't on account of his pain," countered Estelle. "Pain caused by ulcers brought on by worry when his ma was arrested for holding up that liquor store across from the Farberville airport. She was nigh onto eighty at the time, and everybody figured she'd up and die in the county jail."

"Did she?" I asked obligingly.

Ruby Bee banged down a piece of cherry pie in front of me. "No, she escaped through a ventilation shaft and was never seen again. That's what drove poor Collera to his untimely death." She put her hand on her chest. "I'm feeling those palpitations again, Estelle. Do I look pale?"

"You're as rosy as a tomato," I said as I leaned over the bar and plucked a fork out of a bin. "Of course, if you think you're having a heart attack, I'll be happy to call an ambulance. They charge more than six hundred dollars to come all this way, and simply being admitted to the emergency room is liable to cost—"

"Mind your mouth, Miss Nightingale. Maybe I was experiencing a bout of indigestion brought on by fretting about you. I don't believe you've explained where you were last night and earlier today."

I tucked into the pie while I could. "Last night I went to a movie," I said between mouthfuls, "and this morning I directed traffic in Emmet while deputies chased chickens. A truck driver took that sharp curve at the edge of town too fast. Let me tell you, there is nothing uglier than a half-mile chicken slick."

"A movie?" said Estelle, wiggling her eyebrows. "All by yourself?"

"Yes, Estelle, all by myself except for a hundred horny teenagers who were attempting to have sex despite the armrests—or because of them. I wasn't sure. This morning was more exciting, though. Want to hear how one of the deputies snatched up what must have been a seriously constipated chicken and found himself with a face full of—"

Ruby Bee grabbed for my plate, but I scooted it out of reach. "No," she said, "I reckon we don't. I can't believe you're not more interested in this computer lab that Lottie's hoping to set up. Everybody in town's buzzing about it. I stopped at the Satterwaits' produce stand this morning to see if they had any lettuce, and they couldn't talk about anything else."

I gazed blandly at her. "I myself am entranced with lettuce. Even while I was ankle-deep in chicken guts all morning, the only thing running through my mind was endive. You wouldn't believe what a handful costs in Manhattan. Down here, you could buy a used pickup truck and have enough money left over for a half-pint of whiskey to stick in the glove compartment."

"I hope you ain't planning on a grilled-cheese sandwich anytime soon," she said grimly as she began to wipe the bar with a rag.

A tactical retreat, or at least a tactful one, was called for. "I really do think this computer lab is a good idea. More and more colleges are requiring students to bring their own personal computers. I'm not sure how many of the local high school graduates can afford them, but at least they'll be familiar with the concepts. Has the school board made a decision?"

"No, and nobody seems to know why he's so all-fired agin it. He being Jim Bob, that is. According to Lottie, the money can't be spent for anything else. Roy came by for lunch and said he didn't have any problem with it. I guess you know that Peteet's convinced he's being visited by aliens on a regular basis, which is why he hardly ever leaves his house without wrapping his privates in aluminum foil. Haven't you ever wondered why he rustles so much when he moves around?"

"I guess I've never noticed," I said, hoping my wince was not visible.

"It's hard to miss. Anyway, Lottie went over to his house this morning and promised him that he could communicate directly with his friends by using"—she turned even rosier—"his antenna and a computer. That's two votes right there. Yesterday evening Mrs. Jim Bob didn't sound like she'd dug in her heels. I just don't understand Jim Bob's attitude."

Estelle took a sip of sherry. "Idalupino says he has a computer at the supermarket, and spends a lot of time doing things on it. Maybe he's afraid it'll come back to haunt him."

"I don't see how," said Ruby Bee.

The Internet explosion had taken place while I was huddled in my apartment, stalking roaches and reading travel brochures. Computers had appeared in the sheriff's office a while back, but they had not resulted in greater efficiency, or anything else, for that matter. The dispatcher, LaBelle, had told me on occasion that she had a direct link with the FBI files, but I'd had no reason to find out if indeed she did. Liquor-store holdups do not require access to a national databank, but merely a bit of common sense and, more often than not, a day or two of patience before a relative turned. Blood may be thicker than water, but money's a great decoagulator when a reward is on the counter.

"I don't understand it well enough to offer an opinion," I said as I polished off the pie. "When does Lottie hope this will happen? School is out in less than two months. It'd make more sense to start surfing in August."

Estelle glanced over her shoulder in case CIA operatives were hiding behind the jukebox. "She has a dozen computers in boxes in her garage. Earl Buchanon is planning to lay the foundation for the portable classroom tomorrow morning, and the electric co-op and telephone companies have work orders."

In spite of my resolve, I made a face. "And the school board wasn't notified in advance?"

"Not exactly," muttered Ruby Bee.

Estelle popped a pretzel in her mouth. "But we told

Lottie that you'd be happy to have a word with Jim Bob. You're the chief of police, after all."

"And what does that have to do with the price of pot in Peoria?" I asked as I tossed the fork into a sink of brown water. "Am I supposed to hang out in the lab and arrest those students clever enough to figure out how to find porn sites despite Mr. Bailey's best efforts? Sheriff Dorfer's not going to let me fill up the county jail with goggly-eyed teenagers."

"Maybe not," she conceded, "but Lottie's counting on you to change Jim Bob's mind. She has thousands of dollars' worth of computers in her garage, and her drainage is iffy. One heavy rain and she might as well kill herself. You wouldn't want that on your conscience, would you?"

Ruby Bee loomed in front of me. "Lottie embroidered your first communion dress, Arly, despite her failing eyesight. I know for a fact that she soaked her fingers in ice water every night just so she could finish it. Those rosebuds were enough to make a blind man weep. What's more—"

"I'm going," I said. "I doubt I'll convince Jim Bob to so much as blow his nose, but I'll try. In the meantime, construct a plywood pyre and see if you can get Lottie to schedule some free time."

Someone may have demanded an explanation as I walked across the dance floor and out to my car, which was supplied by the town council and therefore marginally functional. As was Lottie, who currently had what might well be major-league contraband in her garage. The fine line between enthusiasm and zealotry had been compromised, and I wasn't pleased to be cast as a co-conspirator.

I was still growling under my breath as I drove out

Finger Lane and turned between the J and B brick pillars that heralded what Mrs. Jim Bob assured one and all was the finest house in Maggody. The competition wasn't real keen; outside of some seventy-year-old farmhouses with homespun charm (but not indoor plumbing), the best we had to offer in rebuttal were the clones in the subdivision over by the high school. Three bedrooms, one and a half baths. I'd often speculated on how one took a half-bath.

Mrs. Jim Bob met me at the front door with all of her usual warmth. "I wasn't expecting company. Are you selling something?"

I forced myself to envision Lottie dousing herself with gasoline. "I thought we might discuss this computer-lab business."

"I suppose it can't hurt," she said as she stepped back and gestured for me to come inside. "Lottie was up here earlier, and I must say she made her case. As long as the teacher can block out pornography, I don't see why we shouldn't make the Internet available to our youth. They don't need to go out into the world with the word 'redneck' tattooed on their foreheads."

I was as surprised by her sentiment as I was being escorted into the living room. Mrs. Jim Bob and I have experienced clashes worthy of a seismographic alert. I could not remember when she had last offered a reasonable response.

For a fleeting second, I wondered if one of us had taken a turn toward sanity, then sucked it up and said, "Is Jim Bob in favor of the computer lab, too?"

"Lottie showed us her figures." She sat down and began to pluck at a crocheted doily on the armrest of the chair. "He conceded that she had included utilities in her budget, and it really won't cost much to run the telephone lines to a portable building behind the gym. I personally have no interest in the Internet, but I think the idea of Brother Verber offering a daily dose of inspiration might spread the gospel to those lost souls in danger of eternal torment." She paused in case I needed a minute to figure out exactly which one of us might qualify as a charcoal briquette. "After Lottie left, Jim Bob and I got down on our knees in this very room and prayed for guidance. As far as I could tell, the Lord has no objections to the Internet, as long as it's not used to tempt the weakest among us with vile images."

"Well, then," I said lamely, "as long as you and Jim Bob are in favor of this, I'll go tell Lottie that the matter's been decided."

"You'd better go by the SuperSaver first."

"Jim Bob's *not* in favor? I thought you just said that he is."

She resumed picking at the doily as if it were a blister. "His mind might have wandered during our prayer session. I don't rightly know why he's upset about having a computer lab at the high school. You'll have to ask him yourself."

The things I do for a grilled-cheese sandwich.

~~~~~~~~~~~~~~

Eula Lemoy eased back her curtain so she could take a good look at the mobile home on the other side of the road that curled through the Pot O' Gold. It was hard to tell if the Lazarus fellow was there or not; sometimes he parked his nasty, smoke-belching motorcycle behind his unit and sprawled in the mud to tinker with it. Whenever she caught sight of him doing it, all she could think of was Raz Buchanon's pedigreed sow.

There was no movement in his kitchenette or living room, but that didn't mean he wasn't sitting on the sofa, scheming to do Satan's work. Eula had tried to be neighborly when he first moved in, taking him a tuna casserole and a generous slice of coconut cake. All he'd done was look at her before closing the door in her face. Ever since then, she'd felt his icy eyes on her whenever she was hanging laundry on the line or walking down to get her mail from the row of boxes at the front gate.

Not that he ever got any mail in his box. He never had any visitors, for that matter. His curtains were always drawn at night, but Eula was sure she'd have heard if somebody knocked on his door. Privacy was not a luxury enjoyed at the Pot O' Gold. Miz Whitbread, who lived next to him, had said the exact same thing just that morning when she'd come over for coffee. Of course she was deaf as a fence post, but there wasn't anything wrong with her eyesight when she remembered to wear her bifocals.

He was up to no good, Eula thought as she let the curtain fall. Nobody lived in the mobile home park by choice. She herself had been born and raised in Maggody, and raised some children of her own in a house out by the low-water bridge. All four were off in other states these days, calling on her birthday and sending scarves and talcum powder at Christmas. When Bernard had died of pneumonia back in . . .

The date escaped her. She went into the bedroom and picked up a photograph of Bernard all puffered up in his army uniform, grinning like a mule with a mouthful of briars. A good twenty years ago, she realized with a jolt of sadness. After the war, he'd found a decent job at the post office and worked his way up from route carrier to supervisor. It had been respectable back then. These days, it seemed like a goodly number of postal workers were "disgruntled." Bernard had always been, well, gruntled with his bonuses and promotions.

It occurred to her that Lazarus might well be one of that sort. Maybe he'd gone into work one day and found a picture of himself taped on the wall with a notice that he was on the FBI's Most Wanted list. The only thing he could do would be to go into hiding in a remote place like Maggody. She'd noticed right off the bat that he had the stare of a psychotic killer. Or worse.

She sat down on the divan and hunted through the pockets of her housedress for a tissue, doing her best not to imagine him creeping toward her bedroom window in the dark of night. He'd probably have a stocking over his head in hopes she wouldn't recognize him, but short of his having a haircut, she'd see right through his pathetic disguise. He'd have no choice but to slash her throat in her own bed. How long would it be before someone found her body in a pool of blood?

Miz Whitbread was in even greater danger, since she wouldn't hear him easing open her door and tiptoeing down the hallway to her bedroom. On the other hand, it wasn't likely she'd recognize him if her bifocals were on the nightstand. He might spare her life.

Eula realized she was as damp as a sponge. She sat back and fanned herself with the latest issue of *TV Guide* while she tried to figure out what to do. According to a show she'd seen a few months back, psychotic killers sought out their victims when the moon was full. For the moment, she and Miz Whitbread were safe, but only for a matter of days. Once the full moon rose over Cotter's Ridge, they would be at his mercy.

Unless, Eula thought with a tight frown, she herself took steps to protect them. Steps like finding the box where she'd packed away Bernard's gun twenty long years ago. She seemed to recall dumping in some bullets at the same time.

Ruby Bee took a mug of beer and a cheeseburger to the trucker in the last booth, made sure there was a squeeze-bottle of ketchup on the table, and came back to the bar with a thoughtful expression. "Do you recall what Leona said right before they left last night?"

"How we ought to hire Gwynnie?" said Estelle, determined to prove her memory was a sight better than most, present company included.

"No, about Jessie Traylor not being reliable. If you ask me, that was an odd remark."

"Did somebody ask you?"

"We are not on some television game show where you have to answer with a question. I almost thought Daniel and Leona were referring to a baby-sitter, but their son, who's twenty-five if he's a day, lives in Sallisaw—and if the rumors are true, shares an apartment with a man named Hilary."

"That's the silliest thing I've heard in all my born days. Next you'll be talking about football players named Suzanne and Carolyn. Besides, Elsie Buchanon heard he moved out to California to learn how to be a pastry chef."

"I think that says it all." Ruby Bee glanced at the

trucker to make sure he was still occupied with his food, then lowered her voice to a hoarse whisper. "But why would Jessie Traylor be out at their house by himself?"

Estelle chewed on a pretzel as she searched her mind for a way not to acknowledge she'd missed what might have been a vital clue. "I suppose I was too concerned about the poor girl to pay any heed. The only thing I could think about was how she was out there on her knees scrubbing Leona's kitchen floor. It was all I could do not to burst into tears right there on the spot."

"So now you're a social worker?"

Estelle conceded defeat. "What do you think she meant?"

"Well, if they took in a foster child, no one's breathed a word about it. Elsie always tells me what's said at the Missionary Society after they've prayed for the heathens in Africa and started in on coffee and cinnamon rolls. If Leona has done something charitable, you can bet the farm Elsie would have heard all about it. It just might be time for me to tackle the pantry. With Gwynnie's help, it shouldn't take more than a day. Maybe I'll close for half an hour to drive out to the Hollifleckers' place and see if she can oblige me."

"What about him?" asked Estelle, jabbing her thumb in the direction of the trucker.

"Royce," Ruby Bee called in her sternest voice, "finish up and be on your way. The exterminator's coming to fog the barroom. You don't want to be leaving a pretty widow, do you? The way your brother leers at Sharlene, I suspicion her bed won't be cold an hour after your funeral. Something might be going on at this very moment."

The trucker jammed a cap on his head and made a

timely exit. Ruby Bee waited until she heard his rig roar to life, then took off her apron and hung it on a knob. "I suppose you're thinking you'll come along."

"For the ride," Estelle said airily. "I hear tell the dogwoods and redbuds are real pretty out that way. I can sit in the car while you talk to Gwynnie."

"Whatever you want to do is fine with me."

"I wasn't asking for your blessing. If you don't want company, say so."

Ruby Bee collected her purse from a drawer. "Come on, Estelle. I swear, every spring you get all prickly like a rash."

"While you stay bad-tempered all year round," Estelle said as she slid off the stool. "It so happens that something downright tragic happened to me nigh on thirty years ago this month. When I'm inclined to tell you, I will, so don't go pestering me about it. We all have our secrets, don't we?"

Ruby Bee was trying to think of hers as they drove toward the Hollifleckers' house. There wasn't much she hadn't told Estelle, from how Arly's father disappeared that rainy night to her flirtation with a drygoods salesman the year Arly started third grade. But now it seemed Estelle had been holding back. "Downright tragic" had been her exact phrase.

So many possibilities were flitting through her mind that she realized at the last moment that she'd reached the turnoff. "Sorry," she said as she hit the brake pedal and squealed around the corner like a NASCAR driver. As much as she hated to admit it, it made her feel just a bit giddy, like a heroine in the Saturday matinee serials she doted on some forty years ago. Not that it qualified as a secret, of course.

Estelle pretended not to notice. "What do you recollect about Jessie Traylor? Didn't his ma end up in a sanitorium?"

Ruby Bee put aside her meanderings and focused on the subject at hand. "No, she ran off with some drunk that worked at a body shop. Jessie's father might as well have been a Buchanon, considering how shiftless he was. He was at the state prison for assaulting a waitress at the Dew Drop Inn when he was killed. Jessie squeaked through high school three or four years ago, and last I heard, works at a factory over in Farberville."

"Living in the family house?"

"I seem to think so. Would you like to know his shoe size and blood type?"

Estelle grimaced. "Why're you getting so snippety?"

Ruby Bee parked in the Hollifleckers' driveway. "I beg your pardon, but I was not being snippety. I just don't appreciate being treated like the local almanac. Jessie comes into the bar once in a while, not bothering anybody or doing anything more than putting a quarter in the jukebox and having a beer. He's on the shy side, but so are plenty of other folks. Beelzebubba Buchanon can't so much as look you in the eye if you speak to him, which ain't saying you might want to. If nothing else, you might catch a glimpse of his nose hair."

"Do you want me to sit here and pray for your forgiveness or do you want me to come to the door with you?"

"Let's not squabble," said Ruby Bee, feeling somewhat remorseful despite the fact Estelle had been keeping a secret from her for thirty years, which was a long time, thank you kindly. "I'll ask Gwynnie about helping with the pantry, and you can see if she can do some work for you later on. I'm not overly fond of Daniel and Leona, but I hate to let the girl suffer on account of them."

Estelle figured it was as close to an apology as she was going to get, so she magnanimously got out of the car and followed Ruby Bee up the steps to the porch.

Gwynnie opened the door before Ruby Bee could push the bell. "Miz Hanks, how nice of you, and Miz Oppers, too! Leona's at the supermarket just now. Is there something I can do for you? Can I offer y'all ice tea and cookies? Please come in and sit down. This is like really sweet of you to come by. Leona will be so sorry she missed you. Daniel's at work, but he'll be pleased to hear how you dropped by. Would you rather have coffee? I can make lemonade if you'd like."

Ruby Bee exchanged pointed looks with Estelle, then smiled. "That's all right, Gwynnie. I was just wondering if you'd like to work for me toward the end of the week. It won't add up to more than five or six hours, but I'll certainly pay you minimum wage."

"You don't have to pay me anything," Gwynnie said, turning soulful brown eyes on her, "but maybe you should on account of Daniel. I'll have to find a baby-sitter, though. Should I call you?"

"Baby-sitter?" said Estelle.

"I can't hardly leave a two-year-old to fend for hisself, can I? Dahlia Buchanon acted like we could switch off a couple of days a week. It'll be easier for me to take Chip to her house than for her to bring the twins here. What's more, I don't think Leona'd be in favor of a houseful of crying babies. She's real indifferent when it comes to babies. You'd think she wouldn't be that way, considering she used to have one, but you never know, do you?"

Estelle eased around Ruby Bee and took Gwynnie's elbow. "This is the first we've heard about this baby. Is he yours?"

Ruby Bee might have voiced disapproval at the rudeness of the remark if she hadn't been so interested in the answer. "I think I would like a glass of ice tea, Gwynnie, if it's not too much bother."

"Oh no," she said. "It's mighty lonesome out here. Daniel's at work all day, and Leona spends most of her time at the county old folks' home reading the Bible and supervising arts-and-crafts projects. When she's here, she keeps to herself in a little room way at the back of the house. Chip and I watch a lot of talk shows in the afternoons. After I've cleaned up the supper things, Daniel helps me with my GED studies while Leona writes letters and reads."

Ruby Bee and Estelle trailed after Gwynnie into the kitchen. There was no baby in sight, but a stuffed animal and a few plastic blocks were scattered on the floor, and the remains of a peanut butter sandwich had been smeared onto the surface of the dinette table.

"Chip's taking a nap," said Gwynnie as she began opening cabinets. "Do you want sugar? Leona uses that artificial sugar, but I'm sure she has the real stuff somewhere. Should I make coffee? Are you sure? I don't mind." She spun around. "Or lemonade? I'll fix it from scratch. Leona bought lemons yesterday."

"Calm yourself," Ruby Bee said gently. "Maybe you should sit right here and take a few deep breaths. You sound real tense."

Gwynnie recoiled as if she'd been doused with a bucketful of cold water. "I do? Gosh, I'm sorry, Miz Hanks. I was thinking you might prefer lemonade. I shouldn't have . . ."

"Come here," murmured Ruby Bee, wrapping her arms around the girl's shoulders. "You're doing fine. You and Estelle and me are going to sit down at the table and have ourselves a nice visit."

Estelle nodded. "We don't need tea or coffee or lemonade, Gwynnie. If there's anything you want to tell us, you can just let your hair down, 'cause all we want is to be your friends. We're apt to be older than your mother, but that doesn't mean you can't talk to us."

Tears were slithering down Gwynnie's cheeks as she sat down at the dinette. She took a paper napkin out of a holder and wiped her nose. "That's real kindly of you, but Daniel and Leona warned me to keep my mouth shut. I've been living here most of a month, but last night was the first time they took me anywhere. They let Jessie come over some evenings. We have to stay in the living room, though, and Daniel makes sure he's gone home before ten o'clock. I might as well be living in a convent." She scooped up the teddy bear and clutched it in her arms. "It's pretty obvious I'm not qualified for that, though," she added wryly. "Leona prays for my soul ever' night over supper."

Even though Estelle had asked for frankness, she had no idea how to respond to it. She glanced at Ruby Bee, who looked like she was once again in the throes of palpitations, then squeezed Gwynnie's hand. "Are you here because of having a baby?"

"Yeah, I guess so. The high school I was going to has a program for pregnant girls, but when I began to show, my ma sent me to a gawdawful strict place over in

Mississippi. They badgered me night and day to sign adoption consent papers. When I refused, they kept me in isolation for four solid months. The only time I was let out was on Sunday afternoons, when the church ladies came with used clothing and smarmy smiles. I hated all of them, and I wasn't going to sign away my baby on their say-so. The first time I laid eyes on Chip, I knew I could never let anyone take him from me. My ma was so mad that she had to be argued into taking me back. It didn't work out, so Daniel and Leona agreed to keep us until I pass the GED. Everybody tells me I should be grateful."

It occurred to Ruby Bee that had they been in a movie, the kitchen door would have burst open and Leona would have stormed into the kitchen and started screaming at Gwynnie. As it was, the only sound was the ticktocking of the clock above the refrigerator. It wasn't deafening by any means, but it seemed to grow louder and more insistent, until Ruby Bee could swear her heartbeat had fallen into rhythm with it.

Estelle pulled a napkin from the holder and blotted her forehead. "Well, Gwynnie, it sounds like you've got everything under control. Once you've passed the GED, you might consider a career as a cosmetologist. You can find a lot of satisfaction in sending away a client who's feeling as pretty as a peahen."

Gwynnie's eyes filled once again with tears. "I can't afford training, not with the cost of rent and baby-sitters. About all I can do is sign up for welfare."

"What about Chip's father?" asked Ruby Bee, aware she needed to tread real softly. "Doesn't he have to pay child support?"

"He died before Chip was born. He was out riding

around and drinking with his buddies, and the car went into a river. His parents refused to admit he was the father. I suppose rich people can demand paternity tests and all that, but I talked to some lady at the legal-aid clinic and she just laughed, same as the social worker did. I aim to take care of Chip all by myself. I'm his mother, come hell or high water." She stiffened and gave them a horrified look. "Pardon my French. My ma's not the best person in the world, but she made sure I went to Sunday school every week no matter what."

Ruby Bee felt a sudden infusion of warmth in her veins, like she'd just slipped down into a bathtub of bubbly hot water. "You have no call to worry, Gwynnie. Estelle and I are gonna take care of everything."

Not everyone at the table shared her feeling.

3

Meanwhile, back at the ranch, or at least at the duplex in Farberville rented by Justin and Chapel Bailey, a storm was brewing like a yeasty batch of beer.

Chapel waited until Justin came through the living room, coldly observing him as he staggered under the weight of a box filled with dog-eared, heavily highlighted textbooks that would never be opened again. Those belonging to Justin had been, for the most part, obsolete before he'd finished the pertinent class—or even begun it. Hers were mostly forays into feministic analysis of didactic studies of urban language patterns, whatever that meant.

"This town of Maggody is not on any map I've found thus far," she said loudly, which was pretty much how she said anything when she was annoyed. She was very annoyed. "I was under the impression we would have a discussion before a decision was reached. We are equals in this relationship, Justin. I told you before you moved in that everything would be a fifty-fifty proposition, from the dirty dishes to the utility bills."

"So?" he said as he dropped the box by the door, alarming their neighbors, who were into nuclear disarmament and had stockpiled cases of food and bottled water under the back porch.

"Major lifestyle alterations are joint decisions, too. They're not arbitrary whims based solely on what you want. You know perfectly well that I've been hoping to get into Dr. Covey's seminar. This is the first time he's offered it in three semesters."

Justin sat down at the opposite end of the sofa. As soon as he'd stopped wheezing and could trust himself to speak in a reasonable voice, he said, "It's a twenty-mile drive, Chapel, and the seminar will only meet once a week. There's no reason why you can't take it."

"What am I supposed to do the other six days?"

"You can find something. Nothing says you have to sit around the trailer park."

Chapel ran a hand through her lemony hair, its color only slightly surreal. It was so frizzy, however, that in the sociology grad lounge it had been the cause of much jovial and irreverent conjecture regarding bolts of lightning, forks, light sockets, and exotic drugs. Her pugnacious features and wiry body ensured all such remarks were made only after she was well clear of the lounge.

"Wow," she said, "like I can wade in creeks and learn how to make soap from wise old mountain women. I can even join the local book club, as long as we can afford a subscription to *Reader's Digest Condensed.*"

"One year, and then I'll be in grad school. You're acting as if we've signed a permanent lease in purgatory."

"Hell's more like it," Chapel said as she began to rip the peel off an orange in a way Justin found obscurely disturbing. "What's more, you haven't been accepted anywhere. Who knows how long we'll sit in a trailer and sink into mindlessness? What shall I look forward to after mastering the art of making soap? Watermelon pickles? Green tomato relish? Dowsing for dollars?"

"Did something happen today?"

She stuffed an orange segment in her mouth. As juice dribbled down her chin, she said, "Armenia is pregnant."

Justin stared. "Isn't Armenia a . . . ?"

"Lesbian? What difference does that make? Is she unworthy of raising a child? Her relationship with Malinda is a good deal stronger than anything we've ever experienced. I can't remember when either of them has come alone to the Sunday evening potlucks at the Unitarian student center." She filled her mouth with another piece of orange and chomped down with enough vigor to send pulp splattering onto the carpet. "I, on the other hand, can't remember when you last came home in time to go with me, much less sleep with me. I find myself wondering if you're asexual, Justin, or simply more enamored of your databases and megabytes than you are of living entities. Have you taken to masturbating with your mousepad?"

"Chapel," he began angrily, then caught himself and sat back. "You knew when we met that I'd have to spend a lot of time in the lab."

"Is that where you are every night until midnight? I called last night and nobody answered."

"I thought you went to the potluck."

"On my way home, I drove by the lab. I didn't see any lights. When I got home, I called."

Justin was still struggling with his temper. "Dr. Mertzell asked me to come over to his house to help him install a new scanner. I need his letters of recommendation for grad school. Hell, I would have gone there if he'd asked me to clean out his gutters. I was home by eleven. Do you think I'm fooling around with all those hot little sorority girls in my freshman labs? I should be flattered."

Chapel looked at the stains under his armpits, at his glittering forehead that added ten years to his age, at his protuberant eyes and acne-scarred complexion. Her expression softened. "No, Justin, I trust you. I was just nonplussed when Armenia and Malinda shared their news with me. I hugged and kissed and made all the right noises, but afterward, I sat in the car and cried."

"We talked about this before we got married," Justin said. "We'll have a child after I finish grad school."

Chapel wiped away what might have been a tear, and her voice was low as she said, "I know we did."

"Then it's settled." He picked up the box. "For the next six months, I'll work on applications to grad school. You can take the seminar and catch crawdads in your spare time. A year from now, we'll be packing for Boston or Berkeley."

"I guess so," Chapel said without enthusiasm, thinking of the glow on Armenia's face. There was no discernible swell to her belly, but it would come with a blessing from the Earth Goddess. At twenty-six, Chapel knew her biological clock had a long way to go before she needed to set the alarm.

Still, she'd married Justin because she understood the importance of genetic strengths. He was not attractive in a physical sense, but his intelligence was formidable. Her goal was a child who could, and would, burst forth with the brilliance she had painfully acknowledged was lacking in herself. Her child, and to some extent his (although nurture would contribute to nature), would redefine the currently simplistic concepts of human existence through intense exposure to the humanities and science. He or she would not be born with a silver spoon, but with an appropriate sized violin in the crib, a daily dose of literature, charts and maps on the wall, and C-SPAN, or at least CNN, on a regular basis. While others read Dr. Seuss to their infants, she would read Balzac and Baudelaire.

It was not the time to mention that she'd tossed out her birth-control pills three months previously. If and when, she told herself, she could handle the situation.

I went into the SuperSaver and headed for the cubicle that served as Jim Bob's office. Had served, it seemed. After a perfunctory knock, I opened the door and gazed with some confusion at a sofa that would have been rejected at a thrift shop and a couple of threadbare easy chairs. No desk, no file cabinet, no fax machine, no precarious piles of manila folders. To make matters worse, Kevin Buchanon was sprawled on one of the chairs, sucking on a can of soda while his Adam's apple bobbled like a tennis ball bouncing into a fence.

"Where's Jim Bob?" I asked.

"You mean like his office?"

"Yeah, Kevin. Last time I was here, this was his office."

Kevin thought long and hard. "Well, he moved his office last week. I mean, he didn't move this, 'cause it's still here."

"I can see that," I said through clenched teeth. "Do you have any clue where he might have relocated the contents of his office?"

" 'Course I do. I'm the one that hauled out his desk. I thought I was never gonna get it through the door. My back's still throbbing something awful. Dahlia had me soak in the tub for more'n an hour, but—"

"Where can I find him?" I asked, speaking slowly and deliberately in words of one syllable, since Kevin was not a polysyllabic kind of guy.

"Jim Bob?"

"Do you think I'm looking for Elvis?"

Kevin's eyes shifted uneasily as he pondered my question. "Elvis died more than twenty years ago, Arly. Estelle Oppers may have claimed to have seen him in that casino over by Tunica a few months back, but that don't make it so. Between you and me, Estelle's kinda flighty. Even my ma says that. I'd hate to repeat what my pa says."

I took a deep breath. "Please don't. Where is Jim Bob's office?"

"You're wanting to see Jim Bob?"

All of this might have been noteworthy had it not been quite so typical of all my exchanges with Kevin, whose brain was insulated with steel wool. What brain there was. I gave myself a moment, then said, "Yes, Kevin, I'm wanting to see Jim Bob. Do you know where he is right now?"

"Sure do," he said with a grin that gave me a distasteful glimpse of his teeth. "He's most likely in his office unless he went off somewhere. He usually tells us afore he leaves. Whenever that happens, Idalupino oversees things. She's a sight worse than Jim Bob when it comes to barking out orders and acting like she hung the moon. That ain't to say Jim Bob's always mannersome, especially when it comes to the work schedule. When I told him that Dahlia and me wanted to take computer lessons, what he said was enough to flip-flop a body in its grave. You'd have thought I'd said we wanted to start holding up liquor stores."

"Like Collera Buchanon's mother?" I asked, despite myself.

Kevin gave me a sober look. "You got to admire somebody with that kind of ambition. Going on eighty like she was, and still—"

I'd pretty much run out of tolerance. "Where can I find Jim Bob?"

"What he did was put up a partition in the employees' lounge. We can get to the restroom okay, but he dint leave much room for furniture and the only window's on his side. I don't reckon he's figured out we're using this, and I shore don't want to be here when he gets wind of it. He's awful busy with his fancy computer, though. Melda sez he won't even notice if there's a fire unless we fetch him."

"What's he doing on the computer?"

"Gosh, I dunno. He sez he puts in orders and keeps track of hours and deductions and things like that. It doesn't seem to work so good. Last week Melda got a paycheck for seventeen thousand dollars, and she hadn't even worked overtime. She wanted to cash it and leave the county, but Idalupino convinced her otherwise. I sure could use a paycheck like that."

"Cashing it could get you in serious trouble," I said. "Will you please take me to Jim Bob?"

Kevin gulped down the dregs of his soda and stood up. "You should have said so in the first place, Arly."

If I'd had my gun and a bullet, or even my radar gun, which I like to pretend emits flesh-vaporizing death rays, I would have plugged him between his bony shoulder blades as he led me to the back of the store. Ignoring his bleats, I went through what was left of the lounge and opened a door emblazoned with a sign that read: "Don't Bother."

"I presume the sign's telling folks not to bother to knock," I said to Jim Bob as he sprang to his feet. He'd been hunched in front of the computer on his desk; I'd had only a momentary glimpse of the screen before he blocked it, but boobs are boobs—and these were doozies.

He bared his teeth at me in what he may have thought was a smile of sorts. "What it means is don't bother to ask, 'cause the answer's not gonna be to your liking. That applies to you, too. Now that we've got that clear, you can run along. I'm busy with the payroll."

"That was one of your employees?" I said as I sat down and made myself comfortable. "I don't recall her bagging my groceries."

He turned around and punched a button on the keyboard, sending the pornographic image into the void. He resumed his seat and gave me a wary look, since we both knew anything I dropped to Ruby Bee and Estelle would be common knowledge within a matter of hours. "It ain't anything worse than an issue of *Penthouse*," he said, attempting to sound amiable, if not apologetic. It was likely that visions of Brother Verber's next sermon were flitting through his mind—as well as Mrs. Jim Bob's suffocating disapproval. His peccadilloes had cost him the price of several pink Cadillacs and a boggling amount of new upholstery. "No need to go talking about it," he added. "All kinds of junk mail comes in ever'day."

"So I saw," I said sweetly, even though it was clear who had the upper hand for the moment. I'd never categorize

Jim Bob as a sacrificial goat, having too much respect for the caprines of this world, but damned if I wasn't going to take advantage of the situation. "What's your problem with Lottie's proposal?"

He ran his hand through his stubbly gray hair. "I'm just not sure it's for the best. Maggody's a quiet little town. You should know, since you get a generous salary for doing nothing more than running speed traps and lecturing teenagers about littering the banks of Boone Creek with beer cans and condoms. Maybe it ought to stay that way instead of hurtling itself into places like the Internet. I don't want to see happy hour at Ruby Bee's replaced with a web site."

There were many words I could (and often did) use to describe Jim Bob, but "sentimental" was not one of them. I stared at him, giving him plenty of time to squirm, before finally saying, "Do you believe Mrs. Jim Bob's going to find out what all you've been doing with this computer?"

"What if she decides we should have one at home? This Justin Bailey ain't gonna control access on it. There's no telling what she might stumble across, and I don't want to be in the country when she does."

"Can't you delete your . . . participation?"

Jim Bob gave me a forlorn look, still under the delusion I was feeling flickers of sympathy. "I reckon you don't know much about the Internet, do you? I went into a chat room a few months back, and—"

"Chat room?" I echoed, imagining the Taj Mahal suite at the motel next to the Dew Drop Inn. I'd never set foot in it, mind you, but I'd heard tales of an enormous Jacuzzi, faux marble columns, brass elephants bearing silk flower arrangements, and a swing with a red plush cushion. I could easily place Jim Bob there in the company of his last girlfriend, the infamous blond bimbo Cherri Lucinda Crate. Chatting.

Yeah, sure.

He snickered at my expression. "On the Internet, fer chrissake. Folks just join in a conversation on the screen, typing their responses. Most of them are likely to be teenagers, from what the little pustules write. Every now and then you run across someone of a more mature disposition and agree to exchange photographs and the like. I didn't realize they could make copies and stick 'em up like flyers for a cyberspace church supper."

"I can't imagine your wife browsing through porn sites."

"There's ways to search for things," he said morosely. "Those goddamn high school brats'll have theirselves a field day if they find"—he gulped—"certain photos."

"Why don't I have a word with Justin about this? Maybe he can do something to keep them from searching for graphic displays of your lily-white ass. You know something, Mr. Mayor? If we don't get this computer lab at the school, I may buy one for myself and learn how to use it. Heaven knows I have plenty of free time, since all I do these days is run speed traps and lecture teenagers. I read somewhere that you can print images right off the screen. Is Mrs. Jim Bob in the market for new wallpaper?"

"That smacks of blackmail, Miss Chief of Police. I could fire you on the spot if I were a mind to." He snapped his fingers (a knack not all Buchanons have mastered). "That's all it'd take and you'd be history."

I suspected he'd prefer to turn me into an anthill of

pulverized dust. I shook my head. "No, I'd be unemployed. That way I could stay up all night playing with my computer and learning how to do mysterious things. I can hardly wait to start expanding my horizons. You didn't share any frontal poses or intimacies with farm stock, did you? I'm not sure I could handle those in the wee hours of the morning."

His yellow eyes slitted like those of a particularly irate water moccasin. "You got no call to say things like that."

"I was just asking, for pity's sake. Roy might have a heart attack if I started screaming at three in the morning. I assume you wouldn't want that on your nonexistent conscience." I sat back and waited for a moment. "The way I see it, Jim Bob, is that you'd better give Lottie the okay. I'll speak to Justin, doing the best I can not to implicate you personally. In the meantime, I suggest you hustle back to this chat room and see how much damage can be undone. You've got about three days."

"Three days!" he screeched, rocking back in his chair so far that he almost went over. "Lottie's got to find these fool computers. The portable classroom can't be moved until there's a concrete slab. The boys at the electric co-op and the telephone company ain't sitting around, twiddling their thumbs and . . ." His eyes were now so slitted I doubted he could see much of anything, including my expression. "Already done, ain't it?"

I shrugged. "You want to call Lottie or shall I run by the high school and tell her the good news?"

"Whatever," he growled as he turned back to his computer. "Tell her, don't tell her, or throw yourself under a school bus. It's all the same to me. Next time you drop by and see the sign on my door, pay attention to it."

"See you and the missus at the first class," I said cheerily, then went back through the remains of the employee lounge. In the store proper, Kevin was industriously mopping the floor with scuzzy brown water, and Idalupino was bent over the drawer of a cash register, flashing glimpses of her cleavage to Nikita Buchanon, who was surely a second cousin once removed or a first cousin twice removed, or even her stepbrother. Consanguinity's not a clan priority. When your family tree has no branches, all there is to do is shinny on up.

I didn't much want to track Justin down in Farberville, but I wasn't at all confident that we could discuss the situation in private if I waited until he and his wife moved into the Pot O' Gold. Eula Lemoy has the eyesight, if not the brains, of a vulture. If I so much as drove past her trailer, Ruby Bee would be demanding a full report within the hour. I have no qualms about telling lies to my mother, but she's often shrewd enough to dredge out the truth.

I headed for the high school.

~~~~~~~~~~~~~~~

Brother Verber gazed out the window of the rectory at the trees lining the banks of Boone Creek. There was something almost poetic about them, he told himself as he took a gulp of sacramental wine and wiped away a tear. They were bleak, just like he was. Their leaves had withered and been blown away by gusts of winter wind. So had his.

He stood in his pajamas and robe, his toenails increasingly riddled with fungus, his corns throbbing, his molar turning a most disturbing shade of black, his sciatica sending twinges down his leg. Love, he thought, genuine and perfect love, had not been sent his way. Accreditation from the mail-order seminary in Las Vegas had given him a divinity degree, but not fulfillment.

He sank to his knees, put down his glass of wine, and lifted his eyes. "Lord," he began, "I realize you've pretty much ignored me so far, but I'm thinking now is the time to do something to prove myself worthy of your favor. Thing is, I ain't sure what it is. I stopped subscribing to certain magazines a while back, and I haven't watched a single talk show since that one featuring women that had sex with their husbands' mothers, though you got to admit it was mildly entertaining."

The Good Lord failed to respond.

Brother Verber cinched the belt of his bathrobe. It was clear that his slate was clean for the time being, in that lightning hadn't struck the rectory. One could almost think that the Good Lord was smiling down on Willard Verber, his humble servant and eager gofer when sin was at hand and satanism on the rise.

"So what do you think about this Internet thing?" he asked, staying on his knees out of piety as much as the difficulty he was experiencing as he futilely tried to push himself up. "You have any thoughts on this?"

The Good Lord wasn't jumping in.

With a grunt, Brother Verber made it back to the sofa. He himself, as leader of the flock and defender against wickedness, knew what lay ahead for his lambs, should they frolic, like the innocents they were, onto fresh green pastures riddled with land mines.

He was in the throes of torment when someone commenced to pound on his door. He gulped down the last of the wine, stuck the glass under the couch, and rose with the dignity befitting his position, which in his opinion, was pushing sainthood, if not the main selection of the Martyr of the Month Club.

"Why, Sister Barbara," he said as he opened the door and stepped back, "what a fascinating surprise this is. I do hope everything's well with you."

"It's the middle of the afternoon," she said. "Is there a reason why you're still wearing your pajamas?"

"Of course there is," Brother Verber replied, wiping his forehead with the cuff of his bathrobe. He toyed with hinting at the onset of a disease along the lines of tuberculosis or hepatitis, then cast aside deceit and lowered his head. "I have been in battle with Satan hisself. I have been begging the Lord to arm me so I can go forth into combat. I have to provide leadership to the community, even when I myself am not sure which path is the righteous one."

"What's got Satan riled today?" she asked as she sat down and made sure her skirt was properly covering her knees.

"The Internet," he said with a soulful sigh. "My little congregation's never been exposed to cable, much less the possibility of pornography." Inspiration struck. "So I'm in my pajamas because I've spent all day thinking about Sunday's sermon. I'm a virgin when it comes to the corruption out there. How can I warn folks when I don't even know what they're up against? I've been racking my mind, but I can't seem to come up with a biblical passage dealing with this, Sister Barbara. When Paul wrote his epistles to the Corinthians and Galatians, he didn't send 'em by E-mail."

"Obviously not. I had a long talk with Lottie this

morning and decided to vote in favor of this computer lab at the high school. The students would most likely be better off taking penmanship and rhetoric, but times have changed."

Brother Verber gazed uneasily at her. "You're in favor of this? What about Jim Bob?"

"Jim Bob is about to change his mind," she said. "We have prayed over it. Arly went by the supermarket to make sure he agreed."

"So it's gonna happen," he said, sliding down on the sofa. "I might as well pack my bags. No telling where I'll end up—in a homeless shelter, hunkered in a culvert, or, most likely, tucked away in a drawer at a mortuary, a toe tag dangling like a Christmas ornament. Sister Barbara, I just want you to know how—"

"What are you talking about? This is a computer lab, not an inquisition. There's no reason to think this will have any effect on you, Brother Verber. You'll write up Bible verses and the topic of your next sermon, along with the dates of Sunday school pageants."

He snuffled. "If only . . ."

Mrs. Jim Bob edged away from his thigh, which was pressing against hers. "If only what?"

"I'd been born a hundred years ago, when the pious citizens of a town like Maggody looked for spiritual guidance from the leader of their congregation, not from some blasted computer in a trailer. I'm here to offer counseling and pray with them, but now they'll find someone on the Internet that'll absolve them of their sins without ever suggesting they ought to drop a dollar or two in the collection plate." He pulled a handkerchief from his pocket and wiped his eyes. "Ain't none of them going to seek my help, Sister Barbara. You just watch the number of folks at the services dwindle. I won't even be preaching to the choir, 'cause there won't be anybody except for Elsie McMay."

Mrs. Jim Bob winced. "And she can't carry a tune any further than she can a potbellied stove."

"Before we know what's happening, the roof of the church will commence to leaking and the floors to buckling. The Wednesday potlucks will be nothing more than the odd green-bean casserole and a plate of brownies."

"Mice, roaming freely."

"Or even rats," he said damply. "Once they've got free run of the church, what's to keep them from invading the rectory?"

She caught herself before she patted his shoulder, which might have set off a torrent of misery. "It's not all that bad, Brother Verber. I'll make sure that everybody in the Missionary Society understands the importance of attending services on a regular basis. The pews won't be empty."

"Are you sure?" he asked as he blew his nose, then thrust the wadded handkerchief in his pocket.

Mrs. Jim Bob was averse to sinking into such sins as vanity, but she saw no choice. "I'm sure."

4

I'd done all I could to bring the millennium, as in computer literacy, careening into Maggody like a brakeless semi. Once Jim Bob buckled under, the school board voted its unanimous approval, with the exception of Peteet, who'd last been spotted walking in a distinctly bowlegged manner toward Boone Creek. Over the last couple of days, I'd gone into Farberville twice and knocked on the door of the Baileys' apartment; most likely they were out scouting for cardboard boxes and friends eager to spend a day of manual labor in exchange for a keg of beer.

Been there, done that.

There'd been activity behind the high school gym. Telephone and electric lines had been laid. Seekwell Buchanon had run Joyce Lambertino's car into a ditch to avoid sideswiping a cement truck, but everybody'd survived and the foundation had been poured without ceremony. Half the senior class had scratched their initials in the wet concrete, but that was to be expected (mine were on the sidewalk outside the gym). Lottie Estes had come by Ruby Bee's to discuss interior decor in the not-so-very portable building that had been hauled over from the elementary school. Since no one seemed to know what colors went nicely with the World Wide Web, beige carpet and blue gingham curtains had won out. Justin was to preside from a desk Lottie had found in the storage room in the high school basement. Ruby Bee donated a beer mug and a handful of sharpened #2 pencils. Millicent McIlhaney brought by several arrangements of plastic flowers. Roy Stiver contributed an antique swivel chair, leather-backed, carved armrests and all, that had once graced a now defunct savings and loan. Elsie McMay dropped off a calendar with depictions of puppies and kittens; Ruby Bee'd accepted it with a nice smile, then set it aside, since it was from 1984. Based on the barroom buzz, I suspected more than one citizen was polishing an apple in anticipation of the big day.

I, on the other hand, hadn't so much as purchased a can of applesauce for the teacher. I'll admit I was curious about all this Internet hype, but it reeked of the very world I'd abandoned in order to escape. Lowbrow (no reference to the Buchanons) appealed more than high tech. Cable would have sufficed.

Sheriff Dorfer had been keeping me busy with a spurt of truck thefts, and I was dutifully writing up dry, useless reports when the telephone rang. I eyed it with what might be described as heartfelt aversion. Having made progress with the paperwork, I was not excited at the chance to tackle a domestic disturbance or a gory wreck. Or my mother, who called several times a day to ask me what I was doing, when I'd show myself for the daily offering of meat and potatoes, or how I planned to hook a nice man and settle down before I withered on the vine like Perkin's eldest.

None of her questions were multiple choice.

I picked up the receiver. "Arly Hanks here."

"We got us a problem," snarled Jim Bob. "Get your ass over here and deal with it."

"Housewives running wild down the aisles with shopping carts? Should I bring my radar gun?" I hesitated as I caught the sound of wailing in the background. "What's going on?"

"Beats the hell out of me. From all the commotion, you'd think we found the image of Jesus on a head of cabbage in the produce department. Half the women in the store are carrying on something fierce. You want to keep your job, Chief Hanks, you'd better keep the peace, too!"

With his customary charm, he slammed down the receiver. I applied a fresh coat of lipstick and buffed my badge on my shirt cuff. Although it occurred to me that Brother Verber might be the one to call in situations involving botanical icons, I ambled down the road toward the SuperSaver, checking the sky for signs of celestial heralds.

A few hawks were drifting over Cotter's Ridge, and a sliver of silver much higher suggested an airplane was transporting lucky souls to some distant destination. Other than that, all I could see were low-lying clouds, spitting out a few drops of rain but without any sort of commitment. Maybe, maybe not.

Whatever was happening inside the SuperSaver had not spread to the parking lot. Raz Buchanon was loading bags of groceries into the back of his pickup, while Marjorie, his pedigreed sow, sat impassively in the passenger seat, headphones tucked under her expansive pink ears, drool looped below her jowls, eyes closed in what might have been porcine ecstasy. At no time in the most distant of futures did I want to be informed of her audio preferences, be it the Beach Boys or a books-on-tape rendition of *Charlotte's Web*. A very tight-lipped Eileen Buchanon was thrusting a cart in front of her as she searched for her car. Despite the sporadic rain, Millicent McIlhaney and Elsie McMay were deep in discussion over the tailgate of Millicent's station wagon. I'd heard rumors about Darla Jean's latest escapades with the track team, so the topic was not challenging to guess. Darla Jean, to put it diplomatically, was into pole-vaulting.

Inside the store, things were less tranquil. The sound I'd heard over the telephone was coming from the cubicle, where several of the checkers were huddled around someone whose distress was less than subtle. Kevin was brandishing a mop near the door as if to smack an unseen gangster. Dahlia was white-faced and mute behind the double stroller, but its occupants were screeching either out of fear or amusement.

Jim Bob grabbed my arm. "About time you got here."

I consulted my watch. "About ten o'clock, actually. What's going on?"

"Gawd, I dunno. That girl, the one making most of the stink, she says someone kidnapped her little boy. We've been up and down every aisle looking for him, but if he was ever here, he's long gone. Kevin checked the restroom, lounge, and cold storage."

"What about the loading dock?" I asked.

"I didn't just get off the watermelon truck, fer chrissake," Jim Bob said, looking a bit gray despite his belligerence. "He must have wandered out the front door while she was looking at tabloids or something. I ain't responsible when a dumb-ass parent can't bother to keep track of her kid."

"Who is this parent?"

"Some girl that's been shopping here for a few weeks. Staying out with the Hollifleckers, Idalupino sez. Maybe you ought to call Leona to come over and shut her up. If she's gonna go on caterwauling, I might as well close up and go fishing the rest of the day. Crappies always bite on cloudy days."

I remembered the girl we'd met after the school-board meeting. "Why don't you go look at naughty pictures on the Internet while I find out what's going on?" I said as I veered around him and went into the cubicle. The girl was the doe-eyed, conceivably anorexic, back-woods princess in search of a job. I doubted she'd find one as long as mascara dribbled down her cheeks like strands of tar.

"Okay," I said, garnering glares from the checkers as I propelled Gwynnie into a corner, "calm down and talk to me. Your child has disappeared?"

"Yes," she snuffled. "He was right there by the cart, but then I went back to swap the yellow onions for white ones, and when I came back, he was gone. I raced all over the store. What are you gonna do? He's not but two years old! He's so trustin' that he'd go off with anybody. What if—"

"One thing at a time." I held my hand at waist height. "This tall, I suppose. Hair?"

"Blond, eyes dark."

"What's he wearing?"

"Oh gee," she said, groaning, "a red shirt with white stripes on the shoulders, and blue shorts. Blue sneakers, probably with the laces untied. Chip likes to tug on 'em and . . ."

"One of these women will find you a place to sit down and bring you a tissue. I'll send the rest of them out to search the parking lot while I double-check the aisles and the back rooms."

"And if you cain't find him? What am I gonna do?"

"We'll find him," I said firmly.

"Please promise me you won't call Leona and Daniel," she said. "They're all the time telling me what an awful mother I am on account of Chip spitting cereal at breakfast and fussing at bedtime. I swear to God I wasn't away for more than a few seconds. I just thought he'd gone back to the cookie aisle. He loves his animal crackers, and he was real pissed because I wouldn't buy him a box. All he did this morning was wet his pants, but Leona told me that I had to discipline him. He's not but two years old!"

I shoved her into Idalupino's arms before she flung herself into mine. The remaining checkers agreed to systematically scour the parking lot, looking not only between rows but under vehicles as well. I sternly ordered Dahlia to take her babies outside and allow them to serenade the county until the search was concluded.

Jim Bob having mysteriously (or perhaps fortuitously) evaporated, this left me, Kevin, and a few bewildered shoppers. I made sure no one had a two-year-old tucked underneath a box of raisin bran in his or her cart, then told everybody to come back later. Once the store had emptied, I turned to Kevin. "Let's do this slowly and carefully. We'll go up and down every aisle in case this child is hiding behind boxes of soap flakes or bags of dog food. After that, we'll make sure he isn't curled asleep on a produce crate in the back. Give it your best shot, Kevin; you may turn out to be a local hero if you find him."

"Do you think I'd be on the six o'clock news?" he asked with a gulp.

"Oh yes," I murmured. "Put down the mop."

"But what if some horrible pervert is lurking in the shadows? You dint even bring your gun, Arly. He could come rushing at us, and the only way we could save the baby would be if I whacked him upside the head and—"

"Put down the mop, Kevin."

"If it was Rose Marie or Kevvie Junior, I know what I'd do," he said as he reluctantly dropped his mop. "Rip his ears right off his head, I reckon. Yank out his tongue and stomp it on the floor. That's what fathers'd do, you know."

I patted his arm. "And you're one of the best, Kevin. Now, let's find Chip. You start with the produce aisle."

When we'd done all the aisles and met at the picnic tables by the delicatessen, I was beginning to feel a bit panicky. We searched the employees lounge and Jim Bob's new office, the restroom, the cold storage filled with crates of vegetables, and the meat locker. Kevin and I shouted Chip's name until we sounded as though our throats had been scraped raw with emery boards.

I was hesitating by the door of the lounge, wondering if it was time to call the sheriff's department, the FBI, or even the Mounties, when a blond-headed toddler in a red shirt with white stripes on the shoulders came stumbling into view. No fanfare, no fireworks, no network anchor.

"Dada," he burbled.

He was less pleased when I grabbed him up. "Chip!

Where were you? Are you all right? Did anyone hurt you?"

He was so much less pleased, in fact, that he began to cry, and with daunting volume. Unable to do anything to calm him, I carried his wriggling body to the cubicle.

Gwynnie snatched him from me. After a minute, both of them quieted down and she said, "Where was he? Is he okay? Did somebody—you know—molest him?"

I wiped baby seepage off my face. "I don't know, but he appears to be unharmed. His clothing is intact. He sounded fine when he appeared."

"From where?" she demanded.

"I don't know. We searched pretty thoroughly."

"Thank gawd he's okay. That's all that matters."

I sucked in a lungful of air and exhaled it slowly. "I need to know what happened, Gwynnie."

"I don't know," she said as she nuzzled the grimy lines across his neck. "All I was doing was shopping. Leona gave me the list this morning, along with some cash." She flapped a piece of paper at me. "Tomato sauce, skim milk, low-fat ricotta cheese, white onions because they're cheapest, bell peppers—"

Chip raised his wet, blotchy face to stare at the list, then began to howl as if he were mortally offended by the very premise of such a dietary regime. The noise evoked the image of an emaciated wolf dying on a distant hilltop, bereft of mayonnaise, cream, and a pat of good old-fashioned butter.

I sympathized.

"We might ought to go," said Gwynnie. "Chip's sort of upset. He gets like this when . . ."

"I need to ask you some questions," I said, trying not

to wince as Chip took it up another octave or two. "Why don't you come by the PD later?"

She tightened her grasp on the child until he had no choice but to subside into hiccupy gasps. "I will when I can, but I got lots of chores waiting me and I'll have to fix supper afterward. All he did was wander off and give us a scare. Maybe I got a little crazy on account of thinking I saw—" She clamped down on her lip.

"Yes?" I prompted.

"Somehow or other he must have got outside. A passerby opened the door for him and he came back in. He's fine, and all he needs is some animal crackers and a nap. I thank you kindly for coming like you did."

She gave me a trembly smile over her shoulder as she went out into the parking lot. Millicent and Elsie nodded at her. Marjorie did not deign to turn her head.

I was trying to figure out what had happened, when Ruby Bee rushed into the store.

"A baby's been kidnapped?" she said. "You got to do something, Arly!"

"He's in his mother's arms," I told her gently.

"But Francine said Elsie said—"

"Gwynnie has taken him home. He got away from her and she became anxious. He came back of his own accord. No harm, no foul."

"You sure of that?"

I felt an unpleasant tickle up my spine. "What do you mean, Ruby Bee?"

"I saw that man what calls himself Lazarus slinking around the corner of the building while I was coming across the road. If he had this poor innocent child for even a moment . . ."

"Exactly what did you see him do?" I demanded.

"He was acting like that sickly fox that skulked around Perkin's pond, chewing on the ducks and coughing up so many white feathers all over his front yard that you'd think it was a Bing Crosby Christmas movie. He, meaning Lazarus, cut across the parking lot and went behind the Suds of Fun. I can't tell you after that, but he looked mighty furtive, if you know what I mean. You ought to do something before he molests more children."

I held up my hands. "As far as any of us know, he hasn't molested anyone. You sound as if you're ready to rally a lynch party, for pity's sake."

Ruby Bee had the decency to lower her eyes. "He just has that look about him."

"What look?"

She rallied. "Well, he's living in the trailer park, for starters. Why would anybody what didn't have to choose to live there? What's more, he doesn't have a regular job or any visible means of support. He doesn't get any disability checks from the government. Most everybody else out there does in some form or fashion."

"Would that imply that Eula Lemoy is checking his mailbox on a daily basis?"

"She may have taken a gander now and then," Ruby Bee admitted. "She has to be careful, you know. He's living right across the road from her. What's more, there's another fellow that moved into the unit down by the back fence. Eula ain't the 'Welcome Wagon' lady at the Pot O' Gold, but she's entitled to protect herself. She hinted pretty darkly that she's doing just that."

"What does that mean?" I asked grimly.

"How should I know?"

"Does she have some sort of weapon?"

"Reckon you ought to ask her yourself."

I caught her arm before she could turn away. "Does she have a gun? The last thing we need in Maggody are pistol-packin' mamas in housedresses and pink sponge curlers. We're not in some urban ghetto with rampaging street gangs. I don't want anyone to get hurt."

Ruby Bee gave me a mulish look. "Then ask her yourself. Now if you'll kindly remove your hand, I need to get back before the dumplings turn tough. Unlike some folks that feel free to spend their days reading travel magazines, I have a living to make."

She darted off, leaving me to eye the checkers, who were heading toward their cash registers. Customers were returning into the store. Muzak was lulling us with a saccharine version of a Beatles hit. If there'd been a crisis of monumental significance, it had dissipated like morning fog.

I decided it might be time to have a word or two with the mysterious new resident at the trailer park. Afterward, I would have several words with Eula, who was likely to be as dangerous to herself as anyone else, if she was, as Ruby Bee had implied, armed.

My car squeaked in protest as it bumped across the cattle guard at the entrance to the Pot O' Gold. I had no idea if the embedded bars were meant to keep cows in or keep them out, having rarely encountered livestock within the city limits. Since there was no adjoining fence on either side of the gate, it seemed to me that just about any animal could enter or leave as it wished. Looking at the rows of rusty, mud-splattered trailers, I knew which I would have preferred.

Eula's homestead was easily identified by the clothesline laden with dingy underwear and thin cotton blouses. Her blinds were drawn, but I had little doubt at least one of her eyeballs was glued to the glass.

I parked in front of the trailer across from hers and sat for a minute to figure out what I thought I was doing. When nothing came to mind, I got out of the car and knocked on the flimsy storm door. "Mr. Lazarus!" I called. "I'd like to speak to you."

"Come around back, then, unless you want to conduct this in public," said a churlish voice. "Might entertain my neighbors, and gawd knows they could stand it. They've been keeping track of my farts and belches for more than a month. Let's give 'em something with substance."

I went around the trailer and found my would-be perp hosing down a very large motorcycle. He was wearing threadbare jeans, a camouflage jacket with bulging pockets, and leather boots with steel-tipped toes. All in all, he was dressed for a brawl.

I was not in the mood to oblige him.

"Lazarus?" I said, although Estelle's description had been on the button: greasy, shoulder-length hair, disturbingly intense eyes, and the overall ambience of someone long off his medication. Just what Maggody needed, I thought, wondering if I myself needed something more along the lines of backup.

"Who are you?" he asked.

"Chief of Police Arly Hanks." I stopped as I heard giggles from the road. Darla Jean McIlhaney and Heather Riley, two of Maggody's less intellectually endowed high school girls, came around the corner of the trailer and stumbled into each other in their haste to catch themselves.

"Arly," breathed Darla Jean. "What are you doin' here?"

"What are you doing here?" I asked.

Heather licked her lips. "Selling ads for the yearbook. For only ten dollars, you can buy a space to congratulate the graduating class. You want to buy one? Your ma always does."

Darla Jean backed away. "Come on, Heather, Arly's probably arresting him or something. Let's try Miz Lemoy across the road. She bought one last year."

Once they'd scuttled out of sight, I said, "Nice to see you're becoming a valued member of the community. Before too long, you'll be taking covered dishes to the Wednesday night potlucks and volunteering to mow the grass at the county old folks' home."

"Be still, my heart. I've been thinking ever since I got here is that the only thing missing from my life was a cop. Now it seems I got myself a right cute one."

"Lucky you," I murmured. "Mind if I ask you a few questions?"

"Do I have a choice?"

"Not really." I sat down on a concrete block below the back door. "You were over at the SuperSaver a few minutes ago, right?"

He dropped the hose. "My comin's and goin's any business of yours, Chief Hanks?"

"This is a small town, in case you hadn't noticed. Everybody's business is my business. I'm not keeping track of your bodily functions, but there was an incident at the SuperSaver. You were seen in the vicinity."

"Doin' what?"

I made an attempt to lighten up, although something

about him was making me edgy. "Nothing serious. A witness mentioned that you came around to the parking lot from the back of the building. I'd like to know what you were doing and if you saw anyone else."

"You think I was doing something illegal?" he said as he went over to the faucet and turned off the water. "I am a simple man, Ms. Hanks. I have turned away from worldly desires, and abandoned carnal indulgences. I'm merely an itinerant poet, a scribe of humanity's foibles, an historian of the inevitable decline of civilization as the rain forests are decimated and the skies befouled by noxious fumes. Our bodies have been tainted by polluted water and chemically sullied food. I write what I see, but I send my words into the stratosphere so that I can never be accused of allying myself with the parties destined to destroy the planet through the wanton waste of wood pulp."

He'd lost me, for the most part, although I did stand up in case I needed to restrain him. "Look, Lazarus," I said evenly, "all I'm asking is if you were behind the SuperSaver a few minutes ago. Save your sermons for Sundays."

"A day of rest for the myopic."

"We're talking about today. Were you there?"

"Why do you want to know?"

I wondered if I could take him. He was a good three inches taller than I, but pound for pound, we were about equal. His face was pasty and his eyes were bloodshot. Despite his bold posture, he was having trouble holding my gaze, and his hands were so trembly that he couldn't have held much else.

"I want to know if you were there," I said. "Answer the question."

"What if I was?"

"A little boy disappeared about an hour ago. He's safe and sound now, but I need to find out if anyone might have entered the supermarket through the back doors. We tolerate a lot of eccentric people here in Maggody, but no one—and I mean no one—endangers a child. Why don't you show me some proper identification?"

"I have cast away all vestiges of the police state," he said, sidling away from me. "I ask for nothing, and therefore require nothing from Big Brother and his confederates. There is no longer any record of my birth, nor will there be of my death. My only legacy will be my poetry swirling into the sky like embers from a bonfire. That which you call God will embrace it."

Maggody has a remarkably high percentage of weirdos per capita, due for the most part to the Buchanon clan. Diesel still lives in a cave on Cotter's Ridge, surviving on squirrels and rabbits. Amber Waves has not come down from her treehouse in over sixteen years; the number of sightseers (or voyeurs, if you will) dwindled after she took to dumping her chamber pot without warning. Peteet, as I'd been reminded, shelters his privates with aluminum foil, although it was hard to imagine what superior life forms might want with his sperm. Buchanons were not the only contributors to the statistics. Merle Hardcock, who is thought to be at least eighty years old, had gone through a phase wherein he fancied himself to be Evel Knievel and built a ramp to jump Boone Creek on his motorcycle. Wet dreams, so to speak. Although she'd recanted afterward, Dahlia had declared she had been impregnated by almond-eyed aliens and cried for the better part of a week. Brother Verber remains perpetually obsessed with the notion that satanists are performing perverse sexual rituals somewhere within his self-ordained diocese. Not even Ruby Bee and Estelle could cut the mustard, so to speak, if tested by psychologists in starchy white jackets. And, okay, maybe I'd seen Elvis a few months back.

Definitely time to test the drinking water.

I turned on my less-than-charming cop persona. "If you can't show me proper identification, then I have no choice but to take you to the sheriff's office, where you'll be detained until we can track down your record. I hear the food's okay but the mattresses are thinner than tortillas. It's up to you."

"Are you accusing me of something?"

I was exasperated enough to accuse him of provoking earthquakes, sinking the *Titanic*, and anything else that came to mind. "Just show me a driver's license, a canceled check, a birth certificate, or a damn magazine with an address label. Work with me, Lazarus. I have no desire to spend the afternoon at the Stump County jail. Sheriff Dorfer will start asking about reports that are overdue, and I'll be almost as miserable as you will. Then again, eventually I'll leave. You'll spend quality time with Big Brother's less-evolved kin. Trust me—they work there."

He sat down on the worn leather seat of his bike. "All I want is to be left alone so that I can walk in the woods and explore my intrinsic spirituality. The cash I've saved pays for rent and utilities. There's nothing left over for luxuries like food."

I realized where we were going. "And the Dumpster behind the SuperSaver provides that?"

Lazarus shrugged. "I can usually find some bruised fruit and vegetables. That broad that owns Ruby Bee's Bar

& Grill, as in your mother, sets out packages wrapped in foil every now and then. She's gonna give everybody in town a coronary if she doesn't cut back on the grease. High cholesterol is a primary cause of heart disease, you know. Lard's more dangerous than a gun."

"I'll mention it," I said dryly. "The Salvation Army has a shelter and a soup kitchen in Farberville. They're nice people who can help you get into a substance abuse program and then arrange some kind of vocational training. Don't you think you might be better off—"

"I do not abuse drugs, Ms. Hanks. You may not approve of my current lifestyle, but, frankly, I don't approve of yours."

"Mine?" I echoed, surprised. "You don't know anything about me, buddy boy. What's more, it's none of your damn business."

"My position exactly."

I felt my face turn warm as I glared at him. "Then just answer my questions and I'll leave you in peace. Were you behind the SuperSaver earlier this afternoon, and did you see anyone approach a blond-haired toddler?"

"Certain interpretations are beyond my control."

At some level, I knew I was losing the skirmish, if not the whole damn war, but I advanced on him. "It's a straightforward question that requires little more than a simple answer. As I said earlier, I don't want to haul you over to the sheriff's department in Farberville and destroy the rest of what might otherwise have been a perfectly agreeable day. Take a moment to commune with the woodland deities or whomever, then describe your actions over the last two hours. If you don't cooperate, you may find yourself with a boyfriend tonight."

Lazarus shook his head. "I've never been accused of doing loathsome things to children. All I want is to be left alone. I'll admit I was pawing through the discarded produce behind the supermarket. I found some salvageable lettuce and a particularly fine potato that I intend to have for dinner. I have broken no laws. You may believe I'm certifiable simply because I have repudiated certain societal norms in order to seek a more quixotic overview of reality. Frankly, my dear Ms. Hanks, I don't give a damn."

5

Mrs. Jim Bob sat at the dinette in the rectory of the Voice of the Almighty Lord Assembly Hall (which may have sounded more swanky than a silver trailer parked under a clump of sycamore trees, but that's all it was), chewing on a pencil as she envisioned what might be necessary to insure success in an arena fraught with the potential for unseemly behavior. Her posture was erect, her eyes atwitch with calculation, her lips curled with humble awareness of her talent for fastidious attention to detail, along with her uncanny organizational skills. She was not president of the Missionary Society for no reason. "I have a very nice punch bowl and more than enough cups and plates," she said, "but I'm sorry to say I see no way around the necessity of using paper napkins."

Brother Verber himself could have used one at the moment. His forehead was damp, and his hands were so clammy that he was battling the urge to wipe them on his knees as she stared at him. He took a subtle swipe with a handkerchief, then beamed at her as befitting his position as her spiritual guidance counselor, if not her assistant caterer. "No one's gonna complain about paper napkins," he said encouragingly. "We use plastic knives and forks every Wednesday night at the potluck dinners, and nobody's ever said a word. The Lord blessed us with all varieties of synthetics, from polyester to things like Styrofoam and paper cups and balloons and . . ."

He was perilously near mentioning condoms, when— praise the Lord—Mrs. Jim Bob cut him off. "The way I see it is that I'll acknowledge Lottie's involvement, then invite you to say a prayer to protect our youth from the corrupting influence of pornography. After that, we'll all have coffee and cookies while we get better acquainted."

"That sounds mighty fine," Brother Verber said, wondering if he should pull out his lime green leisure suit to prove to her how much the Lord loved plastics. He was loath to preen, but he knew he cut a fine figure in it. Why, when he'd put it on and gone strutting into dens of iniquity in case members of his congregation were sliding into sin, several of the ladies had been real complimentary about his taste, one going so far as to describe him as a "margarita pinup boy." The aerosol hair had been less successful, what with the ladies thinking they might run their fingers through his tresses. A goodly portion of said tresses had ended up between their fingers, creating the unfortunate impression he had a nest of spiders on his head. It seemed several of the ladies had a thing about spiders.

"This reception's in the vestibule?" he asked.

"Tomorrow evening right after the first class. This will give us an opportunity to evaluate the young man and his wife. I know that I voted in favor of the computer lab, but I have reservations."

He gulped. "Where?"

"In my heart."

"I knew that," he said as he forced himself to dismiss all

thoughts of a budget motel with a bed that'd jiggle for fifty cents. "You still think they might be bringing in images of naked women? Sister Barbara, we cannot allow this. Our youngsters are already tempted by Satan hisself most every weekend on the banks of Boone Creek, right through winter. I've found blatant evidence of behavior that would make you cringe with disgust. Moses might as well have brought those tablets into the high school gym and smashed 'em on the floor right in the middle of a pep rally."

"I suppose," she murmured, looking at her list. "Lottie has given me the names of those signed up for this adult class. As soon as I get home, I'll start making calls to let them know about this little reception. It seems to me we're all entitled to take a close look at Justin and Chapel Bailey before we just hand over the power to control our moral standards. They could be Democrats, you know, or even atheists."

"You don't think . . . ?"

"It's possible. That's why you and I are gonna be in that computer lab every evening during the classes. I don't see how we can keep an eye on the high school students, but we can make sure that Satan isn't sending subliminal messages to the likes of Kevin and Dahlia."

Reeling with something akin to terror as he envisioned said couple in the very claws of Satan, Brother Verber resorted to mopping his forehead. "Subliminal messages?"

"I read in a magazine how images can be flashed in front of you so fast that you don't even realize that your brain is recording them. They used to do it in movie theaters to trick you into buying popcorn."

"And now they're doing it on the Internet? Selling popcorn—and worse?"

"I don't know why not. We're gonna be linked to places all over the world. We may have the Smithsonian Museum on the one hand, but we may have darker forces, too. I know I'd sleep better if Justin Bailey can convince me that I won't be subjected to split-second messages encouraging me to rip off my clothes and commit wanton acts."

"Wanton acts?" croaked Brother Verber, his throat constricted with panic as he envisioned the unthinkable, only some of which involved Sister Barbara and her blessed endowments of femininity. "You think everybody in Maggody is on the brink of diving into the abyss of depravity? I think we'd better kneel together and seek the Lord's guidance, Sister Barbara. I am beside myself with concern. All I have is my certificate from the seminary in Las Vegas, and most of their lessons involved establishing a tax-exempt house of worship. I should pull out my Bible right this minute and seek—"

"This is no time to get agitated. I will take it upon myself to determine if these college-educated people are the sort we want to join our community. Lottie may have her classroom and her computers, but I assure you that I'll have the last say." She put aside her pencil. "I am, after all, Mrs. Jim Bob."

Brother Verber nodded distractedly, his mind racing as he imagined Eileen Buchanon leaping up from in front of a computer, shrieking in ecstasy as she whipped off her blouse and even going so far as to undo her brassiere. Earl dropping his pants to display his manhood. Dahlia tossing aside her tent dress to expose three hundred pounds of undulating flesh. Eula holding up her skirt as she danced on the desk. Sister Barbara herself flashing firm thighs and undeniably jaunty breasts. The portable classroom literally rocking as the bowels of hell erupted beneath it.

It was too much to bare, so to speak.

"Tell me more about these so-called subliminal messages," he begged. "I won't be upholding my duty as a moral figurehead if I don't know what all to expect."

Mrs. Jim Bob picked up her list. "Expect about a dozen folks tomorrow night at eight-thirty in the vestibule. Make sure the card table's sturdy. My punch bowl was an inheritance from my great-aunt. I'd had my eye on her silver tea service, but that went to a cousin over in Batesville. I'd be real surprised if she didn't pawn it on her way home." She paused, thinking dark thoughts about Batesville white trash, then said, "I'll trust you to come up with something decent."

Brother Verber wheezed an assurance, although, for the record, he hadn't the foggiest idea where to find a card table, sturdy or otherwise.

----~~~~~~~~----

I should have hauled Lazarus over to the Stump County jail and demanded that he be booked for irritating me, which surely qualified as a high crime, or at least a misdemeanor. I should have detoured long enough to disarm Eula Lemoy and give her a stern lecture about handgun safety. And I should have taken the next flight out of the Farberville airport to any destination at least five hundred miles away. While crammed in steerage, my knees under my chin, a cabin attendant determined to make my flight pleasurable with a complimentary beverage and six honey-roasted peanuts, I could have used the time to consider the wisdom of coming back to Maggody. In all reality, you can come home again. You can also poke yourself with a rusty nail.

When I got back to the PD, I started a pot of coffee and called the sheriff's department. "Hey, LaBelle," I said politely, "how are you today?"

"Fine, thank you, if you don't count the fact that my sister-in-law just ran off with a Rotarian."

"Excuse me?"

"I seem to think he was selling used cars out by the highway to Siloam. His wife happens to be a member of my church. I don't know what I'm supposed to say this Sunday when she prances up in her tacky pink maternity dress and asks me what's going on. I'm not hardly my brother's keeper, so why should I be expected to be my sister-in-law's keeper? I can't even keep a Chia pet alive for more than a week."

"Maybe this is the time to drive up to Branson and have a nice Sunday brunch," I suggested.

LaBelle snuffled. "I am not the sort to abandon my responsibilities. If I don't tackle the sixth-grade Sunday school class, no one will. Unlike some folks that have no compunction about running off to places like New York City, leaving their mothers to toss and turn like—"

"Is Harve there?"

"You want to speak to him?"

"That would be the reason I called, LaBelle," I said with commendable restraint. Although LaBelle is Harve's cousin, she has many a Buchanon lurking in her lineage.

"What's your problem, missy?"

"My problem is that I want to speak to Harve. If I have to go into Farberville and come bursting through the doors like a crazed Roto-Rootarian, I will do so. Your hair will never be the same."

"I swear, you must have been raised in a barn. All I was doing was sharing my concerns, but you up and—"

"Harve?"

"Oh, all right!"

She put me on hold for a good five minutes, but eventually he came on the line. "You got any leads on those truck thieves? That justice of the peace out in Hasty is carryin' on like a stuck pig. All they did was take his four-wheel out of his front yard while he was at church, but you'd think they'd hog-tied his granny and left her in her skivvies on the porch swing." He exhaled noisily. "Not that either of us wants to envision that. Soaking wet, she don't weigh but eighty pounds, and she's ninety-seven if she's day. You ever seen a sweet potato that's been left in the back corner of a cabinet for six months? 'Puckery' don't begin to describe it."

"No, I don't have any leads, but give me a break, Harve," I said as I rocked back in my chair and gazed, as I was inclined to do, at the water stains on the ceiling. One of these days I'd end up with a deluge of Spackle on my face, but, hey, life's ripe with potential.

I told him what had or hadn't occurred at the SuperSaver, then added, "I need you to run a motorcycle license plate for me. Based on our less-than-satisfactory interview, I think the guy's likely to be harmless. However, I'd like to confirm he isn't a convicted child molester who served a few hours of his sentence and is out here on probation."

"You just said the little boy wasn't harmed."

"I know I did," I said, "but Lazarus was seen in the

vicinity, and he made me uneasy. There are lots of unsupervised kids in the trailer park. Will you please run the plate and get back to me?"

"I can have him picked up for questioning if you're all this concerned. I can't promise you we'll return him in good shape, though. One thing my deputies don't tolerate is child molesters. A goodly percentage of 'em have to be taken by the emergency room before they can get booked."

"I don't think he did anything. He was evasive and decidedly peculiar, but those aren't crimes. Run the plate—okay?"

Harve chuckled. "Anything to cooperate with a fellow law-enforcement agent. You planning to visit chop shops any time soon?"

"Hell freezing over any time soon?" I responded sweetly, then replaced the receiver and headed for the back room to fix myself a cup of coffee. I was stirring in powdered creamer when the door of the PD banged open.

Ruby Bee came skittering in, her face flushed as if she'd just peeked inside Raz Buchanon's bedroom window and learned once and for all what went on between him and his sow on a Saturday night.

"Half the town's been trying to call you," she said between labored gasps. "Gunfire at the Pot O' Gold! I tried to warn you, but you wouldn't listen! Eula's likely to be dead by now. Estelle's down by the cattle guard, but she swore she wouldn't set foot any further until you got there. For once, you'd better take your gun!"

"Gunfire?" I said.

"Like when people shoot guns at each other. You want to yammer about it or get yourself over there?"

"Who's doing the shooting?"

Ruby Bee yanked the cup out of my hand. "Estelle is there, Arly. I don't know why, but she is. What do you aim to do about it?"

"I don't have a clue unless you tell me what's going on," I said as I backed away from her. "Why don't you take several deep breaths and explain?"

"Listen here, missy—get yourself over to the trailer park right this minute!"

I was propelled into my car. I drove to the Pot O' Gold and stopped at the arch.

Estelle popped up like a resident groundhog. "Thank gawd you're here," she said, hanging on to my car as if it were an ambulance on a battlefield strewn with bodies. "People are killing each other. Any minute now they'll be hurling grenades. After all these years, you'd think the Pot O' Gold would be a quiet, respectable place to live, but—"

"Why are you here?" I demanded.

Estelle straightened up so she could look down her nose at me. "I did not come by to snoop, if that's what you're thinking. I just thought I'd remind Eula that I'm having a discount on manicures next week, this being a slow time and all. It was such a nice day that I thought I'd walk, despite the arthritis in my knees. It can happen no matter whatever your age is, I'd like to point out. It's never too early to take preventative measures. I'm planning to carry a wide variety of all-natural herbal remedies that—"

"Let's go back to bullets and grenades. Is Eula taking potshots at her neighbors?"

"Somebody is," Estelle said grimly. "You can hear it from here."

And I could. The shots were sporadic, but fairly persistent. There were no indications of more significant explosives. "Do you have any idea what's going on?" I asked.

She shook her head so hard her hair swayed. "Like I said, I was just out taking a walk when I realized what I was hearing. I ran across the street to the pool hall to call you, but your line was busy. I finally called Ruby Bee and told her to fetch you at the PD. I didn't know what else to do."

"You did just fine," I said as I studied the road into the Pot O' Gold. No children were riding bikes or playing catch. The swaybacked aluminum chairs were unoccupied. Doors were closed, curtains drawn. The haggard dogs that usually skulked in the weeds surrounding the trailers were elsewhere. Perhaps wisely so.

I caught Estelle's wrist. "I'm going to see what's happening. If I encounter a problem, I'll honk my horn. That's your signal to call the sheriff's office and request support. Don't let LaBelle argue with you—okay?"

"I don't think that's a real good plan. What if you get shot or something? There you'd be, seeping like a slab of raw meat, while Lazarus makes his escape. He could be in the next county before Harve Dorfer shows up."

"Got a better plan?" I said, hoping she did.

She shrugged. I gave her a crooked smile, then drove into the war zone. The gunfire was not emanating from Eula's or Lazarus's units. Johnna Mae Nookim and her brood had moved out a year or so ago, according to Ruby Bee; the unit appeared to be unoccupied. The late Jaylee Withers's trailer had so many tricycles and bicycles outside it that a platoon of pint-sized clowns might have taken up residence.

Not that I was in the mood to be entertained, had any of them ventured outside.

I kept on driving, albeit slowly, all the while coaching myself to dive like a loon if need be. Courage is best left to miniseries heroines confronted by terminal diseases; I had no intentions of sacrificing myself for a drunk with a deer rifle.

Which is what I found at the trailer closest to the back fence. A guy most likely in his early twenties, with unkempt brown hair, baggy jeans, a T-shirt too faded to be read, and a discolored John Deere cap, stood on the small patch of grass, taking shots at a line of beer bottles set on the top rail of the fence. My dear friend Lazarus was observing him from beneath the shade of a sickly pine tree.

I got out of my car and approached cautiously. "What's going on?"

Lazarus took a swallow of beer. "Don't distract him. He's up for an Olympic medal, or so he thinks. It's like the triathlon or something. After he blasts enough beer cans, he's gonna swim Boone Creek and then run to the Missouri line."

"Who is he?" I asked as I watched the guy reload the rifle.

"Name's Seth," Lazarus told me. "I don't reckon I know how he achieved Olympian status, living here and all. He moved in a couple of days ago, and now he's going for the gold. Commendable, if you ask me."

The rifle fired and a beer bottle splintered into the pasture beyond the fence.

"Gotcha!" said the alleged athlete, who was visibly unsteady on his feet (and possibly elsewhere). "Don't the rest of you go thinkin' you'll be safe any time on account I'm gonna blow ever' last one of you to Kingdom Come.

Ain't no point in beggin' for mercy, neither. I drunk you, and I have no choice but to kill you so you can't testify against me."

I moved in. "It's illegal to fire a gun inside the city limits," I said as I grabbed the barrel of the rifle.

"City limits of what?" he replied with an unfocused stare. "Who are you, fer chrissake—the beer angel? As you can see for yourself, most of them are doing just fine. I ain't hit no more than two of them this whole time. Now if you'll just let loose and back away, I feel the Lord is with me."

I tightened my grip as he tried to pull the rifle free. "I realize that there's nothing beyond the fence but a pasture and some scrawny cows. Believe it or not, you're still within the city limits. The circuit judge takes a real dim view of citizens engaging in activities that may threaten the well-being of their neighbors. Firing a weapon is right at the top of the list."

"This ain't a weapon," he said. "This is my cousin Kyle's new Remington. He brought it out so I could try it."

"Where is he?"

Seth sniggered like a fifth-grader. "He got some chili fries at the Dairee Dee-Lishus, but they didn't agree with him. Last time I went into the trailer, he was clutching the toilet for dear life. You're welcome to go on in if you want. Now if you'll kindly remove your hand, I'd like to—"

It took little effort to remove the rifle from him. I gave him just enough of a shove to send him sprawling on his butt. "Let me see some identification," I said.

"You say that to all the guys?" drawled Lazarus. "Is the Pot O' Gold the local version of a singles bar? I'm a

Capricorn, if that matters, and I just love to take long walks in the rain."

I tossed the rifle in the backseat of my car and grabbed Seth's ankle. "Start explaining."

"Kyle ain't gonna like that. He only bought it day 'fore yesterday at a gun show in Springfield. Claims he paid a hundred dollars, but as far as I can tell, the sight's way off. If he thinks he can get a deer with that piece of crap, he might as well close his eyes."

I realized the guy was far too drunk to offer anything marginally coherent. My choices were, alas, to leave him in the muddy grass or haul his sorry ass into Farberville, book him, and fill out yet more paperwork. You never see cops on television filling out paperwork, but bear in mind the show's only on once a week. The other six days of their fictitious existence are occupied with paperwork. High drama it's not.

"How old are you, Seth?" I asked, my foot planted on his back as I felt his back pockets for a wallet.

"Twenty come May."

"And your last name?"

"Smith." He wiggled free and sat up to give me a wounded look. His features were even, his hair hacked off at his ears, his complexion comparable to raw biscuit dough. A jagged scar on his forehead and a bump on his nose suggested he'd been in a fight or two. I had a feeling he hadn't fared well, but the justice of the peace's granny could have gone a round or two with him and come out on top.

Rather than scoff, I merely said, "And what are you doing here?"

"Far as I can tell, I'm sitting in a puddle. I had a couple

of beers too many, okay? You can take the rifle if you want. Kyle ain't gonna like it, but I figured out a long time ago that you don't always get what you want."

He clambered over and got on his knees, forcing me once again to grab his ankle. "We're not done, Seth," I said. "I need to see some identification."

"She's into that," contributed Lazarus. "Seems we need passports to live here. You'd almost think it was some police state where citizens are shipped off for spittin' on the sidewalk."

"Which sidewalk would that be?" I said as I exerted enough force to put Seth face down in the mud. "Do I have your permission to search your trailer?"

"Aw, hell, search whatever you want."

I told him and Lazarus to stay where they were, then went into the trailer. I did a quick perusal of the front room, finding nothing more incriminating than pizza crusts and pieces of calcified pepperoni, clearly the breeding ground for the next generation of houseflies. The effusions from the bathroom gave credence to Kyle's purported whereabouts. I cranked open several windows and then went down the hallway to the bedroom.

There were no sheets on the stained mattress, and the blanket was shabby. Dirty clothes were piled in one corner; they were more apt to decompose than ever see the interior of a washing machine at the Suds of Fun Launderette. The closet held only a few wire hangers and a muddy pair of sneakers that had never been endorsed by a prominent athlete.

I went over to the dresser. On its surface were wadded gum wrappers, a filthy comb missing half its teeth, a tube of hemorrhoid ointment, a scattering of change, and a wallet that looked as though it had come from a discount toy store.

I forced myself to pick up the wallet, then made my way back to the living room, ignoring moans from the bathroom. Seth's current financial resources totaled twenty-eight dollars (plus the change). Unsurprisingly, he had no credit cards. His driver's license, issued only a month ago, was made out to one Seth Smitherman. On the other hand, he hadn't lied about his age. His given address was a post office box in an Arkansas town that I did not recognize, which was not surprising. Within the state confines, one can visit London, Paris, and Rome—and also Bugscuffle, Hogeye, Morning Star, and Evening Star. One can find Romance in White County and meet one's Waterloo in Nevada County.

I tossed aside the wallet and looked around. The tiny television set was supported by a spindly aluminum frame. The prints on the walls had come from the same outfit that sold to motels. The kitchen sink was filled with dirty dishes. The refrigerator, if opened, would shriek of botulism. The carpet crunched beneath my feet.

Okay, I told myself as I stood up, I was dealing with nothing more than an unexceptional specimen of *redneckus arkansawyer*. Some went to the White House, some to the state prison. Flip of a coin.

I left the wallet on the coffee table and went outside. "You have a job?" I asked Seth.

Bless his heart, he was still young enough to be intimidated by authority figures. "Guttin' chickens in Starley City," he said. "I'm gettin' minimum wage and benefits, and iff'n I make it for another thirty days—"

"Queen Elizabeth will adopt you," inserted Lazarus.

"You reckon? Considering where I've been at for the last two years, fuckin' Buckingham Palace might be a nice change. It'd be something to have a butler bringing me clean towels for a change. I don't recollect when I last had clean towels. That's not asking so much, is it?"

He was many things, drunk and vulnerable being predominant. I had no desire to gather him up and haul him into the nearest rehab clinic, but I will admit to an ill-defined sense of futility. I had no idea where Lazarus was coming from, but I suspected Seth was coming from an overwhelmingly dysfunctional background. I doubted that he could hold down a job that required making change. The odds that he'd end up in front of a judge were better than fifty-fifty.

"Why did you rent this trailer?" I asked him. "Why did you come to Maggody in the first place, for that matter? Couldn't you have found a place in Starley City?"

He propped himself up. "I got my reasons."

I spun around and glared at Lazarus. "What about you?"

"He puts it so eloquently. All of us have reasons for doing what we do. You got reasons, Chief Hanks? From what I heard tell, you went off to Manhattan and attended fancy cocktail parties every night. You saw more Broadway shows than I saw episodes of *The Brady Bunch*. What're your reasons for coming back? You think being in the position to push around the likes of Seth and me is gonna help you find yourself? Shootin' fish in a barrel might prove easier."

I realized my fists were clenched. Since I was supposedly the person in charge of the scene, I took a moment to put my gut reaction aside and remind myself of my obligations as a professional.

Yeah. No pain, no gain.

I stared at him. "You seem to think you know why I'm here. Why don't you tell me why you are?"

It was possible, although not probable, that he was going to provide an answer, when Seth began to heave up every last thing he'd had to eat for, as far as I could tell, the last month. His trajectory was formidable.

"Later," I said to Lazarus as I headed for my car.

When I glanced back, he was hauling Seth to his feet. An admirable chore. I've never been able to sort out the saints from the sinners.

6

Ruby Bee's Bar & Grill was locked up tighter than a
tick on a mule's butt. After a moment spent listening to my stomach growl while I considered this
unanticipated turn of events, I realized it was the first
evening of the computer classes. I suppose I should have
signed up, but I hadn't. There were already way too many
things on the list of things I should have done, including
but not limited to learning how to stir-fry, investigating
the obscure surcharges on my bank account, subjecting
my body to a gynecologist, and packing my suitcase to get
out of Dodge while the gettin' was good.

Wyatt Earp may have been tall, but life's short.

I swung by the Dairee Dee-Lishus, bought a sack of
tamales, and retreated to my apartment to watch the
news, weather, and sports. None of it was exciting,
although I was pleased to learn no insidious cold fronts
were creeping in from Oklahoma. Baseball was as exciting
as watching ice cubes melt.

I unwrapped a tamale, then opened a can of beer and a
book, in that order. Happily disregarding the dribbles of
orange grease on my chin, I immersed myself in the
exploits of an amateur sleuth with a teenaged daughter
who spoke in capital letters. The plot was less than credi-

ble, but at least there were no cats cluttering up the crime scene.

I was so engrossed that I yelped when my door banged open. Ruby Bee and Estelle came charging in, both of them a good deal more villainous than any perp on the printed page.

"I reckon you were too busy to bother with the class," said the former, eyeballing the beer cans on the floor. She didn't comment on them, but, being my mother, she didn't need to.

The latter was zooming in on the tamale wrappers. "I hope you got lots of Pepto-Bismol on hand. You ain't a kid anymore, Arly. You eat like that and you're liable to stay up all night with heartburn. Trust me—I thought I'd curl up and die after I ate that store-bought cherry cheesecake the other night. I don't know what I'll do if I hear that commercial about how nobody doesn't like Sara Lee. I'd just as soon she steer clear of me in the future."

"What was going on at the Pot O' Gold?" demanded Ruby Bee. "Estelle said she waited for the longest time, then went on home. I called Eula, and she said the gunfire stopped a couple of minutes after you drove by."

"Just a kid trying out a deer rifle." I opted for a diversion before details were demanded of me. "How was the class?"

Ruby Bee began straightening the comforter on my bed. "It's hard to say. Jim Bob looked like he'd been dragged through a car wash on his way there, but he held his tongue. Mrs. Jim Bob and Brother Verber kept peppering Justin with questions about filthy pictures to the point he said he'd find some for them if that was their only goal in attending. That didn't go over real well.

These pillowcases are a disgrace. Remind me to buy you a set next time I go to Wal-Mart."

Estelle swept aside the tamale wrappers and sat down. "As you'd suspect, Kevin and Dahlia had their troubles. I don't think Justin's ever tried to teach folks like them. There were times I swear he was on the verge of tears. Gwynnie was right nice about helping Jessie Traylor, who's mannersome but was out buying a cheeseburger when the Lord passed out brains. Eileen was there, but not Earl. I suppose he was baby-sitting the twins, though that's hard to believe. Sooner or later, he'd have to change a diaper. He probably had to call his sister over in Muskogee to find out how to operate the adhesive tabs."

I edged an empty beer can under the sofa. "And the two of you? Did you behold the ceiling of the Sistine Chapel as Lottie promised?"

"Have you ever considered getting a vacuum cleaner?" countered Ruby Bee as she perched on the corner of the bed, which was now ready for a drill sergeant's inspection. "The dust in here is enough to clog up a sink. You had an awful time with allergies when you were growing up, you know. I can't count the number of nights I held your face over a pan of hot water while you whistled like a teapot. One time I got so alarmed I drove you to the emergency room, but they—"

"Told you to take me home," I said. "They also refused to amputate when I had an ingrown toenail. Shall we continue?"

"It was kinda frustrating," Estelle said, nibbling pensively on a pumpkin-hued fingernail. "At one point this message came up on the screen that accused me of performing an illegal operation. Me, if you can believe such a thing! Well, I was all set for federal agents to bust into the classroom and drag me away in handcuffs. Justin said not to worry, but I don't think I'll sleep well tonight. How could I do something illegal on the very first night? It was all I could do to 'boot up,' whatever that means."

"What did you learn how to do?" I persisted.

Ruby Bee abandoned her lecture on environmental hazards. "We made up E-mail names and sent messages to each other. Dahlia managed to send something to Kevin that made his ears turn so red I was waiting for them to catch on fire. Gwynnie sent me a real sweet note saying she could help out with the pantry tomorrow. Are you sure you can't do anything for her, Arly?"

"I'm sure," I said levelly.

She continued. "Things were a good deal more strained at the Assembly Hall afterward. Some folks may live in nice houses and drive expensive cars, but their mamas never taught them manners. We were all drinking punch and nibbling cookies when Daniel Holliflecker barged into the vestibule."

"Unlike some who take every opportunity to barge into my apartment?" I asked.

"I am your mother, young lady, and Estelle has been like a godmother to you for"—she frowned—"thirty years. That would have made you six years old. For your birthday, I gave you a pretty little yellow bicycle Roy found at a flea market over in Hasty. You recall that, Estelle?"

"Don't reckon I do."

Ruby Bee hesitated, then resumed glaring at me as if I'd spent the evening decapitating dolls. "If we don't have a right to drop by and visit, no one does. It's not like you were entertaining a caller."

"Then let's not think about that," I said. "What did Daniel do? He didn't bite off Gwynnie's head, did he?"

Estelle snorted. "He came darn close to it. All she was doing was sitting with Jessie in the corner. What with Mrs. Jim Bob watching them with her beady eyes, they weren't even holding hands. Daniel grabbed her arm and dragged her out the door, all the while griping at her like she'd been arrested for shoplifting at Kmart. Jessie lingered for a bit, looking like he'd been punched in the particulars. I've seen starving pups with more spirit."

"Then," said Ruby Bee, passing on my latest batch of sins in order to upstage Estelle, "in came Justin's wife, all gussied up in a long skirt and a see-through blouse. Not one soul doubted for a second that she was braless. The last time I saw a display like that was when Chicklet Buchanon did a striptease under the stoplight to celebrate Nixon's resignation."

"Must have been before my time," I said.

"To get on with the story, Jim Bob choked so hard on a mouthful of cookies that I thought Mrs. Jim Bob was gonna pound him to death, which, based on her expression, might have been in the back of her mind. Brother Verber was as speechless as he's ever been in his born days. Justin tried to hustle her out the door, but she wasn't having that."

I frowned. "Her name's Chapel, right?"

Estelle cut in. "Well, she's not anything you'd associate with church. Her hair's so yellow it'd shame a daisy, and I think it's obvious no competent cosmetologist has touched it in a long while. I can't begin to think where I'd start if she marched into my front room—and march she would, without so much as calling for an appointment. I'd just as soon have Collera's mama show up at my door."

I longed to fetch another beer out of the refrigerator, but I lacked the inner strength to deal with their disapproval. "What exactly did she do?" I asked, trying not to sound too weary.

Ruby Bee seized the stage. "Nothing much, come to think of it. She was real peeved because the water hadn't been turned on at their mobile home, which I guess anybody might have been. Justin told her that she was supposed to have made arrangements. She got all teary and said she didn't know who to call. Lottie promised to see to it in the morning. Jim Bob was still trying to stuff his eyeballs back in their sockets when Mrs. Jim Bob announced that the reception was over and done. Brother Verber was trying to persuade everybody present to attend services on Sunday when Estelle and I took our leave."

I pointed at the clock above the television. "And would you look at the time? I don't know about you two, but I need to be up at dawn in order to defend Gotham City from a double-fisted plague of locusts and frogs."

"There are times," Ruby Bee said, "when you don't make a whit of sense. This appears to be one of them."

"Do you really think so?" I called plaintively as they left, then returned my attention to hot tamales, cold beer, and the odd body or two.

Dahlia buttoned her nightgown and picked up a hairbrush off the bathroom counter. "Don't think I didn't see you staring at her," she said as she struggled with the daily accumulation of tangles. Being the mother of twins precluded much attention to grooming during the day; back when they'd been courting, she'd put on lipstick for Kevin, who'd darn near wept as he described her lips as ripe, juicy cherries. These days, she might as well have worn a paper bag over her head when she crawled into bed.

"I was thinking," he said, flat on his back, his hands entwined behind his head, "that we ought to put some kind of beepers on Kevvie Junior and Rose Marie in case they wander off."

"How are they gonna wander off? Neither of 'em can walk."

"One of these days they'll learn."

Dahlia plumped her pillow. "One day they'll be practicing their multiplication tables in the kitchen. Then, before we know what's happening, they'll be dressing in tight jeans and sneaking off to drink moonshine. Rose Marie'll get pregnant by some carnival worker, and Kevvie Junior will get caught stealing cars and be sent to the state prison. Now, if you don't mind, I figure I'll try to get a few hours of sleep."

She took her rightful half of the bed and yanked the blankets across her.

Kevin sat up. "What's upsetting you, my lustful goddess? We have a home, babies, a steady income—"

"You were staring at her. It's a miracle you didn't forget where you were and start slobbering all over her like a hound dog. Even your ma saw how you were behaving. She patted my arm more than once."

"Are you talking about Chapel Bailey? I have to admit she was asking for attention, but that ain't saying that I did more than notice. Dahlia, you oughta know by now that I'd bring you a pocketful of stars if I could. You're the mother of my babies. Coming home after work is like crawling into a cozy cave. All day long, I think about how much I love you." He was right on the cutting edge of winning over her heart when he added, "But her knockers were something."

Dahlia jerked away what few blankets Kevin had recovered. "That's it! I am gettin' a divorce tomorrow. You may claim to love me, but I see the lust in your eyes when you look at other women. I know I ain't a supermodel, or even a medium model, but it's gonna take me some time to get my figure back. How many women on the inside of *Playboy* magazine can fry up a pork chop? You just answer that, Kevin Fitzgerald Buchanon!"

"I ain't never seen the inside of—"

"Pack your bag right here and now," Dahlia said. "Once your sorry butt is parked at your parents' house, maybe we can talk. I will not be the object of ridicule."

Kevin was so bewildered that he was floundering for a response. "But, Dahlia, my dearest, your pork chops are heaven on earth. Why, your cream gravy—"

She flopped over and pulled what had until seconds ago been his pillow over her head. "I already told you, Kevin. Don't be here when I wake up in the morning. I ain't sure what I'll do, but I have a feeling it won't be something Kevvie Junior and Rose Marie ought should see."

"Dahlia," he whimpered, "what's wrong?"

"I can't hear you, so be on about your business. Whatever you don't take with you will be on the porch tomorrow afternoon. You'd better come get it before Raz notices. My granny used to say he had the stickiest fingers in Stump County."

Kevin considered poking her shoulder, but he could tell from her demeanor that it might just be best to let her have her way for the moment. She was mystifying, and her moodiness lately had left him so dumbfounded that he never seemed to know what to say. She'd been up and down most nights for a good five months, breast-feeding one or the other baby in the rocking chair by the window overlooking the back pasture. As much as he loved them . . . well, there were some things he couldn't do much to help her with.

But, he thought, as he crept out of bed and pulled on his pants, all he'd done was notice Chapel Bailey's nipples poking through her blouse. He hadn't said anything, or even lunged at them like he had at his dearly beloved's on the porch swing one summer night when it seemed half of Maggody was lurking behind the bushes at the end of the sidewalk.

Brother Verber would be the first to accuse him of having lust in his heart, Kevin thought while trying to find his shoes in the dark room. But how could anyone ever replace his love bug? Dahlia was all he'd ever wanted since that first encounter in the back of the convenience store, aptly known as the Quik-Screw. His mouth got all dry as he allowed himself to relive what had taken place on a sunny afternoon while customers complained and Jim Bob kept banging on the door. Had it been one of those Kodak moments, Kevin would have been the first to buy prints.

~~~~~~~~~

"This less-than-fascinating exploration of blue-collar culture is over," Chapel said as she considered how much of the cutlery to take. Two of each, perhaps—one for her and one for the child she might be bearing. Justin deserved to eat with his fingers like a troglodyte, stuffing red meat in his mouth, but she was not about to clutter up her future with superfluous accouterments. "Feel free to burn my books," she added as she slammed closed a drawer. "For that matter, burn my bras at the next social at the church. That ought to satisfy those pigs with their condescending sneers. Use the fondue forks."

Justin was less than comfortable on the lumpy couch that was standard issue with the double-wide. "Come on, Chapel," he said, "you have to admit you showed up in provocative clothes. These people didn't venture down from the trees all that long ago. You had no call to dress like you did."

"I was defining myself."

"As what?"

"Can't you see what I am?"

"All I see," Justin said patiently, "is a thousand dollars a month plus expenses while I teach these people how to send E-mail to each other. I apply to grad schools; you take the seminar. Twelve months from now, we'll be packing up our stuff."

"If I stay here, twelve months from now I'll be wearing hair rollers to the supermarket and cookin' up a mess of ripe roadkill," she retorted. "And don't think for a minute that I didn't see you keeping an eye on that scrawny girl. She was keeping an eye on you, too, even though that boy was hanging all over her. Is she taking this class?"

"Yes, and I'm going to be polite to her, just like I am to everyone else in the adult class. I don't see why—" He stopped as someone knocked on the door. "You expecting company?"

"Yeah, I invited all the degenerates in the trailer park to come by for an evening of illegal drugs and spontaneous sex. Why don't you welcome everyone while I find my leather G-string?"

"Give it a break, Chapel." With some trepidation, he opened the door.

Gwynnie's face was flushed and her eyelids were swollen. "I'm sorry to bother you, Mr. Bailey, but you seemed so nice and I don't know where to turn. As much as I'd like to cram my clothes in a suitcase and hitch a ride to the next state, I got to think about my little boy. He ain't but two."

"Why don't you come inside?"

"I saw the way your wife was glaring at me like I was nothing but a dirty diaper," she said, "and maybe that's all I am. I wouldn't feel right coming inside. Do you think you could sit out here with me for a few minutes? I'm so scared I could wet my pants."

"Scared?" he echoed.

"It's kinda complicated," she said, tears beginning to spill out of her eyes. "I promise I won't take much of your time, but if I don't talk to someone, I don't know what I'll do. Maybe Chip'd be better off being an orphan. I can't let things go on like this."

"Go out and talk to her," Chapel said as she headed for the bedroom.

He wasn't at all sure what to do. "She says she's scared. Maybe both of us should talk to her."

"I don't think that's what she has in mind."

Justin held his breath until the bedroom door closed rather emphatically. "Are you sure I'm the person you should be talking to, Gwynnie?" he asked in a low voice.

"I only met you a couple of hours ago. Isn't there someone else you can trust?"

Gwynnie shrank away from the door. "If I'm causing you grief, say so and I'll leave. I don't know where I'll go, but it's none of your concern. Like you said, it's only been a couple of hours. You got no reason to worry about me. There's more than one way to leave Maggody."

He stepped outside and eased closed the door behind him. "You're not talking about harming yourself, are you?"

"I don't know what I'm talking about, Mr. Bailey. I'm confused and I'm scared. I don't want your wife to get upset. I just need someone I can trust." She sat down on the edge of the concrete slab. "I got to think of my boy, Chip, but at the same time—"

Justin squatted behind her, desperately trying to recall what he'd learned in his sole psychology class (a smattering of social sciences having been required, which was how he'd met Chapel in his sophomore year). "You have a son named Chip?"

"It might have been for the best if I'd let him be adopted right after he was born. I have this awful feeling that something's gonna happen to him, and it'll be my fault."

"What's wrong, Gwynnie?"

"Daniel, for starters. You saw how he acted tonight. Everybody knows I ain't a virgin, but Chip's father was the only boy I ever . . . was intimate with. Daniel makes me feel like a slut." She hung her head. "I wasn't voted most likely to get laid, you know. My ma's boyfriends were all the time pinching my ass and whispering nasty things, but I never paid them any heed. I made a mistake, Mr.

Bailey, and I'm facing up to it as best I can. All I need is a friend. I could tell the minute I met you that you're the kind of person that can see me for what I am—or want to be."

"I don't know what to say," he said honestly. "I'm not real clear who Daniel is, for that matter, or what kind of person you think I am. The one thing I'm not is a therapist."

Gwynnie wiped her eyes as she looked over her shoulder at him. "Daniel is Leona's husband, so he's kind of my uncle. Some nights he comes into my bedroom and stands over the bed, looking down at me. I keep my eyes closed, but I can hear him breathing. If you've ever been abused, you'd know what I'm talking about."

"Isn't there someone to call?"

"No one's ever believed me so far, and I don't see why they'd start now. I may lack a diploma, Mr. Bailey, but that doesn't mean I'm worthless. I have emotions like everybody else. I shouldn't say this, but when I first laid eyes on you tonight, all I could see was a knight in white armor. You'd never let anyone take advantage of your wife, would you? You'd defend her, no matter what." She hiccuped in a way he found oddly touching. "I hope she appreciates that. I know I would."

"Gwynnie, I don't know how to help you. If this man is menacing you, you should tell the policewoman, or Miss Estes, or the woman who runs the local bar, or even Brother Verber. He may not be the quickest to master the basics on the keyboard, but surely he's had training in matters like this."

"Any one of them would carry tales back to Daniel and Leona," she said as she stood up. "I was hoping you'd understand how scared I am. I'm sorry for wasting your time, Mr. Bailey. Please tell your wife how sorry I am for disturbing y'all. It'll never happen again."

Justin caught her shoulders. "You need help, Gwynnie."

"I know I do," she said, sniffling. "It's not your trouble, though. I'll do whatever it takes to stop the abuse, even if it means . . ." She seemed to wilt into his arms, like a daffodil caught in an unseasonable cold snap. "Make sure somebody looks after Chip. Maybe you and your wife can adopt him when the time comes. He's real fond of chocolate milk and stories at bedtime. Make sure you don't let shampoo get in his eyes when you give him a bath. Even though it's supposed not to sting, he gets real upset."

"Gwynnie?" said a male voice from the darkness. "I was thinking that was you. Is everything all right?"

She deftly extracted herself from what Justin had begun to view as an embrace, unpremeditated, but not necessarily objectionable on his part.

"Jessie?" she responded.

The young man ventured onto the patio. "I was just taking a walk when I heard voices. I wasn't sure if it was you or not. After what happened earlier, I was kinda surprised your uncle didn't lock you in the root cellar for the rest of the night."

"He would have if there was one," she said with a rueful laugh. "He said he'd come after me with his belt if I ever spoke to you again, Jessie, so maybe you'd better go on."

Jessie retreated a few steps. "Can't you help her, Mr. Bailey? She's got no one else. I'd try to do something, but

I ain't nothing but an ignorant peckerwood living from one payday to the next. You got a college degree. You're smarter than most everybody here in Maggody."

Justin bit back the urge to ask who among the limited population might not fall into the "most everybody" category. "I don't see what I can do," he said, all of a sudden considering the wisdom of standing on the lit patio should a car come down the road, headlights off, its driver cradling a shotgun in his lap. Or a lynch mob comprised of fierce-eyed fathers and brawny, witless brothers. Even at seventeen, Gwynnie might well be jail bait, depending on the statute.

"Gwynnie," he said in a hoarse voice, "you'd better get on home. You and Jessie need to avoid each other until things calm down. Don't sit next to each other in class, and be careful not to leave at the same time."

"Maybe he should skip classes for a few weeks," she suggested. "I'm pretty sure Daniel's gonna deliver me to the door and wait outside to fetch me. It'll be hard on both of us, Jessie, but I'm real fond of my backside."

"That would be best," added Justin, who'd last had his nose punched in third grade and still broke out in hives when he saw a teeter-totter. Computer geeks might spit and sputter over the latest program operating system, or even the merits of new browsers. They did not, however, raise their hands except to snatch pens out of their shirt pockets in order to scribble their conjectures on pads of yellow paper. As far as Justin knew, there'd been no crimes of passion in Silicon Valley.

7

After a couple of days, Harve got back to me about the license plate off Lazarus's motorcycle. It was legally registered to a more mundane Nicholas Brozinski, who'd been convicted four years previously for possession of a controlled substance. He'd dutifully twiddled his thumbs in the county jail for six months. No other priors, no suggestion of anything that might raise the hairs on the back of my neck. According to the record, he'd been a model citizen since then.

I'd had Harve check on Seth Smitherman, my hapless drunk. Seth's record was more timely, but equally unimpressive. He'd recently completed eighteen months for grand theft auto, and was, as far as the authorities believed, no longer a menace to society. This explained the new driver's license and lack of credit cards (although he might have been preapproved for platinum at a fantastic introductory rate, had telemarketers been able to call him during suppertime at the state prison). Kyle, whoever he was, had failed to come by the PD to pick up his rifle, which was just as well; I'd delivered it to LaBelle with a veiled hint that it might be used against rogue car salesmen. She failed to see the humor.

Even though I was pushing my luck, I'd run Jessie

Traylor's name by Harve. Not so much as an unpaid parking ticket blotched his record. Although Eula Lemoy's name had crossed my mind, I decided she was not likely to have outstanding warrants for anything more serious than overdue library books.

Ruby Bee and Estelle were kicking ass on the Internet, although neither would have described it in those precise terms. Whenever I ventured into the bar and grill, they were much too busy scrutinizing their notes to nag at me. Eileen had been with them on several occasions; the conversations regarding URLs and browsers might as well have been in Kurdish or Swahili. Brother Verber had tacked up a poster on the front door of the Assembly Hall that invited potential worshippers to contact ass_hall@maggody.com for information about specifics of the weekly services.

The sun was shining and the sky was blue when Raz Buchanon banged open the door of the PD and interrupted my relatively pleasant reveries. Not one angel could dance on the head of a pin if Raz were anywhere in the vicinity. His shapeless overalls and beard were encrusted with decades of accumulated filth. What hair he had hung to his shoulders in oily lanks. I did not need to close my eyes to envision myself in a pasture ripe with cow patties; Raz carried the redolence with him (and possibly the patties in his back pocket).

"We got us a problem," he said as he plunked down in the chair across from my desk and crossed his arms.

"You and I have a problem?" I said, feigning astonishment. "Does Marjorie know about this?"

"I reckon I'm here on account of her," he said. His cheek was bulging with a wad of tobacco, but he'd gotten the message long ago that I did not cater to spitters. He'd also learned to leave his sow outside in his truck. "It ain't like I care what other folks do, long as they keep their distance so I can go about my business."

"How is business, Raz? Revenuers any closer to finding your still?"

His eyes narrowed. "I ain't got a still, and iff'n I did, those sumbitches won't find it for another twenty years. Cotter's Ridge is a mighty big place—and downright dangerous lately. Diesel's taken to prowling, 'specially when the moon's out. Perkin saw him gallumping through the pasture on all fours, nekkid as the day he was born."

"And here I am fresh out of silver bullets."

Raz gave me a baffled look. "You been here so long you're beginning to think you're the Lone Ranger?"

"Maybe," I said with a sigh. "Diesel's eccentric behavior hardly rates a mention in the pool hall. Now if he was back to lurking on the bluff, throwing rocks at chicken-truck windshields, I would agree that at least one of us has a problem. I don't know why it would upset Marjorie, though."

"She has a delicate disposition," he said as he went to the door and loosed a stream of amber-colored spit. "She gets all bumflustered when Diesel takes to howlin' down behind the barn. She ain't et much of nuthin' for the last three days."

"It shouldn't hurt her to lose a few pounds, Raz. She's not what I'd describe as 'svelte,' even for a porcine princess with such an impressive pedigree."

"Mind your mouth afore I mind it for you, missy. I suspicion I know why Diesel's acting like this. He's plum tuckered out of eating nuthin' but rabbits and squirrels, so he's hunting for something different. I ain't one to mince words. You'd better tell Elsie McMay to keep her cat locked up at night. Same goes for Miz Whitbread and that pissant critter she calls a dog. I got rats in the barn bigger'n that—and a sight prettier."

"Surely not," I said, shaking my head. "Coons and possums, maybe, or even rattlesnakes—but not house pets."

"He probably figgers they're less stringy. Based on my own experience, I cain't argue with that."

I'd had enough. "Okay, Raz, you've done your civic duty. I'll spread the word. Why don't you run along and make sure Marjorie's not breaking out in a cold sweat over the idea of being served up with candied apple rings?"

"There's sumthin' else," he said, studying his shoes. "It's real likely he took some jars I hid in Robin Buchanon's old shack a few days back while I was movin' particular objects over to another clearing on the ridge. They weren't there but a matter of hours, but when I went back for 'em, half a dozen was gone. I ain't saying Diesel's likkered up, but he might could be for the next week or two."

Stone sober, Diesel was a threat. Drunk, he was apt to be a rampaging Godzilla chewing on more than bushytailed rodents. Winter was on the wane, and a wide variety of people would soon be hiking on Cotter's Ridge, from senior citizens in L. L. Bean wear to boy scouts in high-top sneakers.

"Dammit, Raz!" I said as my fist hit the desk. "If Diesel hurts someone, it's your fault. How could you leave a load of 'shine where he could find it? I ought to take you over to the sheriff's department and have you booked for reckless endangerment. You might as well have given him a loaded weapon!"

"I dint give him anything," Raz protested, hauling himself to his feet and hitching up his overalls. "Ain't my fault he's a thievin' bastard."

I cut him off before he could shuffle out the door. Despite the very real jeopardy of sending swirls of lice into the air, I poked his chest. "How could you be so stupid? Did it ever cross your pea-sized brain that Diesel watches you every last second when you're on the ridge? Why wouldn't he have known where you left the jars? Tell me that, you sorry piece of—"

"Let's not get personal. Marjorie's all jittery as it is. I'm gonna take her home and settle her down on the sofa so we can spend the rest of the evening watchin' the *Planet of the Apes* movies. They have a soothing effect on her. You might consider doin' the same. Marjorie may not be the only one with PMS these days."

I barely stopped myself from going for his throat. "What did you say?"

"Reckon you heard me just fine," he said as he went out the door.

I threw myself down in the worn cane-bottomed chair and tried to decide whether or not to call Harve with the news that we had a problem. I doubted I could get helicopters, or even a search team. No, I'd have to wait until Diesel actually attacked some innocent nature-lover, at which point Harve would hold a press conference on the courthouse steps and promise to send a posse with baying bloodhounds. Not that I believed for a moment that they could track down Diesel any more than I believed they'd stumble across the lair of the dreaded Easter Bunny.

~~~~~~~~~~~~~~

Jessie Traylor managed a grin as he came into Ruby Bee's Bar & Grill and sat down on a stool midway down the bar, but anyone with half a mind could see he was hurting something awful. "Afternoon, Miz Hanks," he said.

Ruby Bee smiled at him. "Nobody's called me that in forty years, except for slick-tongued folks on the telephone wanting me to sign up for their long-distance companies. How 'bout a beer, Jessie?"

"A beer sounds real good."

She filled a mug and slid it to him. "You're acting like a hound what stuck his muzzle down a skunkhole. Got a problem?"

"I 'spose so," he admitted, then wrapped his hands around the mug and stared at the dwindling foam. "It's Gwynnie. Before the computer classes started up, she was saying how she loved me and wanted me to be Chip's pa. We talked about running off, but—"

Ruby Bee held up her hand. "Jessie, you ought should be aware that Gwynnie's in the kitchen."

"No, I ain't," said Gwynnie as she pushed back the swinging doors. "Jessie Traylor, you have no business gossiping about me like this. Whatever I said is nobody's concern but ours. Maybe you think you should call the newspaper and tell them how you unbuttoned my blouse after Daniel and Leona were in their bedroom, or the other night when you expressed interest in taking my panties home as a souvenir. Might be we can appear on one of those afternoon talk shows that features trailer park trash!"

"Gwynnie," he groaned, "you know I wouldn't never

say anything bad about you. You seemed to like me just fine until this computer man came along. Yeah, he's going to earn more money than I ever will, and live in a two-story house and drive a convertible, but that doesn't mean he's set his cap for you. He's got a college degree, and you don't even have your GED."

"He's got a wife, too," Ruby Bee said in a low voice.

Gwynnie's face was bathed in an unnatural hue as she stood next to the neon beer sign. "I know that. The only reason I've been talking to Justin is because he's smart and might be able to help me find a way to go someplace where I won't have to lie awake all night. Daniel's taken to threatening to whip Chip over ever' little thing." She leaned across the bar to gaze earnestly at Jessie. "I can't risk so much as being in the same room with you. It's not just me that might have to suffer the consequences."

Ruby Bee was appalled. "I had no idea things were that bad, Gwynnie. If you don't feel safe, then you and Chip can move into the motel at no charge. Y'all can stay in the unit right next to mine. That way, if Daniel shows up, he'll have to deal with me first. The very thought of him taking after that sweet little baby of yours is enough to make me sick."

Estelle came out of the ladies room. "I couldn't help overhearing," she said with no trace of apology in her voice. "I'm not one to butt into people's private affairs, but it seems to me that we ought to drive you to the Hollifleckers' house so you can pack your things and bring Chip back here. The Flamingo Motel ain't the fanciest place in town, but it's clean and safe."

Ruby Bee glared at her. "You think Mrs. Jim Bob's gonna offer Gwynnie her guest room? The motel rooms out back may not have wallpaper and maple four-posters, but there's not a blessed thing wrong with them. You know darn well I had the carpets shampooed in the fall. Just last month, the exterminator came and sprayed for fleas." She glanced at Gwynnie. "I have it done every spring."

"I don't recollect you installing an ice machine," Estelle countered.

"Why would I install an ice machine?"

"Folks might want ice."

"Folks might want lima beans, too," snapped Ruby Bee. "Should I install a lima-bean machine as well?"

Estelle picked up her glass of sherry before Ruby Bee could get to it and pour it down the sink, which she'd been known to do when provoked. "You might ought to cut back on your medication. Arly'd be real distressed if she heard you carryin' on like this."

"She'd be more distressed if she had to arrest me for manslaughter," Ruby Bee muttered as she began to swipe down the bar.

Jessie grabbed Gwynnie's hand. "I bet Ruby Bee might agree to baby-sit if we took off for a few days and got married in Eureka Springs. We could have a weekend in a real nice bed-and-breakfast with fancy curtains and perfumed soap. Some of them have private hot tubs right there on the balcony."

Gwynnie pulled her hand free and moved away from him. "The last thing on my mind is splashing around in bathwater, Jessie. There's a court order that says I have to live with Leona until I'm eighteen. That's two months from now."

"A court order?" said Ruby Bee, putting aside her

dishrag. "What judge would make you live in the same house with a man like Daniel?"

"It's kinda complicated. You're really, really sweet to offer to let me stay here, but I have to think about what's best for Chip and me." She plucked a napkin from a metal holder and wiped her nose. "I put down new shelf paper in all the cabinets but the two on the far side of the range. It's getting late. I'd better pick Chip up at Dahlia's and start fixing supper. I can finish up tomorrow if you want."

Estelle's face was almost as red as her hair. "This court order is nothing but malarkey! We are not about to allow you to spend another night cowering under the blankets, worried sick that your baby might be hurt."

Gwynnie held up her hand. "It ain't that bad. Daniel doesn't drink so much during the week, and Leona usually keeps him under control. The troubles don't start until the weekend, when both of them . . ."

"Leona, too?" gasped Ruby Bee.

Jessie looked as though he wanted to dive across the bar and sweep her up in his arms like a hero in tights and a cape. "Gwynnie, for God's sake, fetch Chip and stay in the motel for the time being. I don't know any lawyers, but we can find one that will do something about this court order. It might not be a good idea for me to go to the house, but I'll wait here to carry in your suitcases. In the meantime, I can go over to the supermarket and buy some apple juice and animal crackers for Chip. He likes those, doesn't he? That way, when—"

Gwynnie blew her nose and stuffed the napkin in her pocket. "I am not your feebleminded little sister, Jessie Traylor. Don't go telling me what I ought to do!" She shoved her way through the doors into the kitchen. Seconds later, the back door slammed.

Ruby Bee and Estelle exchanged looks, neither of them quite sure what to say. Jessie slumped over his beer, looking as if he wanted to wave his hand at the firing squad and give them the go-ahead to blow him off the bar stool. It's unlikely the jukebox would have survived.

"I ain't got any idea what's wrong," Kevin said, trying not to snuffle on account of his pa watching television in the next room. His pa had made it known a long time back that he didn't tolerate sissies, especially under his own roof. "I go by four, five times a day, and Dahlia seems grateful to see me, but if I so much as hint that we might ought to talk . . . well, I been slapped upside the head so many times I'm seeing double. She don't have any problem long as I change diapers and spoon oatmeal into my darling babies. Soon as I try to persuade her to tell me what's wrong, it's all I can do to skedaddle before the frying pan bounces off my head." He rubbed a scab on his chin. "She got me here with a can of string beans. If it hadn't been empty, they'd be picking teeth out of my sinuses."

Eileen set down a glass of milk in front of him. "So you're planning to live here for the next few years while your wife thinks things over? You're a grown man, Kevin Fitzgerald Buchanon, as well as a husband and father."

"And a damn freeloader!" bellowed Earl, then turned up the volume so it sounded like the wrestling match was taking place ten feet away, endangering not only the porcelain bust of Wayne Newton on the end table (a wedding present from his great-aunt Bernis), but also the clay ashtray Kevin had made at church camp some fifteen years ago. Even though it resembled a lump of dog poop, it held the position of honor on the mantel. Eileen always got misty when she dusted it.

"Pay no mind to your pa," she said. "He knew better than to have that second bowl of chili. I reckon one or the other of us will be sleeping on the couch tonight, but that's none of your concern. You and I are talking about the sorry state of your marriage."

"You think I don't know it?" Kevin said, so overcome with grief that it was all he could do to dunk a cookie in the milk and get it to his mouth. "I was real surprised when my beloved said she wanted to keep going to the computer classes. You've watched her, Ma. All she does is hunker in front of the screen and mumble, like she was whispering secrets. Last night I asked Mr. Bailey what he thought she was doing, but he just shrugged." He blindly fumbled for another cookie. "It's like she's carryin' on with some ghost inside her computer that nobody else can see or hear. Maybe Brother Verber was right when he said Satan might be lurking on the Internet."

"That borders on blasphemy," Eileen said sternly as she snatched away the plate of cookies. "I have to agree that Dahlia's upset about something, but that doesn't mean she's stumbled across the devil's own web site."

Earl came into the kitchen. "I was thinking a meat-loaf sandwich might be just the thing afore the championship bout. The Vegas Avenger is takin' on City Boy Lloyd. It don't get any better than that."

Eileen gave him a look. "You want me to draw you a map to the refrigerator, Earl? We've only lived in this house for thirty years."

"What's wrong with you?"

"You and your son are two of the most helpless folks I've ever met," she said as she untied her apron and dropped it on the floor. "I am tired of being a tugboat!"

Earl's jaw dropped. "You're a tugboat?"

"You heard me! Heaven forbid either one of you can begin to make your way in or out of this particular harbor without me. Has it ever occurred to you that you can fix a meat-loaf sandwich all by yourself, Earl? That big white thing over there—it's the refrigerator. That aluminum contraption on the counter is, last I looked, the bread box. It's been there since you gave it to me on our twenty-fifth anniversary—and what a touching gift it was."

"What's gotten into you?" asked Earl, backing away. "You was complaining about the old bread box."

"There is more to life than meat-loaf sandwiches."

Kevin licked his lower lip. "Maybe you should take an aspirin and lie down, Ma. I'll make you a cup of tea."

She turned on him. "If you knew how to operate the kettle, which you don't. Your pa couldn't fight his way out of a vacuum cleaner bag, and neither could you. I reckon Dahlia can use my help for the time being."

Eileen left the kitchen in a manner that suggested she would not take well to being detained by so much as a pitiful bleat of protest.

Earl glowered at Kevin. "Got any bright ideas?"

~~~~~~~~~~~

"I had a word with Gwynnie," Leona said as she hung up her skirt and closed the closet door. "She claims she hasn't seen Jessie since the reception at the church. She spent the last three days at Ruby Bee's, and has agreed to put in a few hours tomorrow. She'll volunteer in the nursery during the Sunday morning and evening services. In exchange, we'll continue to baby-sit Chip during the computer classes." She made sure her nightgown was buttoned before she sat down in front of the dresser to apply cream. "I wish you wouldn't treat her as if she was a criminal," she said, leaning forward to make sure she dealt with every nook and cranny on her face. In the mornings, she stretched her muscles; in the evenings, she allowed herself the pleasure of a facial massage. Her most private fantasies involved living in a wildly expensive spa, not for a weekend, but for a decade or so, with muscular young men named Sven hovering outside her door.

Daniel was lying in bed, a hardback book propped open on his woefully neglected abdomen. "I do not treat her as a criminal," he said. "I am concerned that she might lapse into behavior that we find unacceptable. Chip didn't appear from a cabbage patch. Obviously, Gwynnie has engaged in fornication. It's our responsibility to see that she does not do so again until she's of age. Once she is, I won't be at all surprised if she begins earning her living on street corners. I know she's your niece, Leona, but you must admit her mother was hardly a positive role model."

Leona grabbed his book and threw it across the room. It crashed against the wall in the way only a biography of an obscure nineteenth-century politician could, which was with a satisfactory thud. "After my brother died, Dolores may have become obsessed with church work, but she never so much as took a drink or smoked a cigarette. She's currently at a mission in Kenya or Kenbabwa or Kenbaziland or whatever they call it these days. They keep changing the names. There ought should be a rule about that."

Daniel had enough sense to remain where he was. "We have living proof that Gwynnie is a disaster waiting to once again occur. She's more willful than any mule in Maggody. She was fifteen when she had a baby, for pity's sake. All she had to do was sign the adoption papers and that would have been the end of it. Don't you know why Dolores decided to do missionary work in Kenya? We're the ones living in shame, while she's off giving smallpox vaccinations and singing hymns in some church in the jungle."

"Living in shame, Daniel? Haven't we been over this time and again for the last month? Gwynnie's reckless behavior in no way reflects on our reputation in the community. Brother Verber hinted just yesterday that I might be selected to organize this year's bake sale. I'd like to think part of our profits will go to Dolores's mission."

"Gwynnie's a time bomb," he insisted.

"Somebody is," muttered Leona as she went downstairs to the living room. She gathered up plastic trucks and a terry-cloth dog, tossed them into the playpen, then poured herself a glass of vodka and retreated to her little room at the back of the house. Her choice of reading material was the Bible. The Book of Revelation was her favorite. There was nothing more exciting than a bloodthirsty apocalypse. Bring on the beast.

———wwwwww———

Life in Maggody was as soporific as anything I could buy over the counter, or even in the back room of the pool hall. The moon had made an obligatory appearance above the ridge, despite halfhearted efforts from clouds to obscure it. If Diesel was on the move, I couldn't hear him. Midges and black flies were still plotting their annual onslaught; we were safe until April showers brought May puddles. The only sounds to disrupt the night were from sexually enthused bullfrogs on the banks of Boone Creek and trucks rumbling through on their way to the Missouri line. I'd been careful to close my curtains so that I would not be exposed to the unremitting stoplight below my window. There was only so much entertainment to be had from the progression of green to yellow to red to green to yellow to red.

I had decided I was well beyond the need for a lobotomy, when the telephone rang. I staggered to the couch, and was in what might be described as a less than professional mode as I snatched up the receiver.

"What?" I snapped, fully expecting Ruby Bee to tell me that she'd found a dead silverfish in a kitchen drawer.

"This is Leona Holliflecker. I just checked Gwynnie's room, and she ain't there. Chip's missing as well."

"Give me a minute." I turned on the overhead light and rubbed the grit out of my eyes. "Do you think something's happened to them?"

"Would I be calling you otherwise?"

I had to acknowledge she had a point. "It's close to midnight, Leona. When did you last see her?"

"After supper, she gave Chip his bath and put him down for the night, then went off to the computer class. When she got back, she came back to tell me she was home and said she was going upstairs. When I stopped by her room on the way to bed . . ."

"So she was there an hour ago?"

"Two hours ago, anyway. Chip's blanket is gone, but not much else. His clothes are in the dresser, and so are hers."

"You didn't hear them leave?"

"I didn't hear anything, but I've been in the back of the house, getting ready for Sunday school. I like to reread the assigned passages so I can make a contribution to the discussion. On my way to bed, I detoured to see the front door was locked, but it was half open. I thought I'd better make sure Gwynnie and Chip were safe."

I forced myself to sit up straight. "It sounds as though Gwynnie grabbed Chip and headed for greener pastures, Leona. She might not have found life in Maggody to be to her liking. The idea is not incomprehensible."

"She would have taken his clothes," she said with a muted belch. "She would have taken hers, too. If she was all that miserable, all she had to do was say so. My sister in Omaha is willing to take them in. She's already got a dozen mangy dogs. What's another two mouths to feed?"

I struggled for a suitable answer, then gave up and said, "Gwynnie's been missing for two hours. I can't do anything tonight."

"You most certainly can. I know for a fact she's been running to Justin Bailey for advice. He may not realize she's underaged, but he has no business fooling around with her. You need to march right over to his trailer and demand to speak to him. If he's not there, the sheriff should be looking for him. I aim to crass pages!"

"Crass pages?"

"I meant to say press charges. I'm so upset my tongue's tripping over itself."

"Leona," I murmured, in the clutches of the classic loss for words.

"If you won't go there, I will," she countered shrilly. "Gwynnie is my niece. She may have had her problems, but I will not abide this teacher taking advantage of her!"

"Don't even think about it," I said as I grabbed for my shirt and jeans. "It's a lot more likely that Gwynnie and Chip are at the bus depot in Farberville. I'll call the sheriff's department and request that a deputy go by. In the meantime, I'll drive around the Pot O' Gold, but I am not going to beat down any doors."

"She's run off with Justin Bailey."

I made a last attempt to reason with her, although I could smell the alcohol on her breath despite the fact that we were talking on the telephone. "You have no cause to think she did, Leona. She's liable to be on a bus, with Chip asleep in the seat beside her. Seventy-two hours from now, you can report her as a runaway. What does Daniel think?"

"I'm not about to wake him up at this hour."

She seemed to have had no reservations about waking me up, I thought as I replaced the receiver. Gwynnie and Chip had vanished no more than two hours ago. For all I knew, she'd stuck him in a stroller and headed out for a long walk. It may have been rude of Gwynnie not to inform Leona, but hardly worthy of an APB. But there had been the incident at the supermarket a few days earlier. Chip was, as Gwynnie had repeatedly stressed, two years old.

I dialed the number of the sheriff's department. Harve and LaBelle were gone for the day, but some smart-mouthed adolescent said he'd make a note of my request to check the bus depot for a teenaged girl with a toddler. I stopped short of suggesting he take a class in civility at the community college—if it were offered, which it most likely wasn't.

It wasn't a requirement at the police academy in Camden, for that matter.

I was dressed and I was wide awake. The stoplight would continue doing its thing as it had since I'd moved into the drafty apartment with a primitive kitchen concealed by a shower curtain and a bathroom that might have disgraced a budget hotel in Calcutta.

Leaving the cockroaches to frolic in my absence, I went down to my car and drove over to the Pot O' Gold. Gwynnie and Chip were not sitting outside any of the dark trailers. If Justin Bailey had fled with her, his wife was not keeping the home fires burning, in any sense of the phrase. Lazarus's motorcycle was parked beside his back door. Eula's clothesline was devoid of unmentionables.

I came to a stop to admire the full moon above the ridge. I wish I could say I came up with some poetic observations, but I was pretty much staring blankly when a heartstopping ululation shattered the serenity of the moment.

Diesel was indeed likkered up, courtesy of Raz Buchanon, my least favorite moonshiner. It was a toss-up, but I vowed one or the other of them was going to be real sorry he'd ever been born.

So many morons, so little time.

8

I knew what was awaiting me when I came into the PD the next morning. I dealt with the coffeepot, watered the yellow fern on my desk, randomly opened and closed desk drawers, waged a gut-wrenching internal debate whether or not to leave the front door ajar (Raz *v.* Mold, which will never make it to the Supreme Court), and finally punched the persistent red eye of the answering machine.

"What the hell's going on out there?" drawled Harve's voice, sounding more peeved than Custer must have been when he led his troops over the crest of the hill at Little Big Horn and realized he had himself a significant problem. "As much as we'd like to cater to your ever' whim, we don't have the manpower to stake out the bus depot, fer chrissake. You got a runaway missing for all of twelve hours now? I got newspaper reporters breathin' hot and heavy over a rash of stolen pickup trucks, not to mention a meth lab in Bedelia and a floater in the reservoir. Before you get all flustered, the floater's been there for at least a month."

"And good morning to you, too," I said as I filled a mug with coffee.

Harve grumbled on. "One of the boys on the night

shift went by the bus depot, but, needless to say, he didn't find any runaway teenaged girls with toddlers. He did chance on a drug dealer we've had an eye out for, but don't go thinking you'll get any credit for it. I hope this doesn't have anything to do with that would-be pervert you're so fired up about. Sounds like you been out huntin' the wiffle bird. Don't call us; we'll call you."

I rocked back in my chair and debated other possibilities. There were no more messages, which led me to think either Gwynnie had returned to the fold or Leona was too hung over to care. I was, however, concerned about Chip's whereabouts.

I let an hour pass before I called the Hollifleckers' house. Leona answered just as I was about to give up.

"Who's this?" she demanded with enough hostility to cause Diesel to freeze in his tracks, if only momentarily. "If you're selling something, I don't want it."

"This is Arly. Have Gwynnie and Chip come home?"

"No."

"Have you thought where they might have gone?"

"As far as I'm concerned, Gwynnie's gone. It's a shame about Chip, but there's nothing more Daniel and I can do. She signed her contract with the devil. I'll keep praying for her, although I doubt it'll do any good. Will we be seeing you at the Missionary Society brunch this morning? Brother Verber let drop that his inspirational message will be about the use and abuse of the Internet. Even though I haven't been going to the classes, I expect to find it very interesting. Mrs. Jim Bob and I may have our differences, but she was right to be worried about our youth. I know for a fact that more than one of the boys in the fifth-period class is finding his way to pornographic material."

"Let's talk about Gwynnie and Chip, Leona. You mentioned a sister in Omaha. Have you called her?"

"There's no reason to do that. Gwynnie's more likely to be headed for Las Vegas. Daniel tried to keep her focused on the GED, but she's not interested in anything but sex. She had Jessie Traylor panting all over her not a week after she moved in with us. I don't put much credence on her story about meeting him at the supermarket. In my day, girls met boys at school and at church, and maybe at the roller rink."

I forced myself to stay on topic, despite the urge to say something that might have been a bit off-color. "Wouldn't Gwynnie have taken more than Chip's blanket?" I asked.

"She was real fond of dressing Chip up in clothes she found at garage sales and consignment stores. I have to admit I was surprised that she left all of them behind. She took the diaper bag and a bottle of apple juice from the refrigerator. It's impossible to tell about toys; they're strewn all over the house. We might as well set a washing machine on the porch and put a rusted pickup truck on cement blocks in the yard. Maybe we can rent some chickens to scratch in the dirt."

"What did Daniel say this morning when you told him?"

"He left before dawn for a weekend conference in Springfield. There wasn't any point in disrupting his plans. Gwynnie's old enough to know her own mind."

"And Chip is two."

Leona remained silent for a long moment. "I'm sorry I called you last night, Arly. Gwynnie may be young, but she knows what she wants and how best to get it. All we can do is let her be, whatever may happen."

"And Chip is two," I repeated.

"She's not going to let anyone hurt him."

As tempting as it was to tear into her with the fury of a hurricane as yet unnamed but destined for the annals of FEMA, I forced myself to take a couple of deep breaths. "She's seventeen, Leona. She can't vote, buy cigarettes, or open her own account on the Home Shopping Network, which we don't get, but may someday. Don't you think you ought to be worried about her and Chip?"

"I am planning to spend the afternoon at the old folks' home, helping them make daffodils out of tissue paper and pipe cleaners. If you want to spend yours hunting for Gwynnie, so be it."

"Okay," I said, then replaced the receiver. They had last been seen less than twelve hours ago; no law-enforcement agencies would take heed for another two and a half days. Which would, of course, give Gwynnie ample opportunity to be three and a half states away. Which might be fine. Leona did not sound as though she were disturbed by the unannounced departure, and I certainly wasn't.

Or maybe I was.

I left the unread newspaper on my desk and drove over to the Pot O' Gold Mobile Home Park. Snotty-nosed children were hurling various things at each other; inquiring minds did not want to know what they were scooping out of polluted drainage ditches. Eula's clothesline flapped harder than the flags in front of the UN building. Dogs looked ready to chew off my tires if I dared slow down. Men in torn undershirts and boxer shorts scratched themselves in the limited privacy of their patios. If ever there were an enclosure that should have been overshadowed by a nuclear power plant, it was the Pot O' Gold. Mutations were already in progress.

Justin and Chapel Bailey were renting a trailer once occupied by Vitrio Buchanon, who'd involuntarily taken up residence in the state prison some five years ago for digging up half the bodies in a private cemetery out past Hasty. He'd claimed to be investigating a miracle cure for impotency, but the county prosecutor hadn't bought it. Pawnbrokers across the county had bought plenty of antique jewelry, however, as well as creepy little nuggets of gold and silver.

I parked, stared down a child with a water gun until he dodged behind a tree, then knocked on the door.

The woman who opened it failed to smile. "We've already had eleven invitations to area churches, from the Assembly of God to the Zion Fellowship Hall. I can assure you that we will not be attending any of them, or yours, either."

"I'm the chief of police," I said, "and the PD can't afford hymnals."

"Good. Arrest that biker down the road. He was roaring around half the night, and every coyote in the county was howling." She gave me a dry smile. "While you're at it, turn off the damn tree frogs."

"You're Chapel Bailey?"

"Arly Hanks, right? Come in and have some coffee. Justin's off fishing. His only encounters with nature thus far have been to pay some kid to mow the lawn. Now he's Stanley Kowalski, survivor of the Stone Age, bearing the raw meat home from the kill in the jungle. If he so much as holds up a dead fish, I'm on the night train to Memphis."

"Not into the rural thing?" I said as I followed her into the living room.

"I throw up when I successfully swat a fly. Milk, sugar?"

"Milk, please."

"Justin told me about you," she said as she handed me a mug and gestured at the sofa. "Women are rarely given your position. Don't you find your gender problematic when confronting dedicated male chauvinism?"

"Nobody's dedicated to much of anything in Maggody." I took a swallow of coffee. "I was hoping to speak to Justin. Do you have any idea where he's fishing?"

"A couple of the high school boys picked him up this morning at a ridiculous hour. He said he'd be back by the middle of the afternoon, so we can rule out Canada and Key West. Other than that, I don't have a clue."

"Has Gwynnie been by today?"

"No."

The flatness of her response stopped me for a moment. All things were possible, but she should have been surprised, mystified, or offended by the question. As it was, I could have asked if she'd seen any birds on the power line.

I changed the subject until I could get a better handle on her. "Are you finding ways to occupy yourself while Justin teaches all the classes?"

"Well, let's see," she said rather sourly. "I declined to join the Voice of the Almighty Lord Assembly Hall, even though I was assured I could work in the nursery three times a week and teach the kindergarten Sunday school class. Leona Holliflecker invited me to attend her Monday morning Extension Club and learn how to make peach preserves, but I passed on that. Lottie Estes wants me to volunteer in the high school library twice a week, but I don't think so. I'm expecting to be offered an apprenticeship to a midwife. I have, however, perfected the art of driving the four-wheel across Boone Creek, spewing crawdads into the woods. My next goal is to persuade Huckleberry Buchanon to build a raft so we can run off to New Orleans."

"Not so happy, huh?"

Chapel grimaced. "Should I be? I haven't had a single conversation requiring words of more than one syllable. Some feral maniac roots through our garbage can every night. Justin rarely comes home before nine o'clock. I spend the days with Oprah, Jerry, Judge Judy, and crude home videos of people crashing into boat docks and being hit in the crotch by projectiles. I would not describe myself as 'happy.' The word 'suicidal' comes to mind."

"I know what you're going through. I grew up here. I spent a lot of time watching moss grow on the tree outside my bedroom window. I used to write stories that featured 'Arly of the Amazon.' I don't think they were very good."

"I'm making too much of it," she said, trying to smile. "Justin promises we won't be here for more than a year. I'm hoping to take a seminar at Farber College this summer, and I can apply for a fellowship in the fall. It just seems as if every time I turn around, I encounter someone drooling—or a crawdad begging to be sent into the top of a pine tree."

"Could be." I put down the mug. "Gwynnie and her child have disappeared, Chapel. I'm under the impression she's been asking Justin for guidance. When was the last time she was here?"

She thought for a moment. "A couple of nights ago."

"Not last night?"

"No. After the class, Justin went into Farberville to drink beer with his friends from the department. I went with him a few times, but I couldn't begin to figure out what they were even talking about. Frat boys fight over women in tight jeans; these guys go wild over esoteric things like systems applications."

"Did he say anything about Gwynnie before he left?"

She shrugged. "He stopped to change clothes, took off, and came home shortly after one. The high school boys pounded on the door at seven this morning. He wasn't pleased, but he yanked on some clothes and went off with them. I suppose he's up to his ass in bass by now."

I gave her a moment to express some concern for Gwynnie and Chip, then said, "Justin didn't mention anything about what he and Gwynnie might have discussed over the last few weeks?"

"I think we can rule out astrophysics and Eastern philosophy."

I stood up. "Will you please ask Justin to call me when he gets back?"

"Without fail," she said as she picked up my mug and headed for the sink.

Her back was toward me as I left the trailer. She clearly felt no sympathy for Gwynnie, but I could understand. My ex-husband had worked late many a night to counsel interns and promising young doey-eyed (but not doughy-thighed) models. He'd ended up with the twelve-piece setting of china, the sterling silver service, a signed Salvador Dali print, and a rent-controlled apartment on the Upper East Side, while I had two plastic plates, a fork and three bent spoons, a one-room apartment over an antiques shop—and a chance of regaining some self-respect.

I had no idea what Chapel's chances were, or Gwynnie's, for that matter. For the time being, there wasn't much I could do for either of them.

————————wwwwww————————

"This is kinda fun," Dahlia said as she dribbled chocolate syrup into a glass of milk. "We ought to rent some movies this evening. We can put on our pajamas and make up a big batch of popcorn."

Eileen shoveled a spoonful of strained beets into Kevvie Junior's mouth, then took aim at Rose Marie, who was more finicky but temporarily affable. "We ain't in middle school, Dahlia. You're married, same as me, and our husbands are fending for themselves at my house. Neither of them is capable of heating up a can of soup. I love these little babies, but they should be spending time with their pa."

"He's been comin' by."

"That's well and good," Eileen said as she ducked a split second before Rose Marie rejected the beets in a forceful manner. "This can't go on. Soon as we get the babies down for their naps, we need to sit down and talk."

Dahlia's chins began to quiver. "I don't want to. You've been real good to come and stay with me, but if you reckon you ought to be heating up that can of soup, I ain't here to stop you."

Eileen did as best she could to throw her arms around Dahlia's broad shoulders. "We'll just rent those movies and have ourselves a right jolly time. There's no computer class tonight, so Earl and Kevin can have their supper at

Ruby Bee's. Soon as Rose Marie here stops sneezing and takes a few more bites, I'll go down to the supermarket and buy the fixin's for a tasty pizza. You'd like that, wouldn't you? Pepperoni and sausage?"

Dahlia wiped her eyes. "I have a fondness for anchovies and black olives."

"Whatever you want, honey," said Eileen, wondering why she hadn't listened to her sister some twenty-five years ago and gone on birth-control pills.

And gone off to California.

—————\wwwwwww—————

"Did you hear?" Ruby Bee demanded as Estelle came clattering across the dance floor. "Gwynnie's run away."

" 'Course I did. Lottie called me while I was doing my nails, and not ten seconds after we hung up, Eula called to say how she saw Arly driving by on her way to Justin and Chapel's trailer. I think there's something going on here."

"Like what?"

"How on earth should I know?" Estelle sat down on her bar stool, although she made it a policy never to drink in the morning, unless it was a cold day, in which case the sherry served to warm her innards, or a hot day, in which case liquids were all that could save a body from dehydration and certain death. On middling days, she figured it settled her stomach and prevented heart disease. Most mornings qualified.

"Did Eula have anything else to say?" asked Ruby Bee.

"Arly stayed for no more than fifteen minutes, then left. Chapel was standing in the kitchen in front of the window. Both their cars were there. She didn't catch sight of Justin, though."

"You think him and Gwynnie ran off together?"

Estelle regarded the ceiling until a glass of sherry found its way to the countertop in front of her. "No, it's mighty hard to imagine. Justin's in his mid-twenties, with a degree, and married. Now I have to say we haven't seen much of his wife, but—"

"We saw plenty of her at the reception."

"That may be," Estelle said pensively as she began to suck the salt off a pretzel, "but I can't recollect anybody saying much against her since then. Lottie claims she's perfectly polite, in a kinda crumpy way. Millicent had a civilized talk with her in the supermarket about the price of two-percent milk. Elsie said she was nice as pie at the Suds of Fun the other night when they were both short of quarters for the dryers."

"So that means Justin didn't run off with Gwynnie?" Ruby Bee broke one of her cardinal rules and poured herself a glass of sherry. "You saw her last night, asking him for help and then purring so sweetly while he tried to undo whatever mess she'd made on her computer. It seems to me she does just fine when he's occupied with somebody else."

"I was accused of performing seven illegal operations," Estelle grumbled. "My only saving grace was that Dahlia managed to do eleven. I don't care what Justin says—any day now we're gonna have storm troopers busting into the classroom. I fully expect to face a firing squad in the parking lot beside the gym. Dahlia will be whimpering, but I aim to look them in the eye while I smoke one last cigarette."

"You don't smoke."

"Not anymore, but in this particular situation, I ain't one to fret about lung cancer or emphysema."

Ruby Bee tucked this into her mental file of things she didn't know about Estelle over the last thirty years. She dearly hoped she wouldn't hear a passing remark about rodeo clowns or lounge lizards in glistening black toupees. "So Arly was out there this morning?"

"Looking grim, from what Eula said. I don't suppose there's any point in calling the PD."

"No, but I was thinking, Estelle, that Eula might just like to have a piece of banana-cream pie to go with her lunch. I've got the briskets and scalloped potatoes in the oven, and the cobblers don't need tending for a good half hour. What say we run over to the Pot O' Gold and have a little visit with Eula?"

Monet Buchanon may have thought he was going to have a beer before lunch, but he was informed otherwise and sent packing down the road while the door was locked. Estelle glanced at the ditch as she drove across the cattle guard.

"Arly didn't seem too upset about the gunfire the other day," she said in a vaguely accusatory way. "Elsie says she believes Arly's more concerned with staying on Harve's good side than she is with upholding the law here in Maggody. LaBelle complains that Arly calls all the time and insists on speaking to Harve on his private line, like they have some special relationship."

Ruby Bee flung open the door of the station wagon, even though they were ricocheting along the rutted road and she was in danger of taking a brief but possibly fatal dive. "I am getting out of here this minute! If you ever so much as set foot inside the bar and grill, I will—well, I don't know exactly what I'll do, but it won't be pretty. Here I thought we were friends, but then I learn you've been keeping things from me for thirty years and repeating slander from the likes of LaBelle!"

Estelle stomped on the brakes before Ruby Bee sailed out, although, for a heart-stopping minute, it was darn close. "I didn't mean it like that. Everybody knows LaBelle's shy an essential vitamin or two."

"Continue," Ruby Bee said darkly.

"Arly went to the police academy to learn how to deal with this kind of thing, and I have no call to second-guess her. I'm sure she's doing what she can according to the law."

"And?"

"I say we go on and see what Eula has to say. Where's the piece of banana-cream pie?"

Ruby Bee turned around and looked at the backseat. "We may have to save it for another visit. Is there anything else you want to say to me, Estelle?"

"I already told you I was sorry. Do you still want to see what all we can find out from Eula, or would you prefer to go back to the bar and deal with Monet? It won't be long before the cobblers are gonna need to be taken out."

Ruby Bee sank back with a scowl. You assumed you knew somebody, she fumed, but then it became plain as the nose on your face (and painful as a spider bite on your posterior) that you didn't. For thirty years, she'd never thought for a second that Estelle would have so much as given LaBelle the time of day, much less passed along gossip regarding Arly.

Estelle parked next to Eula's trailer. "You coming in?"

"I suppose so," said Ruby Bee.

"If you've changed your mind, I can take you back to the bar. I'll go on home and give myself a pedicure. I got in a new shipment the other day, and I've been wanting to try Fuchsia in Your Face."

"If it's on your toenails, how's it in your face? Were you a contortionist thirty years ago?"

Neither of them spoke for a long while. Ruby Bee at last swallowed and said, "We'd better get on with it. The cobblers are baking and I need to open up for lunch afore long. I don't mind losing Monet's business, but I have to pay the bills, same as you do."

"Eula may not know anything."

"Then it won't take us long," Ruby Bee said as she opened the door and stepped into a puddle of scummy water. "I swear, I don't understand how Eula puts up with this."

Estelle found a more prudent path to drier ground. "I don't think she has much choice. She's got her Social Security checks and Medicare. She may get payments from the postal service, but I wouldn't be surprised if all else she gets is a Christmas greeting once a year, three months late."

Eula opened the door as they picked their way across the sodden yard. "Hurry up," she said urgently. "He's been stirring for the last half hour. Any minute he'll come out."

"Lazarus?" asked Estelle as she and Ruby Bee scurried up the steps and made it safely inside. "What's he gonna do?"

"I don't rightly know," Eula said as she sat down and put her hand on her ample bosom. "All I can say is he's right on the edge. I won't be surprised when vans from the television stations flock like starlings out there. Geraldo will be interviewing Miz Whitbread, and Lazarus will be on the cover of the *National Enquirer*."

Ruby Bee risked a peek out the window. "You think so? It looks pretty quiet over there."

"Right now it may," said Eula, "but there was all sorts of commotion last night. He must have come and gone half a dozen times, and at one point, I distinctly heard voices."

"Voices?" echoed Estelle as she peered over Ruby Bee's shoulder. "What were they saying?"

Eula adjusted a pillow and lay back. "It was hard to make out much, but it was obvious they were plotting devilment. I made a point of watching the news today, fully expecting to hear about a string of ritual murders across the county. Charles Manson's neighbors must have felt the exact same way. Remember how he had all those young people to do his dirty work?"

Ruby Bee shrank back, stomping on Estelle's foot in her haste. "Is there anybody else in there with him?"

"I ain't laid eyes on Gwynnie, although I've seen her go in and out on occasion, sometimes in broad daylight. Leona'd have a hissy fit if she knew about it. She wouldn't be the only one."

"But you didn't see Gwynnie last night?"

Eula shook her head. " 'Course, I didn't stand by the window till midnight. My nerves ain't what they used to be. Bernard used to tease me how I never had any problem sleeping when he worked nights at the post office. I didn't let on that I never closed my eyes until I heard him coming through the front door at daybreak."

Estelle may have been overreacting as she limped to the dinette, sat down, and pulled off her shoe to examine her toes. "So what makes you think Lazarus is about to do something?"

"Did you see him loading a gun?" added Ruby Bee, hoping Eula's trailer was bulletproof like the Popemobile.

Eula allowed them to fret for a moment. "Not five minutes ago he came outside and set a canvas bag on the ground by his motorcycle. He's been living here long enough to know those savage little brats steal anything that ain't nailed down. Just the other day they took three of my brassieres and a real nice half-slip my daughter sent me for my birthday. She's the only one that seems to remember these days."

"Why, Eula," said Ruby Bee, "if I'd known, I would have made you a cake with pink carnations. My carnations ain't outstanding, but if you squint, you can see what they're meant to be."

"And I would have given you a free manicure," said Estelle, unwilling to be upstaged by some self-proclaimed patron saint of cake decorators. "You be sure and call me next year and we'll make an appointment. You can have your choice of any polish that catches your fancy."

Eula was about to mention the date when Ruby Bee eased back the curtain and said, "You're right, Eula. He just now came out of his front door, wearing a leather jacket and carrying a helmet. Where do you think he's going?"

"How would I know a thing like that?"

Estelle forgot about her injury as she returned to Ruby Bee's side. "The bag's not big enough for more than a few body parts. If I had to guess, I'd say it's his laundry. He ain't gonna be a hit at the Suds of Fun, if that's where he's going."

Ruby Bee chewed on her lip. "I didn't see him lock the door."

"What does that mean?" whispered Estelle. "I hope you're not contemplating a felony, Rubella Belinda Hanks. Arly's gonna take a real dim view of visiting you on alternate Sundays."

"What'd she say?" demanded Eula.

"Nothing, Eula," Ruby Bee called, then dropped her voice. "Gwynnie and Chip could be in there, either by choice or tied up on the floor. If he's going to the launderette, it'll take fifteen or twenty minutes to get the clothes in the machines and hunt up enough quarters. We could be in and out in a twinkling."

"You are talking about breaking and entering. I am not about to engage in a major felony."

"I am talking about a rescue mission. There are times, Estelle, when the end justifies the means. I reckon this is one of them. If you want to wait here, you and Eula can have a fine time deciding on fingernail polish. Stay clear of the window if you hear sirens, and don't feel the need to disrupt *your* weekends with visitations."

"There's no reason to think Gwynnie and Chip are in there."

"There's no reason to think they're not," countered Ruby Bee, who realized her position was unreasonable but was determined to stay on the high road now that she scrambled onto it. "Eula," she said more loudly, "Estelle's gonna fix you a cup of tea and find out more about your cuticles. I have cobblers in the oven, so I'll have to run along."

Estelle managed to trod on Ruby Bee's heel, tit for tat and all that. "I'd better go with her, Eula. We'll have that cup of tea another time."

"I'd like that," Eula said, her eyes closed.

Ruby Bee and Estelle left, both feeling as guilty as sin. After furtive glances, they dashed across the road and cowered by the back door.

When nothing much happened, Estelle said, "This has to be the craziest idea you've ever had. He could come back any minute. How do you aim to explain what we're doing inside his trailer—assuming we have an opportunity to explain before he kills us dead on the shag? We don't hardly look like real estate appraisers, and the welcoming committee from the Missionary Society brings jars of homemade blackberry jam and coupons from the supermarket."

"Can you live with yourself if you could have saved Gwynnie and Chip? I figure we can do a decent job in under thirty seconds."

"This is worse than when you crawled into the Dumpster. It was a wonder you didn't end up with a broken neck."

Ruby Bee stiffened. "That is not a moment I care to be reminded of, thank you very much. Are you ready, or would you rather sit in the car?"

"I'm ready," Estelle said grimly. "Thirty seconds, and then we leave. Living room, bathroom, two bedrooms, and maybe a hall closet."

Ruby Bee tested the knob. "Like I said, he didn't bother to lock it." She licked her lips. "Thirty seconds is all it's going to take. If we find Gwynnie and Chip, we'll call Arly."

"If we find their bodies, you mean."

"Let's just do it."

They went into the double-wide. Estelle took the living room while Ruby Bee darted into the bedrooms and flung open closet doors. Several piles of clothes caused her heart to seize up, but she had no choice but to prod them. She made a final dash into the bathroom, made sure the stains in the bathtub were innocent, if disgusting, and crashed into Estelle in the hallway.

"What?" she said.

Estelle's voice was so weak it was barely audible. "Motorcycle," she croaked.

Ruby Bee realized she could hear it, too. The sound was a far cry from that of the Popemobile. "Front door or back?"

"Toss a coin. Either way, we're plum out of luck."

"You have a real bad attitude," Ruby Bee said as she grabbed Estelle's arm and dragged her out the back door, which was as good a choice as any. "Now crawl under here and stay quiet."

"Like I was thinking I should stand up and recite the pledge of allegiance?"

"Like you was thinking to shut up," said Ruby Bee, pressing Estelle's face into the mud as a motorcycle sputtered to a halt within a matter of feet.

Circumstances precluded further conversation.

9

Mrs. Jim Bob pounded her fist on the door of the rectory as if it were Jim Bob's flattened face and went so far as to rattle the knob as though other parts of his anatomy were involved, in a manner of speaking. "Open up, Brother Verber!" she shrieked. "I don't care if you're in your pajamas, or your altogether! I have to talk to you right this minute! That'd mean now!"

Brother Verber came hustling around the corner of the Assembly Hall, fittingly dressed in his leisure suit, which he'd taken to wearing lately, although he hadn't quite found the courage to wear it to services.

"What's wrong, Sister Barbara?" he said between gasps (the trousers being on the tight side due to inexplicable shrinkage in his closet). "You sounded like you was being set upon by hooligans."

"It might be better if I was. I'd suggest we sit in the Assembly Hall, but I'm afraid someone might come in and overhear us. As loath as I am to criticize members of the congregation, some of them have ears like satellite dishes."

"They do?" he said as he opened the rectory door. "I would have said most of them are deaf as fence posts. The minute I commence my Sunday-morning sermon, their eyes turn dull like they can't hear a word I'm saying. Earl Buchanon is snoring within seconds. If it weren't for the spellbound attention you and a few others bless me with, why—"

"This ain't the time," she said as she began to scoop up dirty clothes and carry them to the hamper in the bathroom. She owed it to the congregation, and her position in it, to maintain a semblance of respectability on the off-chance some floundering soul might seek spiritual direction and be distracted by underwear on the armchair.

Brother Verber took advantage of her absence to toss several empty bottles of sacramental wine in the trash and put away the makings of a peanut butter and mayonnaise sandwich. "How 'bout a glass of ice tea?" he said when she returned.

"This ain't the time for ice tea, either." She sank down on the couch and pulled a handkerchief from her purse. "Did any of your courses at the seminary include how to perform exorcisms?"

He was so dumbfounded he could barely speak. "Exorcisms, Sister Barbara? You mean heads spinnin' and green vomit and castin' out demons?"

"That's precisely what I mean," she said as she wiped her cheeks. Her eyes narrowed. "Didn't I try to tell everybody about how these computers would let wickedness sneak into our community? Well, let me tell you—it's here! We might as well burn our Bibles and dance naked around a bonfire."

Brother Verber was real sorry he'd polished off the last of the wine, since at least one of them sure could have used a swallow or two. "Who's taken to dancing naked around a bonfire?"

"It's a matter of time. Haven't you sensed the moral decay setting in this last week?"

He tried to think if he'd run into any moral decay lately. "The collection plate was a might skimpy on Sunday, but Baltimore Buchanon was sitting in the back pew, and he's been known to take out more than he puts in. My toilet's started to make a right peculiar noise. Until the plumber showed up and pulled the coon out of the septic tank, I was convinced it was possessed by Satan hisself. I had no choice but to do my business at the pool hall. That ol' boy charged me a dollar every time, which was less than charitable."

Sister Barbara closed her eyes and leaned so far forward he was afraid she might topple off the couch and hit her head on the coffee table. Just to be on the safe side, he clutched her knee.

"That is not what I meant," she said in a tight voice, "and you are cutting off circulation. Last night at the computer lab . . ."

"I sure was heartbroke I couldn't make it, but I felt it was more meaningful to dedicate myself to doin' the Lord's work."

"Like what?" she demanded, snapping back like a string bean and removing his hand. "Did someone pass away at the old folks' home?"

He shook his head. "No, but if they had, I would have been beside the bed, reciting Bible verses to offer comfort and strength. I have brought back many a soul from the brink of death with my tireless vigils. I've been out to pray with old Miz Ripplegram four times now, and she's rallied like clockwork. The very moment I step in the room, she finds strength to continue on life's mysterious journey. Faith is an amazing thing, Sister Barbara. Hallelujah!"

"So where were you?"

Brother Verber found the need to brush dandruff off his shoulders and lapels. "You might say I was ministering to the homeless. There are many destitute women—and men, too—out there on the dark corners in Farberville, begging for spare change just so they can earn the price of a hamburger and a cup of coffee. It likes to break my heart to hear their stories." When she didn't pursue it, he eased back and said, "Now tell me what's troubling you."

"Well, last night I was sitting in the cubicle, reading an E-mail message from my sister-in-law over in Amarillo, when—" She put the handkerchief to her nose. "I don't know if I can go on, Brother Verber. It was so awful."

He was well beyond the confines of simple bewilderment. "Your sister-in-law is consortin' with demons?"

"No, she was telling me about her oldest son's new job when all of a sudden—"

This time he clutched her hand. "Spit it out, Sister Barbara. We're here in the glow of the Lord's house. If you was to go to the window, you could see that neon cross above the door of the Assembly Hall, blinking day and night, telling all the lost lambs that there is sanctuary within the fold. 'Yea though I walk through the valley of the shadow of death, I shall fear no evil.' "

"Do you recall what I told you the other day about subliminal messages and how you can't see 'em?"

"Your sister-in-law was trying to trick you into buying popcorn?"

"Not hardly. What I saw, or thought I saw, was a picture of Jim Bob. Before I could blink, it was gone. I sat there for another hour, staring at the screen, but the only thing I saw was the E-mail from Imogene telling how McCoy is working for some tractor company in Fort Worth."

He nodded as though this had been covered in one of the seminary brochures. "Why, all that means is you're a virtuous Christian wife who never forgets the vows she took to love, honor, and obey. Even though you didn't realize it, you were thinking about him, maybe wondering if he'd like fried chicken and mashed potatoes for supper, or maybe pork chops and black-eyed peas simmered with bacon rind, along with cornbread, turnip greens, and sliced tomatoes topped with a dollop of cream-style cottage cheese, which would make a fine feast for company if you ever were inclined. Your mind was playing a little joke on you."

"I didn't see him wearing the suit and tie he had on for our wedding."

"Something more casual?"

"You could say that," she muttered.

Brother Verber was beginning to put two and two together, although it wasn't quite adding up to four (proficiency in arithmetic not having been a prerequisite of the seminary). "So you caught a glimpse of Jim Bob in his underwear, and—"

"It wasn't *his* underwear, I can assure you, unless he's been leading a secret life. I know over the years he's taken up with Jezebels, thinking he can deceive me with his bald-faced lies. Whenever I catch him, he's always quick to repent and promise not to stray, but outside of taking him to a vet, I don't see how I can stop him."

His hands involuntarily drifted to his lap. "Are you positive you saw this?"

"I most certainly am, for the most part. I believe that when Satan found out we were all going to learn how to use the Internet, he took it upon himself to send these disgusting images so we'd all begin to feel filthy, even though we wouldn't know why. He made the mistake of sending one to somebody who happens to be righteous and unafraid of confronting sin when she sees it. He picked the wrong person, Brother Verber. I've always had a Bible in one hand; now it's time for me to take up the sword in the other."

Brother Verber felt a singular chill. "What do you aim to do with the sword? You wouldn't do anything to Jim Bob, would you? You admitted you only saw this picture for a split second. It was at the end of a long day, and sometimes our eyes play tricks on us. Just the other night I could have sworn I saw an orangutan in the parking lot behind the old Emporium."

"In a lacy red garter and high-heeled shoes?" She stood up and headed for the door. "I am going to ask some of the others in the class if they've seen these missives from Satan. It's not too early to start gathering kindling, Brother Verber."

"For a bonfire?"

"To burn up the portable classroom before Satan can slither out the door and into our homes."

After the door closed, he went to the window and watched her drive away in her pink Cadillac. He had no idea if she was going to Ruby Bee's Bar & Grill, the high school, or to a pawnshop in search of a double-edged weapon. After scratching his head for a minute, he decided it was definitely time to stock up on sacramental wine from the wholesaler on the other side of Farberville.

It would be worth the drive.

———wwwwwwww———

Jim Bob sat back and rubbed his eyes. What he thought he'd seen, imagined he'd seen, had not really seen, couldn't possibly have seen—well, it was nothing more than a hallucination. That's all it could be. He'd never been one to drink before late afternoon, but now was the time, if ever there was, for a pint of bourbon. He was thinking about going out to his truck to get it, when Idalupino came into his office.

"There's this man out front," she said. "He sez he's the distributor that handles paper products. I told him you might be gone, but he—"

"You did good, Idalupino, 'cause I left an hour ago, and you don't know where I went. Tell him to call next week."

"You left an hour ago?"

"Yeah, explain how I went over to visit my granny at the old folks' home. She's been chewing on her extremities, and the doctors don't know what to do. She's down to seven fingers and six toes."

"That's awful!"

Jim Bob closed down the computer and grabbed his cap. "You tell the guy to call and make an appointment. I cannot ignore my obligations to my granny. A baker's dozen tonight, but who can say how many in the morning? Her ability to do simple addition is drying up faster than Boone Creek in August."

He went out the door to the loading dock, tottered

unsteadily down the steps, and climbed into his truck. His hand shook as he found the bottle underneath the seat and took a gulp. A second gulp eased his nerves, and a third came close to calming him down.

He wasn't even sure if anything had actually happened. There he'd been, sending an E-mail to Ldesiree@hot-body.com> when all of a sudden, across his screen, not more than for a fly's fart of a second . . .

The bottle was damn near empty before he allowed himself to give serious consideration to what he'd seen, which was an image of Mrs. Jim Bob, naked as the day she was born, but a sight older. A flicker of thigh, a flash of unfettered breast, the unmistakable self-righteous smirk surrounded by a helmet of hair.

Could a guilty conscience create such a thing?

Problem was, Jim Bob thought as he finished off the bottle and tossed it out into the parking lot, he didn't have a conscience, as Arly had said, guilty or otherwise. There were times he felt kinda bad about lying to Mrs. Jim Bob, but he couldn't up and say he was going over to Tonya's apartment at lunchtime or spending the afternoon with Cherri Lucinda.

What the hell was he supposed to say?

Lottie Estes knocked on the door of Justin Bailey's trailer, then sat down on the aluminum chair on the patio. There was something so wrong, so evil, going on. She knew darn well that her eyesight was less than perfect, but at the same time she knew what she'd seen at the computer lab.

She let her head fall back. No, she reminded herself as she took cleansing breaths like she'd learned to do when

Perkin's eldest taught the class in yoga, she didn't know what she'd seen. It had come and gone so fast that all she could think was that she was protein-deficient. Hadn't her nephew been nagging her about calcium and iron tablets? She'd fully intended to eat an apple a day and all that, but it was hard to get fired up about spinach and calf's liver.

A pack of filthy children ran by, screeching at each other. Lottie, temporary mistress of her universe, willed them to go away. Only Justin could assure her that she had not seen a fleeting image of Brother Verber engaged in a sexual encounter with . . .

She stood up. She couldn't have seen it, and therefore she hadn't. As soon as Justin reappeared, he would offer reassurance that the image had not—never could have—flashed across the monitor.

———∿∿∿∿∿———

Seth Smitherman came close to tugging on his forelock as he came into the PD. "Hope I'm not bothering you, Ms. Hanks."

I looked up from the cosmetics catalog Estelle had forced on me, but thus far had not left me dithering over the elusive subtleties of blue, black, and blue-black shades of mascara, followed by several pages of mink brown, auburn, dark brown, and blue-black-brown. It was making me feel inadequate, at best, as if I had failed in my responsibility to the mascara manufacturers of the world. I did not bat my pathetically unadorned eyelashes. "You here about the rifle?"

"Kyle's been asking about it. Can I sit down?"

"Suit yourself. The rifle's at the sheriff's department,

duly tagged and awaiting the owner to claim it. Changed your name since I last saw you?"

"Yeah, well, I'm just trying for a clean start. I got a job, I'm paying the bills, I ain't stealing anything from anybody. I guess you could say I am ree-habilitated."

"Then welcome to Maggody," I said, struggling for a hint of sincerity. Within the city limits were enough ex-cons to form a Kiwanis breakfast club. One more was hardly noteworthy. "Why did you decide to move here?"

"It's cheap."

"Admittedly, but there's not much action."

Seth gave me a wry smile. "You know damn well I just got out a month ago. The last thing I want is action. I'll do the six months of parole, then be on my way. Don't worry that I'm gonna stick up the supermarket. Canned hams hardly stir my soul like an eighty-nine Grand Am."

"Is it safe to leave my keys in the car?"

His composure wavered, and then collapsed. "I was eighteen, and I did something stupid. I've paid in more ways than you'll ever know. While I was in prison, this preacher came by every week to pray with me and help me find my way. I'm holding my head up now, determined to do what's right."

"Firing a weapon inside the city limits is likely to be a parole violation."

"Kyle brought out a case of beer to celebrate his birthday. Are you gonna report me?"

"No," I said, "as long as what happened the other day doesn't happen again. It might be better if Kyle stays away for the time being."

To my dismay, his eyes welled with tears. "I know that. My parents hate me, and Kyle's damn near the only family I have left. I came to learn in prison to take responsibility, and that's what I aim to do. You can leave the keys in the car, Chief Hanks; I got more important matters to deal with."

"In Maggody?"

"I reckon. By the way, your mother and that red-haired friend of hers are hiding under Lazarus's trailer. You might want to look into it."

"What?" I said as he walked out of the PD.

"This has to be the most gawdawful position you've ever put me in, Ruby Bee," Estelle whispered. "Here we are, trapped like a couple of mudpuppies that—"

Ruby Bee wiggled back to her side. "Hush up, for pity's sake. He ain't gonna sit out there forever. As soon as he goes back to the launderette, we can be on our way."

"Do we know he went to the launderette, or did a voice inside your head tell you that?"

"I believe you came up with that idea."

"I never," Estelle said, hoping the trailers in the Pot O' Gold were hooked up to septic tanks.

"Then it must have been that voice. Right now it's saying that you'd better keep still."

"Ask it if it has any bright ideas how to get out of here."

Ruby Bee sucked in a breath as she watched Lazarus, or his boots, anyway, move toward the door. "This is promising. The minute he goes inside, we'll bolt for the station wagon."

"And get shot in the back?"

"What makes you think he has a gun?"

Estelle squirmed into a somewhat more comfortable position, if such a thing could be had in cold, slimy mud. "Well, he ain't dirt poor. There's a computer on the dinette, with all kinds of oddments and cables that we ain't seeing in the lab. What's more, if you'd ever tried to talk to him in the supermarket, you'd know."

Ruby Bee sniffed. "Have you ever tried to talk to Alcatras Buchanon? Now there's someone who can't tell which end of the zucchini is up."

"Oh my gawd!" screamed Eula from across the road. "Somebody's gotta help me!"

Lazarus's boots stopped. "What's the matter with you, old lady?"

"I am having a heart attack! The pain's enough to make me fall off my porch! I can't catch my breath! You got to take me to the emergency room before I die right here in the Pot O' Gold! They say on television that every minute counts."

"So call an ambulance," said Lazarus.

Estelle grabbed Ruby Bee's shoulder. "We'd better do something!"

"I don't think so," she responded dryly.

Eula turned up her intensity. "There's no time to wait until they get all the way out here. I'm going to lie in the backseat of the station wagon. If you don't know how to find the hospital in Farberville, I can give you directions. You got to drive me there!"

The boots shuffled for only a few seconds. "Okay," he called.

Less than a minute later, the station wagon careened down the road toward the gate. A babble of low voices implied an audience had appeared for the latest display of melodrama, then faded along with the sound of the station wagon. High crimes played better than misdemeanors.

"You reckon Eula was faking?" asked Estelle.

Ruby Bee began to wiggle forward, mindful of the wires and pipes under the trailer. "You know darn well she was at the window before we set foot in the yard. She had a clear view when we dived under the trailer. Maybe she saw something on Lazarus's face to make her think he was coming after us."

Estelle snuffled. "What's this?" she said, holding up a sodden lump that had been caught in her cuff.

"I'd guess it's a dead rat."

Ignoring Estelle's squeals, Ruby Bee maneuvered her way out to the patio. Several kids stood in a group, sniggering, but wisely took off after she growled at them. She was trying to scrape mud off her dress and knees when Estelle finally emerged.

"Did it occur to you that I might be the one having a heart attack?" she said coldly.

Ruby Bee studied her. "Is that a leech?"

Estelle frantically rubbed her chin, then examined the mud on her palms. "I don't see it. Is it still there?"

"No, but neither is your station wagon. What say we go over to Eula's and clean up before we walk back to the bar and grill? Otherwise, we're gonna look like poster children for one of those third-world relief organizations. I am too old to be featured in an infomercial."

Estelle was gazing at Eula's yard. "He took my station wagon. I spent two hundred dollars on the transmission not more than a month ago. I suppose it's still under warranty."

"Let's hope Eula is," said Ruby Bee as she began to

walk across the road. She didn't have the heart to tell Estelle about her hair, which brought to mind the image of a hen caught on a fence post during an electric storm.

It was worthy of a faint smile, but not a comment.

———∿∿∿∿∿∿∿———

"We got us a problem," Raz said as he banged into the PD, accompanied by his omnipresent stench.

I'd been hunting up my keys in order to drive over to the Pot O' Gold yet again, this time to peer under Lazarus's trailer. "I'm busy, Raz. Come back later and we'll debate the scientific evidence concerning the validity of déjà vu."

"I don't know what that means, and I don't care. I found a body up at Robin Buchanon's shack. It weren't there yesterday. I would have said sumthin' if it had been."

"Whose body?"

"How in blazes would I know?" he said, spewing flecks of tobacco. "You got any hazelnut roast coffee? I've taken a fancy to it."

I wondered if I could yank the beard off his face. "Don't think you can come in here and—"

"She wasn't very old, mebbe a sight more than twelve or thirteen, but far from nice and plump. Marryin' age, I suppose, if anybody would have had her. My cousin Joe Dean married one like her, and she upped and died while birthin' their fifth child. There he was, burdened with—"

"Shut up!" I said. "Let's get this straight. You just now found the body of a young woman in Robin Buchanon's shack? Is this what you're saying?"

"What I was saying was Joe Dean's wife—"

I stood up. "Don't make me kill you, Raz. I only have four bullets, but I'm willing to waste one on you."

He had the nerve to turn surly on me. "I was just doin' my civic duty. Iff'n you don't care, neither do Marjorie or me. She's been hintin' she wants to snuffle for acorns down by Boone Creek."

"Are you sure the girl was dead?"

"Deader'n a preacher come doomsday. Her eyes was vacant, her tongue hangin' out, and she'd messed herself awful. Marjorie liked to have turned pea green. Thought about it myself, but I've seen worser. Not a month ago, a cat got caught under the house, and—"

"Raz," I said carefully, "did you see a child anywhere around?"

"Doncha think I would have said so?"

"What were you doing at Robin's shack?"

He shrugged. "I was thinkin' Diesel might come back for more jars, in which case I was gonna blow his sorry ass into the next county. He had no call to steal my 'shine like he did. I got my rights like ever'body else."

"Go outside and sit in your truck," I said. "I'll have some more questions for you after I've talked to Harve."

"Whatever you want," he mumbled as he went out the door.

I was reaching for the telephone when I heard his truck drive away. Having expected as much, I dialed the number of the sheriff's department and snarled at LaBelle until she put me through to Harve.

"Bad news," I began bluntly. "From what Raz Buchanon just told me, he found that runaway girl's body in Robin Buchanon's shack on Cotter's Ridge. His description sounded pretty damn grim."

"He have anything to do with it?"

"I don't think so. The little boy hasn't turned up. I'd appreciate backup as soon as possible, preferably with as many dogs as you can get. Tell 'em to bring sack lunches, because we may be there for a long time."

"You reckon he wandered off?"

"How should I know, Harve? All we can do is search for him unless you have any other bright ideas. Go ahead—I'll make a list."

Harve barked something unintelligible at LaBelle, then said, "Don't go biting off my head, Arly. Les and some of the other boys will pick up a four-wheel-drive vehicle at the state police barracks and be there as soon as they can. I suppose I'd better track down McBeen so he can have a look-see before we transport the body."

I took a deep breath. "Make sure the boys are armed. Diesel got hold of an unknown quantity of Raz's moonshine. He's apt to be a problem."

"Jesus H. Christ," Harve said with a drawn-out sigh. "Anything else you want to add to make my day?"

I decided not to mention Ruby Bee and Estelle's purported whereabouts. Harve was having a bad enough day as it was—but nowhere near as bad as Gwynnie's, if that was indeed who Raz had found in the dilapidated, bat-infested, decaying shack on Cotter's Ridge.

10

The logging trail that wound up the ridge to Robin's shack was no more than a sorry pretense of a washed-out streambed dating back to Noah's forty-day cruise. I had no idea how close I could get, but I was determined to bounce off boulders, if that's what it took. Without a doubt in anyone's mind who'd ever set foot in Stump County (or any of the adjoining ones), Raz was a lyin' sumbitch, but this was not the sort of thing he would have fabricated. The body could turn out to be that of a hitchhiker who'd somehow found her way to the cabin. It didn't seem likely, though.

The night had been cool, the day thus far reasonably warm. There was no way to guess from Raz's description how long Gwynnie—assuming that's who I'd find—had been dead, or how long Chip had had to wander off into the snarly, gnarly brush of Cotter's Ridge. Gullies and bluffs were abundant.

The bottom of the car scraped every few seconds as I jerked the steering wheel back and forth. The town council would not be pleased when they had to replace the oil pan, and maybe an axle or two; repairs might cost three times my annual salary. Bluejays dive-bombed the car, protesting my presence. Squirrels darted in front of me in some sort of rodent kamikaze game. A crow watched as I maneuvered around a fallen tree trunk.

A second splintery barrier ended what hopes I had of getting to the immediate proximity of the shack. I climbed out of the car, paused to allow my heart to stop pounding, and then began to hike up the road. Unlike the seniors in their L. L. Bean boots, I was wearing loafers from high school, although the value of their pennies had tumbled due to inflation. My feet slipped and slid with every step.

It took me a quarter of an hour to finally come around a bend and see the shack. An idyllic rustic retreat it was not. It had been a visual nightmare some years ago, when it had been inhabited by the notorious Robin Buchanon, who'd supplemented her otherwise nonexistent income with moonshine and prostitution. She'd been murdered while hunting ginseng, and her brood of feral children dispersed to healthier environments. No one had ever asked what had happened to the scrawny chickens and rawboned hounds. The outhouse seemed to be leaning at a more perilous pitch than when I'd last seen it; a clap of thunder might be enough to knock it down. What had been a barn was a pile of weathered kindling.

Bring your own marshmallows.

The shack itself had not fared well. The door had fallen off its hinges, and almost all of the tar paper had blown off the roof. Weeds pushed their way through gaps in the porch. The steps had collapsed. Tattered cellophane triangles flapped in the windows.

I sat down on a stump until my breathing steadied. I could hear a cacophony of birds, a truck grinding gears on the county road to the north, and a freight train in the valley beyond the ridge. As I listened more carefully, I could hear insects droning and buzzing.

I could not hear a child.

I wiped off my forehead and stood up. Even though I wasn't into paranormal nonsense, I was half expecting to see Robin step outside and aim a shotgun at my face. She'd never taken kindly to unexpected company, unless it was a customer for either moonshine or her vulgar companionship. I waded through weeds, scrambled up onto the porch, and reluctantly stuck my head through the doorway.

As I feared, Raz's story was true—and there was no doubt Gwynnie was dead. Nature was already beginning to have its way with her corpse. I avoided more than a glance as I went into the back room, ascertained that Chip was not in a corner or under the remains of a mattress filled with bug-ridden corncobs, and then came back into the front room.

A blue canvas bag had been tossed against a wall. I took a quick look inside and determined it was a diaper bag. I put it aside as I heard dogs barking. McBeen, the county coroner, could deal with Gwynnie, and would, in his own sweet time, offer a cause of death. Not my job.

I went back out to the porch as Les, two unfamiliar deputies hanging on to leashes attached to slobbering German shepherds, and McBeen climbed out of vehicles vastly superior to mine. The dogs were in a fine mood; no one else appeared to be.

"Did you ever consider finding a body at the Holiday Inn?" said McBeen as he wiped his face with a crumpled kerchief. "Even if you did, you'd probably drag it out into the middle of nowhere before you had me called in. Do you know what's on TV this afternoon, Chief Hanks?"

I glanced at Les, who shrugged blankly. "No, McBeen," I said, "I've been too busy investigating a murder to flip through the channels."

"Baseball," he muttered. "I hate football and I hate basketball—especially this newfangled women's basketball—and gawd knows I hate hockey. I hate figure skating, too, and golf is about as thrilling as watching molasses drip out of a jar in January. I wait all year for the baseball season to start. I stockpile cases of beer in the carport. The first exhibition game of the season, I move the recliner smack-dab in the middle of the living room, and it stays there until the World Series is over and done. Mrs. McBeen usually finds time to visit her mother for a month or two. Can you guess where I'd prefer to be right now, Chief Hanks?"

The dogs were snuffling excitedly as they came across the stubbly expanse, no doubt finding traces of crimes committed during the tenancy of the last five or six generations of this particularly stunted bough of the Buchanon clan.

"What've we got?" Les asked me.

"Gwynnie Patchwood, age seventeen. No blood or bruises that I could see, but I didn't look closely. That is, after all, Baseball Commissioner McBeen's job. There's no sign of her two-year-old child. His diaper bag's inside, though, and the story's that she took him with her last night."

Even the dogs quieted down as we all looked at the scrub oaks, brambles, pines, and thickets of bloodthirsty thorns. Broken limbs splayed like drunken sentinels. Sunlight struggled through branches still clinging to dead leaves. Foliage rustled as some unseen animal approached, then realized its folly and turned away. A mockingbird trilled a repertoire of curses.

"Aw shit," Les said, pretty much verbalizing everybody's thoughts. "You think to bring something for the dogs to track?"

I shook my head. "No, but there's a blanket in the diaper bag."

One of the deputies was hoisting McBeen's fat butt onto the porch as I came back out with the blanket. "There's most definitely a scent," I said in what might be classified as an understatement. "Can you handle the crime scene, Les? I'd like to help with the search."

"You don't have to do this, Arly."

"Yeah, I do. Be real careful not to smudge any fingerprints on the pieces of glass by the stove. I have a feeling that when we put them together, we're going to have a quart Mason jar."

"Moonshine?" wheezed McBeen as he brushed off his knees and struggled to his feet. "Bad batch? We ran into some last fall that damn near peeled the skin right off a couple of good ol' boys. I'd hate to tell you what it did to their livers. I've got 'em in jars on my desk. Amazing."

"Just do your job, McBeen," I said, then hopped off the porch and joined the deputies. "I assume Harve warned you about Diesel. He's liable to come swinging down on a grapevine or screaming up out of a crevice. Feel free to shoot him, but try not to kill him right off the bat."

One of the deputies, who was perhaps a day or two older than the alleged age on my first fake ID, gulped. "You think he has the little boy?"

"Absolutely not. He's just been living up here so long

that he knows the entire ridge better than you do your own backyards. He may be fine, or he may be totally out of his gourd. Aim for his kneecap, okay?"

The dogs stuck their muzzles in the blanket, then began to drag the deputies around the yard in widening circles.

Les put his hand on my shoulder. "Go on back to town. If the boys find anything, I'll come and get you. We've got seven more hours of daylight, and I can promise you we'll find the little boy if he's anywhere near here."

"His name is Chip."

"Then we'll find Chip. I've got a son not much older, and Deputy Phart's wife is expecting a baby any day now. We're not going to do a piss-poor job and then go for nachos and beer."

"Will you stop by the PD and tell me whatever McBeen has to say in his preliminary report?"

Les squeezed my shoulder before releasing it. "I'll either stop by or call as soon as I get back to the department. Sheriff Dorfer's taking this real seriously."

"So where is he?" I demanded angrily, as well as unreasonably. "The victim is seventeen. Her two-year-old child is missing. Is he too busy pontificating to the press to haul his ass up here and do the job he was elected to do?"

"Go back to town and see what you can find out. This isn't a rest stop on the highway. She must have been told about this place."

I got a grip, albeit slippery, on myself. "I'd appreciate it if you keep me informed. Trying to get through to Harve is harder than making a long-distance call to Siberia." I forced a smile. "Not that I ever have, of course."

One of the dogs took off at a clip, dragging its hapless handler into the brush. Obscenities ensued.

"Probably a rabbit," said Les.

"Probably," I agreed. I was about to set off, when something on Les's body beeped. My eyes involuntarily checked the sky for the mothership.

"Cell phone," he said dryly, having noted my response. He flipped open a plastic thing, muttered into it, and then grinned at me. "Chip's turned up at the emergency room at the hospital in Farberville. His diaper was soggy, but he's unharmed. One of the aides has been in touch with the mother's relatives."

"Who brought him in?" I asked.

Les conversed for another minute. "They're still working on it, apparently. I need to catch the deputies before they stray too far. You can call Harve when you get back to your office. Someone will let you know what McBeen has to say."

I made my way across the sea of weeds, stopped for a moment to admire the four-wheel-drive vehicles that could surmount logs as if they were Tinkertoys, then continued down the road to my antiquated cop car and floored it all the way to the highway.

Oil pan be damned.

The answering machine was flashing as if every rat in the county was determined to sneak its way into my office. I took off my shoes and hobbled into the back room to scrape the gunk out of the coffee pot. The befouled beaches of Prince Edward Sound could smell no worse nor be any stickier.

I started a fresh pot, then hit the button on the answering machine. As expected, the first dozen messages were from Ruby Bee, expressing everything from maternal apprehension to irritation concerning my whereabouts. Unlike Les, she did not possess a cell phone, so I concluded she'd found a way out from under Lazarus's trailer. One of these days I'd have to inquire into that one, I thought as I called Harve.

"Well, you surely caused a stir," LaBelle began before I could do more than identify myself. "Deputy Phart's wife has gone into labor. It's likely to be an hour before he can get to the hospital."

"Let me speak to Harve," I said.

"Why would you think he's here on a Saturday afternoon?"

My lower lip was beginning to throb as my teeth ground into it. "Let me speak to Harve."

"What did you find on Cotter's Ridge? Was it that runaway girl? You heard that the little boy turned up at the hospital, didn't you? The girl at the admittin' desk didn't see who let him off. He was right cheery, though, once they got him a fresh diaper and some ice cream."

"Really?" I murmured. "Harve there?"

"Some relation named Leona went over to fetch him, just like he was nothing more than a bundle of laundry."

"Harve," I insisted.

I was almost sorry that I'd persevered. When Harve came on, he was so sputtery that I had to wait several seconds before he began to make sense (which is not to imply that he was making all that much). I did not want to think about what he was doing to the cigar butt clenched between his teeth.

"I requisitioned two dogs," he said. "Two! That'd be twice as many as one. You know how hard it is to do that?

The chief of police was at his granddaughter's birthday party at one of those places that serves pizza and blaring music in equal batches. He was right testy. The state police promised to send a helicopter up to Cotter's Ridge, equipped with heat sensors and all sorts of queer military stuff designed to find Russian submarines. With my luck, they'll come across a marijuana patch and take all the credit."

"Life's a bitch, Harve."

He may have missed the irony. "Damn straight. At the moment, Deputy Phart's wife seems to be having triplets, and her mother let me know in terms more befitting a sailor that it's my fault he ain't there. What's more, I got an unruly mess of reporters outside the office, all clamoring about this missing baby. Soon as I tell 'em he turned up—or some mouthy hospital employee does—they'll storm the emergency room. I told the Holliflecker woman to get over there and take him out a back door."

"Hardly his fault," I commented.

"I guess not. Les called in, said McBeen thinks it's alcohol poisoning, maybe a suicide. It looks like she got so drunk she choked on her own vomit."

"How ridiculous is that? She makes her way to an obscure destination on Cotter's Ridge, of which she has no knowledge. She carries her child, who's likely to weigh thirty pounds, for at least a mile up a treacherous nonroad. She proceeds to drink herself to death for no known reason, having chanced upon a quart of moonshine that conveniently happens to be there. Heretofore, she's been a caring and responsible mother, but chooses to put her child in a life-threatening situation. Did she assume he would wander off a bluff? Is that why she didn't pack any peanut-butter sandwiches? Believe in fairies, Harve?"

"There's no evidence anyone else was there."

"So how did Chip end up at the hospital?"

Harve rumbled unhappily. "Guess you got a point. She must of handed him over to somebody. Why don't you see what you can ferret out at your end? I'll call you soon as McBeen has something more definite."

I slammed down the receiver and banged my muddy heels on the desk. Robin Buchanon's cabin was hardly a popular tourist destination. It was possible—but not probable—that Gwynnie had stumbled upon it. Until McBeen came out with a preliminary opinion, there was no way of knowing how long Gwynnie had been sprawled on the floor.

A two-year-old was not my notion of an ideal witness, but I decided to find out if Chip had anything to say about his last twenty-four hours. He'd spent the night somewhere, and then been dumped at the hospital. Great-aunt Leona was not likely to be a nurturing support figure. But no matter what I thought of her, she was the next of kin for the time being.

Life sucks, as Chip would learn.

I drove to the house and knocked on the door, then leaned against the railing as I struggled not to envision what I'd seen. The image was nothing I needed to share with Leona. When the door opened, I forced myself to act like a cop.

"Leona," I began, "I have bad news."

"I didn't think Chip was roaming around the hospital for no reason. Gwynnie's a tramp, but she isn't neglectful. Is she in jail?"

"No," I said, then told her about the body at Robin Buchanon's cabin, skirting the graphic details. "The county coroner will let us know by the end of the day how long she's been there, and give us a better idea what happened to her. I think we'll end up with a homicide, though."

Her face turned ashen. "Somebody killed her? Why would anybody do such a thing? She wasn't really a tramp, despite her Patchwood blood. She never hurt anybody, and she was determined to take care of her child. She could have just signed the adoption consent papers and walked away." She paused for a moment. "Are you sure she didn't kill herself?"

"Chip was at the hospital in Farberville. He didn't get there under his own steam, and he couldn't have been there for more than a minute or two before someone found him."

"Was she—violated?"

I nudged past her and went into the living room. "The coroner will make the determination, but I didn't see any signs of it. Can I get you a glass of water?"

"I knew something terrible had happened when that woman called from the hospital. Chip was just wandering around the waiting room with a note pinned on his shirt. Now how on earth would he end up there, all alone? Gwynnie wouldn't have left him."

"I don't think she did," I said gently. "Someone took him there and sent him inside, knowing that he'd get help. Did he say anything?"

"Of course not," she said, sitting down and for the first time seeming to assimilate what I'd said. "Are you sure it was Gwynnie?"

"I saw the body."

"So what am I supposed to do, Arly? Do I have to go to the morgue or call someone to deal with the . . . I just don't know what to do now," she said, beginning to cry. "Gwynnie's mother is in Africa, and I have no way of getting hold of her. Chip's in the back room, playing with his blocks. His father's dead. I feel like I should be making calls, but I don't know who to call. Nothing like this has ever happened. Please tell me what to do."

"Call Daniel," I said. "He can be here in a couple of hours. Once he's back, we'll all figure out what needs to be done."

"Was it that Jessie Traylor?" she demanded.

"Why would you say that?"

"He was here last night, and so angry. Gwynnie went outside and tried to reason with him. I couldn't hear what they said, but I could tell they were at odds. There was no point in asking Gwynnie when she came back inside; she wouldn't hardly give me the time of day these last few weeks."

"Any idea why?"

Leona began to twist her hands. "I don't know for sure, but Jessie was pressuring her to get married. Daniel was dead set against it. He thought Gwynnie needed to earn her GED and find a job."

"Nothing wrong with that," I murmured. "How's Chip doing?"

"There's no point in you speaking to him. I asked him where he'd spent the night and how he got to the hospital, but all he did was babble. He barely knows a scant handful of words. Questions are likely to upset him. Daniel left the number of the motel on his desk. I'd better call him."

"I'll be back later," I said as I stepped over a plastic dinosaur and took my leave. Once on the porch, it occurred to me that I was out of the loop. I wasn't sure who Jessie Traylor was. I knew that Gwynnie had been leaning on Justin Bailey, but I didn't know how hard. Chapel Bailey hadn't been fond of her. Nicholas Brozinski, aka Lazarus, had been roaring around the trailer park the previous night. Eula Lemoy was armed, and therefore dangerous.

Some days it didn't pay to get up.

Make that most days, considering my you-may-qualify-for-food-stamps salary.

I decided my best bet was to swing by Ruby Bee's Bar & Grill and see what I could find out. Richard Burton sought the source of the Nile; I surely could seek out less esoteric information.

The proprietor herself was bustling around behind the bar, doing her best to ignore me as I came across the dance floor. "You have mud on your ear," I said as I climbed onto a stool. "I wouldn't be surprised if you have something worthy of the Centers for Disease Control seeping through your veins. The Pot O' Gold is cited annually by the county health department for violations. Nobody's ever done anything to remedy them, of course. That wouldn't be in keeping with the age-old traditions of arrogance and ignorance. The arch over the cattle guard ought to read, 'We ain't gonna get whatever it is, and iff'n we do, so what?' "

"Your mouth ought to be cited," Ruby Bee said in a most unfriendly voice. "I was concerned about Gwynnie and Chip."

"So you crawled under Lazarus's trailer? Was your next destination the roof of the Dairee Dee-Lishus?"

"It's kinda complicated."

I waited in case she might care to elaborate, then let it go and told her what had happened. "Chip's at Leona and Daniel's house," I concluded. "It doesn't sound as if he suffered any ill effects from this."

Ruby Bee's hostility had evaporated. "That poor girl," she said, swiping at her eyes with the hem of her apron. "I really think she was hoping to do the right thing. She may have been rambling in the back pasture, overlooking the obvious. She was awful ambitious for someone in her position, but maybe that's what you're supposed to be if you want something better for your child."

"Are you referring to Justin?"

She filled a glass with ice tea and set it in front of me. "It was kinda painful to watch in class. She'd simper and carry on, but as soon as he went to help someone else, she'd be clattering away a mile a minute on the keyboard. A few minutes later her screen would be filled with gibberish and she'd be whining for him."

"Chapel told me that Gwynnie was coming by their trailer after class."

"She needed approval. Justin was kind to her." She paused and looked down. "Maybe too kind. After one class, I saw them talking behind the gym. They were standing real close."

"Too close?" I asked softly.

"It was dark. Justin ain't the sort to do something like this. What's more, neither of them has lived in Maggody long enough to know about Robin's shack. Somebody local must have . . ."

"Somebody like Jessie Traylor?"

"Well, he'd have heard of it, but so would everybody

else that grew up around here. He's a nice boy, Arly. He was so smitten with Gwynnie that he begged her to run off with him to Eureka Springs and get married. She could have done worse. He has a steady job and Gwynnie said he was good with Chip."

I took a swallow of tea. "Was he a participant in the computer classes?"

"He came the first night," Ruby Bee admitted, "but then Daniel made a scene at the reception and Gwynnie told him to stay away, or at least that's my understanding. The other night I thought I saw him on the far side of the parking lot, hanging around like he was waiting for her, but I couldn't be sure. And last night, too, come to think of it. There's only the one utility pole by the entrance to the gym. Twenty feet away, it's darker than the inside of a cow."

"Maybe I'd better speak to him," I said as I reluctantly pushed aside the glass. "Where does he live?"

"In that house just past the Pot O' Gold. His pa had a contract with one of the poultry companies, and used to operate a few chicken houses. A windstorm came through, and of course ol' Traylor hadn't bothered with insurance. His wife took off after that. He was killed in prison." She grabbed the glass and dunked it in a sink of water. "I'd better see what I have in the freezer. Times like this, I always believe there's nothing more comforting than a green-bean casserole and a lemon pound cake. Mrs. Jim Bob does a real nice molded pineapple salad with cream-cheese icing. The Missionary Society can provide the ham. I need to make some calls."

"Gwynnie's body isn't even in the morgue."

"Life goes on," said my-mother-the-philosopher, "and

so should you. You take charge of seeing justice is served; the rest of us will look after the survivors."

I tried to remember the Traylor family as I drove toward the house. The name was familiar, but I couldn't recall encountering the parents, and Jessie must have been in elementary school when I made my escape from Maggody. I certainly hadn't dealt with him in my professional capacity, but there were all sorts of folks living peaceably on the fringes. Some of them might be making fertilizer bombs in their garages or crack cocaine in their kitchens, but there just weren't enough hours in the day to conduct periodic door-to-door searches. I did not want to be around if and when all the ponds in Stump County dried up after a particularly brutal summer drought.

Work on it.

The Traylor homestead was held together with spit and a prayer. The yard was dirt-hard. The windows were curtainless, but a few defiant daffodils bloomed along the edge of the house and a planter on the porch was thick with yellow and purple pansies.

I parked behind a pickup truck that was liable to be older than its current driver. Wishing I'd demanded to hear more of Jessie Traylor's background, I went to the door and knocked.

After several minutes, he opened the door and gazed blearily at my badge. "Arly Hanks? You got to excuse me. I'm about to start on the night shift, and I always try to catch a nap so I won't doze off and lose a finger or two." His ears turned red as he realized he was wearing only baggy briefs that threatened to slip off his hips. "Sorry, I wasn't expecting company."

"I need to talk to you about Gwynnie Patchwood," I said.

"I don't see what there is to talk about," he said as he ground his fingertips into his eyes. "She told me to get out of her life. I never made the honor roll, but I know when to take a hike."

"This was last night?"

"Yeah," he said, waving me inside. "Lemme start some coffee. 'Scuse the mess."

He left me in a living room that was far neater than mine. The wood floor was deeply scarred, and the upholstery allowed glimpses of the cotton filling. The walls were barren and in need of a fresh paint job. The mess he'd alluded to seemed to consist of a beer can on a table and a book with a title that implied even dummies could master the Internet.

I went to the kitchen door. "Mind if I look around?"

His shoulder blades twitched. "For what? The only drugs you're gonna find are in the medicine cabinet in the bathroom, and most of 'em have been there for twenty years. I'm old enough to have a six-pack of beer in the fridge."

"You live alone?"

He banged down the coffeepot with such force that he had to grab the waistband of his briefs before he put both of us in a most uncomfortable situation. "Why don't you tell me why you're here, Chief Hanks? Did Daniel and Leona Holliflecker accuse me of trespassing or endangering the welfare of a minor? Gwynnie's not some sweet little schoolgirl in pigtails. She knows her own mind."

"I heard you had an argument with her last night," I

said, allowing him to believe the Hollifleckers were the reason for my presence. "What was that about?"

"You run a mighty tight town if you can go around demanding folks tell you their private business. Did Mayor Buchanon declare martial law?" His hands were shaking as he finished filling the coffeepot with water and took a can of coffee from a cabinet. Brown granules scattered on the counter as he dumped in several scoops. "Aren't you supposed to have a warrant to come charging in here like this?"

"You invited me into the house," I reminded him. "Let's talk some more about last night. A witness saw you at the edge of the gym parking lot. Were you waiting for Gwynnie?"

"I sure as hell wasn't waiting for the ice-cream truck. Daniel Holliflecker may not have to let me inside his gate, but the parking lot's public property. I'm a taxpayer, same as him!"

The kitchen was beginning to feel a little overheated for my taste. "I'm going to the living room, Jessie. Why don't you put on some clothes and join me? If you'll be straight with me, I'll return the courtesy. Otherwise, we may end up in an interrogation room at the sheriff's department. I'd hate to make you late for work."

Five minutes later he came into the living room, dressed in torn jeans. His feet were bare, but we weren't headed for a place where shirts and shoes were required for service. "Listen, Chief Hanks," he said, sitting across from me, "I don't know why you're here. I ain't done anything wrong."

"Then why don't we get this over with?"

"Yeah, okay," he said dully. "I waited outside the computer classroom last night, hoping to talk to Gwynnie. When she saw me, she just stuck her nose in the air and drove off. I came and got my truck, and caught up with her about the time she arrived at the Hollifleckers' place. She made it clear she didn't want anything to do with me ever again. After that, I drove home and drank whiskey."

"So last night was the end of your relationship with her? You were hurt, but did nothing more than skulk back here and drown your rejection in whiskey?"

He scratched his chin. "That pretty much covers it. I've gotten over other girls, and I'll get over her. She's kinda a pain in the butt, always complaining about how she has to do all the housework, cook, and chase after Chip. She wants expensive clothes and a new car and maids and a nanny and all sorts of things I can never give her."

I couldn't argue with that. "So there's no way she and Chip could have appeared on your doorstep an hour later?"

"In my dreams," he said with a grimace. "I stayed up most of the night, coming to terms with things. She won't ever be content with me. Chip might be, but he'll never have the chance to find out."

I gestured at him to sit down next to me on the sofa as threadbare as his dreams, then told him what had happened. He was still hunched over, his face cradled in his hands, when I left.

11

I drove over to the high school and parked by the corner of the gym. The portable classroom was likely to be locked, but I needed some sort of visual image to figure out what had been going on while I'd dedicated myself to sitcoms (did I mention I was *sans* cable?). Yes, I should have leaped on, signed on, logged on, whatever. Maggody could not remain my private asylum indefinitely; the inmates were turned loose way too often. Not even Roy Stiver could survive a steady diet of Buchanons and what seemed to be an unending assault of crazies. He spent four months in Florida every year; I couldn't afford that, but crawling into the storage shed behind Ruby Bee's Bar & Grill for a couple of weeks held appeal, in a musty sort of way.

I'd probably find at least one Buchanon in the rafters to keep me company. Hanging upside down, wings folded.

I was surprised to discover the door was not locked. Feeling as though I was trespassing, I went into the trailer. It was decidedly not the war room at the Pentagon. Nothing beeped or bleeped or shrilled or trilled as I looked at the two rows of cubicles with shoulder-height partitions made of particle board. Unlike similar spaces

I'd seen in offices in New York, none of the desks were decorated with anemic plants or photographs of equally anemic children. Computers took up most of the space on the desks. The chairs had obviously been gleaned from an array of sources.

I was contemplating a blank screen when Brother Verber opened the door and poked his head inside.

"Ain't interrupting, am I?" he said.

"Only if you're planning to commit a felony. I'm really not in the mood for felonies just now."

He came through the door, dressed in a garish green outfit that reminded me of the consequences of a bad meal in Tijuana. "Why, Arly," he said, clasping his hands together, "what a wonderful opportunity for us to spend a few minutes together. Mrs. Jim Bob keeps telling me how sinful you are, but I've always clung to the belief that I could keep your soul out of Satan's clutches. Many are the nights I've prayed for you."

"Are you cruising for converts? You may have better luck when Ruby Bee's cranks up for happy hour later this afternoon. Many a good ol' boy's crying in his beer by seven o'clock, begging his dead mama for forgiveness and wondering how he came to shoot his pappy and run over his dawg."

He made sure the door was closed, perhaps so we wouldn't be overheard by anyone attempting to monitor our conversation via spy satellite. Can't trust those Ruskies, or maybe Belaruskies, these days.

"There are evil things coming through the Internet," he said. "I have an obligation to the members of my flock to make sure that they are protected. I am here to do that for them, just like I can for you. Will you pray with me?

Will you fall on your knees and admit that salvation is within your reach?"

"This isn't a baptismal bathtub, Bubba Verber. It's a trailer. Rumor has it that it was being used to teach sex education at the elementary school last semester."

So I made it up. Big deal.

"God moves in mysterious ways," he intoned with only the faintest hesitation, "as does Satan. I can have no rest until I disarm the devil and herd the strays safely into the fold."

"Yeah, right," I said. "When I arrived, I didn't see any sinners grazing out past the gym. Is there any particular reason why you think Satan's hanging around here on a Saturday afternoon?"

"Satan don't care what day it is. He's looking to do evil whenever he can, even on the weekends."

"What's he doing as we speak?"

Brother Verber's forehead began to glisten. "It's confidential. Anyways, Justin Bailey told us we should all be using the computers when we wanted. I was thinking to put the gist of my Sunday morning sermon on the web site. That way, folks can ponder the implications in advance and be settled on the pews in the morning, eager to shout 'Hallelujah!' "

"And what is the gist?" I asked as I wandered in and out of the cubicles, finding nothing more intriguing than gnawed pencils. "Our Father who art in cyberheaven, hallowed be thy E-mail address?"

"Something along those lines. Our horizons have to expand with this new millennium. Maybe there's no longer room for traditional churches, and spiritual rewards are gonna be found on the Internet. Just the other day I stumbled across a web site that promises a two-bedroom condo in heaven and a bottle of holy water in the here and now, all for nineteen ninety-five. The Voice of the Almighty Lord can do it for half the price, plus your shipping and handling. My calling is to find a way to reach out to all these lost souls surfing the Net in hopes of finding solace."

"Extra for a deck with a barbecue grill?"

"Redemption ain't cheap, as you yourself must know."

"As I must," I said, restraining myself out of some deeply buried sense of Southern decorum. Proper ladies do not swear. They do not kick dogs (except out of sight of the hired help), and they do not lose their tempers unless it is required of them. All Brother Verber was doing was pushing some buttons that Mrs. Jim Bob has already worn clean. "Is the computer lab unlocked all the time?"

"I seem to think Justin locks up at night. He's only running a couple of classes during the day, so he encouraged us all to come by whenever we want. Ruby Bee's up here most afternoons, listing her menu on the web site and exchanging recipes with ladies as far away as Tallahassee. I know for a fact Estelle's found a new source for wholesale cosmetics and has been ordering left and right. I ain't quite sure what Dahlia's doing, but she carries on something fierce. She makes a point of blocking out the screen whenever I come by. She can do that. It's just as well Jesus didn't invite her to walk on water with him."

I stared at him. "Justin doesn't worry that someone might steal the computers?"

Brother Verber gave me a pious smile. "Just because the Lord giveth doesn't mean anyone is gonna taketh away. We live in a Christian community. I never lock the rectory, and I don't hesitate to leave the keys in my car when I go by the supermarket to buy a loaf of bread and a box of fish sticks. Despite my vigilance, never once have I encountered crime in our little community."

Which only meant he'd been too pickled to notice an abundance of murder and mayhem over the last few years in the little "nothing-ever-happens-here" utopia. In need of fresh air, I said, "Put your sermon on the web page, Brother Verber. The more detailed, the better. I'll swing by the Assembly Hall tomorrow morning in case you need crowd control. The parking lot next to the remains of the bank branch can take the majority of the spillage, but after that, I'll just have to kill 'em."

"Kill 'em?"

I rubbed my temples. "A stupid joke. Leona Holli-flecker is a member of your church, isn't she? I think she may be in need of your professional services."

I proceeded to tell him why, then left. Ruby Bee and recipes, Estelle and wholesalers, Dahlia and the sort of dark secrets only she could concoct. I was frustrated by my lack of knowledge about the prevailing activities of practically every last person in Maggody—except me. For all I knew, Raz was purchasing his jars on-line. Diesel might be ordering gourmet ingredients from animal shelters in Connecticut. Petrol was likely to be wallowing in porn at the old folks' home, possibly encountering photos of Mayor Jim Bob engaging in activities I was loath to imagine.

I put another dent in the oil pan as I careened across the cattle guard at the Pot O' Gold. Eula was pinning underwear on her clothesline, but I did not wave. Justin Bailey might be as cooperative as a crappie on a cloudy day, I thought grimly, but he was by damn going to give me whatever it took to divine what was going on in this little obscure corner of the planet. If not, he might find himself in need of shipping and handling.

To hell in a handbasket, as we're fond of saying in these parts.

I pounded on the door of the trailer. I was on the verge of ripping it off and chewing it up when Justin appeared, clad in a towel. Shampoo oozed down his neck, and his eyes were unnaturally red.

"What?" he said, annoyed.

"I need to talk to you," I countered, not caring.

"Right now? I was—"

"I don't care if you were negotiating a peace accord in the Middle East! Go get dressed and come out here."

I flopped down on an aluminum chair on the concrete slab that served as a patio, wondering if I ought to be enforcing a dress code within the city limits. The males were on an unfortunate streak; nothing could save me if the females followed suit and I encountered Dahlia in a thong bikini or Mrs. Jim Bob in hot lingerie. Or Ruby Bee in pedal pushers and sequinned sunglasses, for that matter.

Justin was leery as he joined me a few minutes later. "What's this about?"

"It's about Gwynnie Patchwood. She was found dead this morning on Cotter's Ridge."

"Gwynnie?"

"The seventeen-year-old girl in your computer class. The one who came by here most nights to whimper. She's dead, Justin."

"But how . . . ?"

"That's why I'm here. We'd all like to know."

"Dead?" he repeated.

"Where were you last night?"

He pulled off his glasses and gaped at me. "You don't think I had anything to do with this, do you?"

I leaned back and regarded what sunshine could be seen through the gray clouds gathering above the ridge. "I wish I knew, Justin. Why don't you tell me what was going on between you and Gwynnie?"

"Nothing," he said with an adolescent squeak, as though the very concept of sexual intimacy was alien, if not an abomination. "She was in the class, just like your mother and Estelle and Mrs. Jim Bob and Lottie Estes and all the other participants. She showed up on a regular basis. Some nights she came by the trailer to ask for personal advice. She'd had a hard time. All I could tell her was that she had to look out for herself and her child. I didn't have the resources she needed."

"You weren't flattered by her attention?"

"She was a kid. So maybe I was flattered, but I have my own agenda. I'm focused on getting into grad school, doing research, writing my dissertation, landing a high-tech job, and smiling all the way to the bank. Not that any of us will actually be going to banks in the future; those transactions will be on-line. I had a few students like Gwynnie when I was a teaching assistant at Farber College. Most of them were blond. When they showed up in my office after classes were done for the day, wanting to know what they could do to earn a passing grade, I suggested they study."

I rearranged my butt in the remarkably uncomfortable chair. "And your wife was okay with Gwynnie's interminable visits?"

"Not especially, but you can take it up with her. Chapel has no reservations making her opinion known. Last night, I supervised the lab, locked up, and went into Farberville to see some friends. Gwynnie left at eight-thirty, the same as we all did. She looked like she wanted to talk to me, but Lottie cornered me with some gibberish about seeing things on the screen. I told her to have her eyes tested."

Wishing I could better watch his reaction, I said, "There have been rumors that you and Gwynnie . . ."

It took him the better part of a minute to reply, but he did so forcefully. "Then you'd better verify them, Chief Hanks. She was nothing but a kid trying to find a way out. The only potential husband on the scene is never going to earn more than minimum wage. Other than him, she'd have been stuck with welfare payments and food stamps. Her stepfather abused her, as did a steady stream of her mother's boyfriends, and even dear Uncle Daniel. Maybe you should be questioning him."

I stared at him. "She told you that Daniel was abusing her?"

"She made it clear she was afraid of him."

He hadn't offered any rebuttal to the rumor, but I doubted he would. Ruby Bee had passed along her opinion that Justin and Gwynnie had been—well, consorting behind the classroom, but the source had also been observed hunkering under a trailer in the Pot O' Gold. Said source had thus far failed to explain. For the record, in the past said source (and her cohort in crime) had claimed to see a luminescent extraterrestrial walk on water.

Credibility was an issue.

"What did Gwynnie say about Daniel?" I asked.

"Nothing explicit."

"Can you give me the names of the people you were with last night?"

"No," he said. "I was invited to a party at LaRue's house, but there was some sort of screwup and nobody was home. I tried a couple of more places, then went to the beer garden on Thurber Street. I sat, I drank, and eventually I left. I most certainly did not commit any crime more serious than driving home after having a couple of beers."

"Gwynnie's dead."

"I'm sorry. I didn't kill her."

I wriggled around in the chair. "Then let's talk about these computer classes. Jessie Traylor was kicked out, right?"

"It was his decision not to attend, although he's still using the lab during the day, along with a lot of other people. Next fall, I'll most likely have a full schedule of classes, but for the moment the students come in during their study halls and lunchtimes. I'm working with maybe a dozen of them. A couple of 'em are pretty darn good."

"I'll need a list of their names. Who else?"

"The guy who lives in the last trailer. He's been dropping by to play games on the computer. I tried to get him to come in the evenings, but he won't."

"Did Gwynnie ever come during the day?"

Justin shook his head. "I think she had baby-sitting complications. Why are you asking?"

"She wasn't exactly going to parties or dances at the high school. Her opportunities to fraternize were limited to church and the computer lab."

"All I did was show her how to explore community college and student-loan web sites. I was only trying to help her. I'm really sorry she's dead."

"So am I," I said wearily. "In the morning, drop off a list of everyone who's set foot inside the computer lab over the last couple of weeks, including the janitor."

"That would be Lottie Estes and her feather duster."

I stood up. "Just bring me the list." I took a step, then stopped. "Have you ever heard of someone named Robin Buchanon?"

"I've heard of Jim Bob, Mrs. Jim Bob, Kevin, Dahlia, Eileen, a hair-impaired woman at the supermarket named Idalupino, and what I assume are urban legends"—he looked around—"or rural ones, I guess, about Buchanons who live in caves. That's about it."

"Where's Chapel?"

"She left a note saying she was going to the library at the college to work on her proposal for a fellowship for the fall semester. She needed to photocopy some text that's not available on-line."

"Catch any fish?"

"The only thing I caught is a cold," he said as he went inside.

I was heading out of the Pot O' Gold when Eula came dashing onto the road in a manner reminiscent of the suicidal squirrels I'd encountered earlier. I reluctantly braked for her, as I had for them.

"You got to talk to Ruby Bee!" she shrieked.

"Is she under your trailer? Whatever will we do with her now that she's taken up this new hobby?"

"She's at the bar, but she has something real important to tell you. She's been calling all over town, trying to track you down. I saw you drive by earlier, and I promised her

I'd flag you down and make you promise to get over there as soon as possible."

"Any idea what it is?"

Eula fluttered her hands. "Not really, but it has to do with that girl what was found dead in Robin's shack. Drank herself to death, or so I heard. I for one am not surprised. I've already said a prayer that Leona will never find out about her niece's unseemly behavior. Mum's the word, as far as I'm concerned. I don't speak ill of the dead, or of the living."

Kudzu vines may threaten to overtake the roadside vegetation and tear down the power lines, but the grapevine is far more relentless in Maggody. With Brother Verber and Mrs. Jim Bob gleefully ticking off my every sin, Ruby Bee and Estelle monitoring my daily grind with an eye to romance, and Mayor Jim Bob holding his breath in hopes I would do something worthy of getting myself fired, I might as well have been under perpetual microscopic scrutiny.

"Was this on the local news?" I asked Eula.

"No, but Ruby Bee called LaBelle at the sheriff's department, trying to find you, and then called me. After what I went through earlier, I was entitled. Lazarus was downright rude to me on the way back from Farberville."

"You and Lazarus went into Farberville?"

"You'd better get over to the bar and grill. Ruby Bee's frantic to talk to you."

"On his motorcycle?"

"No," she said, averting her face. "If you're so all-fired interested, ask Ruby Bee. It was her fault to begin with—hers and Estelle's, that is. If you'll excuse me, I got better things to do than stand here and gossip. So do you."

I was still sitting there as she flounced inside her trailer and closed the door. I finally put the car in one of whatever gears it had left and drove toward Ruby Bee's Bar & Grill to determine whatever earthshaking news was to be presented to me not on a silver platter, but more likely on a worn tin cookie sheet.

———∿∿∿∿∿∿———

Mrs. Jim Bob was on her knees in front of the dresser when she heard Perkin's eldest wheel the vacuum cleaner into the bedroom. She hastily rose and smoothed out the wrinkles in her skirt. "You don't need to vacuum in here today. Did you change the sheets?"

Perkin's eldest nodded, perhaps mendaciously.

"Well, then, you can go on home for the day. I am doing an inventory of Mr. Buchanon's underwear on account of a sale at Sears next week. He has been complaining about his lack of matching socks. You wouldn't know anything about that, would you?"

Perkin's eldest shook her head, perhaps mendaciously.

"I'd like to think there aren't any socks behind the dryer. Socks don't grow on trees, as even you must know. It seems like every six months a good half of my husband's socks have vanished, along with several pairs of boxer shorts." She blinked beadily in case a confession was forthcoming, then waved her hand. "You run along. I hope to see you bright and early tomorrow morning at services. The Lord forgives those that admit to their shame, be it fornication or the stealing of socks."

Once she heard Perkin's eldest go out the front door, Mrs. Jim Bob resumed her position in front of Jim Bob's dresser. If she had seen on the computer what she thought she had seen, and she was still pretty much sure she had (except late at night, when she tried to convince herself it had been nothing more than a bizarre delusion caused by sausage past its prime), then Jim Bob had been secretly engaged in a lifestyle that made her sick to her stomach just to think about.

But she couldn't confront him without tangible evidence of his perversity, she thought as she tried to convince herself to pull open the bottom drawer. For once, Brother Verber might have been right when he'd suggested it was all in her mind. She'd seen daytime talk shows where men paraded around in women's garments, pretending to be whores. Images could have lingered, just like cabbage and pinto beans.

Her hand faltered. If she searched his drawers and found proof, then what would she do? She'd have no choice but to throw him out of the house, but actual divorce would violate the sacred vows she'd taken that terminated with "till death do us part." Causing his death would have serious consequences for her presidency of the Missionary Society, and she'd lose all chances of being reelected to the school board in November. She might even be relieved of her duties as administrator of the Sunday school.

What's more, there was no way she could slip a little rat poison in the scalloped potatoes without the Lord taking note and frowning down on her. "Thou shalt not kill" was spelled out with no ifs or buts. Jim Bob paid scant attention to the Ten Commandments, being especially oblivious to the one about committing adultery, but she was a devout Christian who never so much as allowed her big toe to stray off the path that led to heaven.

Nobody in the congregation dared argue with that.

It took her a good minute to finally ease open the drawer. There was, as she'd anticipated, a jumble of socks and T-shirts, along with a box of smelly cigars and several magazines with shameless hussies on the covers. She had expected no better, and was almost feeling relieved when her hand encountered something decidedly silky and lacy stuffed way in the back.

She slammed the drawer closed and stumbled down the hall to her bedroom. Once she'd locked the door and made it to the bed, she forced herself to remain collected. All these years of marriage could not have been a mockery. She'd fried chicken every Sunday, after all, and planted begonias out front, done the laundry, washed the windows once a year, dusted the silk flowers, and saw to it that Perkin's eldest brushed away the cobwebs in the utility room. She'd offered the spiritual guidance in their relationship, but only because of his frailties in matters best left unspecified. There'd never been any doubt in her mind that she would bring him around, or at least wear him down to the point of docility.

But now that she had learned of his depraved secret, was it possible other folks had, too? Could she continue to hold up her head while seated in the front pew of the Assembly Hall while everyone snickered at her behind her back?

There was only one thing to do, she decided grimly. Confronting Satan would not be easy, what with Jim Bob as his witless prodigy, but she had no choice.

"Till death do us part," she said as she went back down the hall to his bedroom. "We'll just have to see which one of us goes first."

Ruby Bee came skittering out from behind the bar as I came across the dance floor. "I have been trying to find you ever since you left!" she said in a whisper that could have carried to the back row of the balcony (had there been one). Several of the diners in the booths looked up, chunks of brisket impaled on their forks. Gravy dribbled on more than one chin.

"I left about an hour ago," I pointed out. "Hardly enough time for an army to invade or an epidemic to break out. Was it necessary to get Eula involved in whatever this is?"

"This is real important."

I caught her arm and propelled her toward the bar. "Then why don't you just tell me?"

"Go on out to number six and see for yourself. Estelle's waiting for you. We figured one of us had to protect the scene. That's one of the things you learn from watching police shows on television."

"The scene of what?"

Ruby Bee gave me a shove. "I don't reckon we can discuss it in here, not with all these vultures in the booths. Go on, Arly. Estelle must be getting antsy by now."

Rather than argue, I went out the back door of the bar and grill and between the two parallel buildings that comprised the six units of the Flamingo Motel. The unit under discussion was the last on my right; had I kept on going straight, I would have been obliged to duck under a barbed-wire fence and take my chances with a frustrated bull.

Estelle met me outside the door. "Thank gawd you're

here! I wanted to call Harve, but Ruby Bee insisted that we wait for you. You know how she keeps all the curtains drawn so the carpets and bedspreads won't fade. Well, earlier she happened to notice the curtain was pushed back kinda crooked and came to straighten it. That's when she realized . . . well, see for yourself."

"Maybe I should do just that," I said, not sure if I'd find Diesel clinging to the light fixture on the ceiling or Jim Bob sprawled in the tub with a bottle of whiskey. I stepped inside. "Okay, the furniture's intact. No blood-splatters on the walls. No heavy breathing or groans. Should I check the bathroom mirror for messages written in blood?"

"Look at the bed, Arly."

"A bit rumpled."

Estelle snorted. "No one has rented this particular unit in months. Do you honestly think Ruby Bee would leave the bed in that state? She's real fastidious about changing sheets and emptying wastebaskets and putting in fresh towels. What's more, she said the exterminator was here not too long ago and she went inside all the units with him to make sure he did a thorough job."

I approached the bed. "Could he have taken a nap after she left?"

"If he did, it wasn't by himself," she said darkly as she pulled back the bedspread. "I'm not of a mind to speculate about these stains."

"Is Ruby Bee's unit unlocked?"

"She gave me the key. Normally, she doesn't bother to lock it unless she's going off someplace, but all these wild stories about Diesel have been making all of us jittery. Elsie won't let Stan out of the house. According to her, all he does these days is lie on the windowsill and watch the robins hop around on the lawn. She feels real bad, but—"

"Wait for me at Ruby Bee's," I said, then nudged her out the door. There were several stains, some fresher than others. I began to pick up on odors other than disinfectant and furniture wax. Urine, I realized, and the same sour stench of vomit I'd encountered only hours earlier. And sexual encounters.

I took a quick look in the bathroom and closet, then went over to Ruby Bee's unit, fixed myself a glass of soda, and sat down on the sofa. Ignoring Estelle, I dialed the number of the sheriff's department.

Harve himself answered. I told him what I'd found, waited out his decidedly unhappy sighs, then asked if McBeen had added anything to the preliminary report.

I heard a match scritch and a lengthy inhalation before he said, "Yeah, a few things. The victim was already dead when she was left in the shack, which would fit in with what you're saying. The lividity indicated she was on her side for a period of hours after she died, but she was on her back when you found her. What's more, there are some nasty bruises on her upper arms and around her mouth. McBeen won't say it, of course, but it looks like someone sat on the girl's abdomen, knees pinning down her arms, and poured the alcohol down her throat. She couldn't have resisted for long."

I winced. "And maybe at the Flamingo Motel."

"Looks like it."

"So it does," I murmured.

"Les ain't gonna like this any more than McBeen did earlier. He promised his wife they'd look at used cars."

"Did Deputy Phart make it to the delivery room before the stork did?"

Harve exhaled. "Stork's on the fourth pass, last I heard. I suppose I'll have to oversee this myself."

"Wow, Harve," I said, "that'll make my day."

He hung up without bothering to say goodbye.

12

As soon as I hung up, Estelle started in with questions, but I cut her off. "The keys to the units are kept in the drawer under the cash register. There are no indications someone forced open the door. What about the key?"

"It seems to be missing. There are moments when Ruby Bee's in the kitchen dishing up food, but it'd be real risky for anybody to go behind the bar. You'd think after all these years I of all people could fetch myself some sherry, but even I don't dare. Dahlia was the only waitress in a long while, and she quit a year ago."

"Therefore?" I said.

Estelle began to nibble what I had learned from the catalog was Tangelo Tang off her lower lip. "Gwynnie did some work in the pantry last week, and just the other day was putting down shelf paper. She was back and forth, looking for scissors or tape or whatnot."

"When's the last time Ruby Bee saw the key?"

"If you want to interrogate your own mother, it's between her and you. Don't go thinking she knew anything about this, though. She may have offered Gwynnie a safe place to get away from the likes of Daniel

Holliflecker, but she would never allow the Flamingo Motel to be used for tawdry romances."

I opened the door so I could watch for Harve. "Give me a break, Estelle. Two or three times a year a truck driver has one too many pitchers of beer and wisely decides to sleep it off. Beyond that, travel agents do not book their clients into the Flamingo Motel, and AAA does not include it in the guidebook. Michelin awards no stars. Ruby Bee knows damn well what goes on out here. She may not condone it, but that hasn't stopped her from accepting cash in exchange for a room key."

Estelle flapped her jaw for a moment, cranking up to what would have been an eruption of self-righteous indignation worthy of Mrs. Jim Bob, then thought better of it. "Well, she didn't give Gwynnie the key, and she's had no call to make sure it was there since the exterminator came."

"So Gwynnie might have taken it as much as two weeks ago?"

"She could have. There's no way of telling. A salesman stopped by a couple of nights ago, but he stayed in number four. Other than that, the units have been empty for six months."

"What precisely did Gwynnie say about Daniel?"

"She was worried that he might be abusive. Ruby Bee, Jessie, and I all tried to persuade her to stay at the Flamingo. She seemed to think we were sticking our noses in her private business. Jessie caught the worst of it, even though he was just trying to help."

This was the second time I'd heard the rumor, but it was of the sort that only two parties could verify. One of them was no longer available. "What did you think when she said this about Daniel?" I asked Estelle. "Did you believe her?"

"I wasn't sure what to think. According to Gwynnie, she had to live with Leona for another two months on account of a court order, so she couldn't get away from him. I can't imagine why anybody'd make up something like that."

"Nor can I," I admitted. I went to the doorway and gazed across the gravel at the opposite building. A regular at the bar might have taken the key, but the threat ran deeper than being caught in the act. None of the locals would gamble on being spotted creeping out of the Flamingo Motel after a liaison. The teenagers took advantage of blanket-friendly spots alongside Boone Creek; the adults preferred the anonymity provided by dumpy motels on the fringes of Farberville and Starley City.

When Harve, Les, and a deputy carrying a very serious-looking crime scene kit finally appeared, I pointed them in the direction of number six. "I know we can't afford DNA testing," I said, "but we may be able to nail someone with old-fashioned fingerprints. It's distressingly obvious that sexual encounters were taking place, as well as . . ."

"Seventeen," said Harve, shaking his head. "Back in my day, the only girls that'd meet a boy in a motel weren't anybody you could introduce to your mama. Girls like that, well, everybody knew they were trash."

"Is this a bulletin from the Jurassic Trailer Park?" I said acerbically. "Girls wore skirts to their ankles and boys chopped wood to earn two bits to take a date to the newest Charlie Chaplin movie? A loaf of bread cost a dime? Jeez, Harve, we ought to have you bronzed. We can put you up outside the courthouse next to the statue of

Jubilation T. Cornpone. It'll be a toss-up which one of you looks more dignified."

"Got health insurance?" growled Harve.

"The city council gave me a box of Band-Aids."

"Extra-wide?"

Risking life and limb—and then some, Les inserted himself between us. "We'll get prints and samples. I don't know if we'll need the mattress, but we will take the sheets. Isn't there someone you should be interviewing right now, Arly?"

"Yeah," I said. "I'll talk to the uncle and see what I think. The bottom line's going to be fingerprints." I paused. "You may have to track down a particular exterminator and get his prints for comparison. Ruby Bee can give you his name."

"Everything we find will be on the way to the state forensics boys this evening," Les said. "We'll be here for at least an hour."

What he meant was that I had an hour to go soak my head, which I needed to do. I'd scraped up bodies thrown from cars that had failed to negotiate the pertinent curve; I'd fished bloated teenaged corpses out of the reservoir on occasion. But it was never easy.

I gave Harve an apologetic look. "I'll go talk to Daniel Holliflecker, then swing back by. If you want coffee or something, Estelle will fetch it for you. If you're not careful, Ruby Bee will be fixing you cheeseburgers and fries."

He relented. "And they'll be the best cheeseburgers west of the Mississippi. You go see what you can find out."

"Could you boys do with coffee?" asked Estelle. "How about some pie? Anybody in the mood for coconut cream?"

I left them to debate the crime-scene menu and drove to the Hollifleckers'. By this time, casseroles and cakes would have arrived in droves. Well-meaning church ladies would be protecting the portal like bronzed Spartan soldiers. Ruby Bee's green-bean concoction was surely displayed in a place of honor, perhaps next to Mrs. Jim Bob's wobbly pineapple-and-cream-cheese delight.

"Why, Arly," said Millicent McIlhaney as she opened the door, "how kind of you to come by. Lots of folks have already arrived, but there's always room for more. Would you like something to eat? I myself haven't had a chance to taste it, but I hear that Edwina's corn pudding is divine. Estelle brought by a very nice loaf of homemade bread and some huckleberry jam, and Ruby Bee can always be counted on, can't she? Your mama never misses an opportunity to offer us a real tasty casserole when troublesome times come about. You must be so proud of her."

"Absolutely," I said as I went inside. "Is Daniel here?"

Millicent's smile wavered. "Not as yet. Brother Verber wanted to wait with Leona, but she said she'd rather be alone."

"I'm going to have to speak to her."

"I believe she's in her sitting room. It's on the far side of the kitchen, out by the back porch. Are you sure you should disturb her in this time of grief? How about some pot roast and garlic potatoes?"

I brushed past Millicent, eyed the tantalizing spread on the dining-room table, and went through the kitchen to a room crowded with bookshelves, stacks of magazines, depictions of martyrs in all manner of painful demise, and a wastebasket containing several empty vodka bottles.

Leona appeared alarmingly limp in a chair in front of a

cluttered desk, but she lifted her head. "What do you want?"

"I need to know more about Gwynnie."

"Somebody killed her."

"Looks like it."

"Chip's gonna be wanting supper before too long. What am I supposed to do when he asks for his mama?"

I sat down on a footstool beside her desk. "Did you get hold of Daniel?"

"No," she said, tearing up. "I called the number and left a message at the desk, but you know how irresponsible these motel clerks can be. His seminar should be winding down for the day before too long. If he doesn't call, I'll try again. There's no cause for you to badger me like this, Arly. I am doing the best I can, just like I always have."

I realized one of the vodka bottles had been emptied in the last hour. "I do know you're doing your best, Leona. I'm just trying to do mine."

She hiccuped. "I should hope so."

"Gwynnie's father is dead and her mother is working at a mission in Africa, right? Are there any brothers or sisters who should be notified?"

Leona stared at a print of a martyr riddled with arrows; he had the flowing hair of a hero on the cover of a paperback novel, but bore an unfortunate resemblance to a pincushion. "Her older brother lives out in California. When she got herself into that whole mess, he made it clear that he didn't want anything more to do with her. Some nights I pray for earthquakes; other nights, I opt for mud slides and fires. Then again, maybe he'll snort alfalfa sprouts up his nose and die a most painful death."

"Perhaps Daniel should make the call," I said tactfully.

"It's my understanding that Gwynnie was under some sort of court order to live here until she turned eighteen. Is that true?"

"We agreed to it. The judge gave her the choice of living with us or going to prison. None of us were real happy about it."

"Prison?"

Leona shrugged. "It would have been one of those minimum-security places, more like a summer camp than anything else. She couldn't have taken Chip with her, though, and he would have been put in foster care. We worked it out with the social-worker lady, and she made her recommendation to the judge. It might have been better if we'd allowed the system to take charge." She swung around to give me an unfocused glare. "Why'd she end up drinking on Cotter's Ridge? She wasn't beaten and locked in the basement at night. Dahlia looked after Chip while she did odd jobs for Ruby Bee. Daniel and I saw to him in the evenings so she could take the computer class. Despite our misgivings, Jessie Traylor came by every now and then to sit on the porch swing with her. Her life may not have been a movie where everybody sings and dances, but she wasn't mistreated. In a few months, she could have upped and done whatever she chose. Why did she do it?"

"Someone did it to her," I reminded her. "What kind of legal trouble had she been in?"

"I disremember the specifics. She and some of her friends stole a car. They had a wreck or the car went off the road or something. It wasn't the first time Gwynnie'd run into problems with the law, and she most likely wouldn't have had any options if she hadn't been pregnant. With the judge's permission, Dolores packed her off to an unwed mothers' facility in Mississippi. Later, Dolores let her come home, but all they did was scream at each other. Two months ago Dolores upped and went off to save the souls of heathens in Africa. If we hadn't agreed to take Gwynnie in, Chip would have been sent to live with strangers. The Patchwoods look after their kin as best they can, even the common ones."

"Would you mind if I take a look at her bedroom?"

"Suit yourself. Take the bedroom with you when you leave. I don't give a rat's ass."

I detoured through the living room and told Millicent that Leona might benefit from something to eat, then continued upstairs. The first room, claustrophobic but clean, contained a crib with a sleeping baby and cloth diapers stacked on a card table. Further down the hall, I looked in at what was likely to be Daniel's office. Glassy-eyed fish leaped on the walls, and a computer was centered on a walnut desk larger than my bathroom. Leona's choice of art leaned toward martyrs in moments of anguish; Daniel seemed to prefer prints of ducks, mostly unaware of guns aimed at their bellies.

Gwynnie had covered her bed with a bright quilt, but her room still felt stark, as if she were an inmate trying to make the best of it until the parole board relented (a relevant analogy). The only books in sight were study guides for the GED, and, unsurprisingly, a Bible. Her drawers were filled with cheap underwear. Her closet held a few thin cotton dresses and skirts. She'd possessed a total of three pairs of shoes: those she'd been found in, a pair of cheap canvas tennis sneakers, and grayish bedroom mules that had gone through more than one molting season.

No ruby slippers for the unwed mother.

I sat down on the bed, trying to remember where I'd hidden my personal treasures at her age. Ruby Bee had never hesitated to search under the mattress, claiming it had to be turned periodically. Drawers were a joke. I'd once taped a poem from a particularly articulate suitor behind the toilet bowl. It took her a day, maybe less, to find it and then read it to me over supper. I'd been so embarrassed that I'd told him to take a hike. Someone who'd attended the tenth high school reunion reported that he owned a pro hockey franchise in Canada and was planning to compete in the next America's Cup yacht race.

Bad choice.

The suitcases in the closet were empty, and the shelf was dusty. I looked underneath the dresser, then removed the drawers to make sure nothing was taped on their backsides. The only items in the light fixture were dead bugs.

Seventeen implied cunning, but of a limited fashion. There was no ledge outside the window on which to leave a shoe box, nor easy access to a niche in the attic. The braided rug on the wood floor did not conceal a loose board. There were no trees within reach from the window.

The one thing that seemed to keep Leona and Daniel at a distance was Chip. Neither seemed to consider him more than a minor inconvenience that came attached to a major one. Whichever of them was the designated babysitter of the hour may have felt obliged to check on him, but it was hard to imagine either of them lingering.

He was breathing peacefully as I crept into his bedroom. A lamp beside the crib provided minimal light. I eased open drawers and fumbled through overalls and folded shirts. I moved on to the closet, where I found the payload in a diaper bag on the back corner of the shelf.

I took the cheap plastic box to Gwynnie's room and opened it. On the top was a pressed carnation, colorless and brittle, most likely a corsage of some splendor in its day. Newspaper clippings featured likenesses of Gwynnie at age four, when she'd found the first Easter egg at a mall, in fifth grade when her class had planted a tree at a nursing home, and in junior high, when she'd been named first runner-up in a local beauty pageant involving produce. A letter from her mother, which I did not read. A letter from her probation officer, warning her that if she failed to comply with the court order, she would lose custody of her child and be remanded into detention. A bookmark with a faded purple ribbon. A report card from sixth grade, asserting that she had potential if she would strive to apply herself.

And then, at the bottom, a flat plastic stick four inches long and half an inch wide. I myself had gone through moments of panic when I'd peed on such a thing and then waited, sucking in my breath until I came close to passing out on the toilet seat. Gwynnie must have stashed it in her box, unaware that the result faded within hours. The only reason she would have done so was for it to serve, mistakenly or not, as proof that she was pregnant. A negative result would have been pitched in the trash.

What I said does not warrant repeating, but it was one of those words you should not say to your great-aunt, particularly on her deathbed.

Gwynnie'd been meeting someone in number six for as long as two weeks, before or after the computer classes, or maybe during the odd moments when Ruby Bee was inside the bar, sloshing gravy on mashed potatoes and slicing apple pies. Jessie Traylor had a house, but Gwynnie might have been too nervous to park in his yard. She most certainly would have needed a haven in which to get cozy with Justin Bailey; Chapel, lacking a schedule, no doubt came and went on whim (and woe to the frogs in Boone Creek when she was whimsical). Daniel was an obvious consideration. Despite evidence that Leona drank herself into an abyss every night, at some unpredictable point she must have roused herself to stagger upstairs.

Gwynnie was beginning to seem less and less the poster child for teen angel. She'd stolen the key from under the nose of her benefactress. Using the motel room for sexual encounters amounted to betrayal of the trust and support she'd been offered. The previous night, seemingly after nine or ten o'clock, someone had met her in the room and killed her, then found a way to transport her body to the shack on Cotter's Ridge. Why had she taken Chip with her to begin with? And who had taken him into Farberville and dropped him off at the hospital?

Certainly not Miss Okrafest, I thought. Based on what Raz had said and I'd observed, her body had been in the shack for several hours before Les had received the call about Chip. Toddlers did not wander in public facilities for more than a minute or two without being scooped up, especially ones with droopy diapers and notes pinned to their shirts.

My head jerked up as I heard a muted whimper from his room. Leona was in no condition to deal with him, and I hadn't heard an indication from downstairs that Daniel had returned. I'd never had a puppy or a kitten; the only creature I'd ever nurtured was a goldfish that I won at the county fair the year I turned seven. It went belly-up the next day. I'd never gotten around to naming it, although I'd been leaning toward "Goldie."

It occurred to me that my best bet was to go downstairs and let Millicent know that Chip was stirring. I replaced the letters and clippings in the box, and was about to add the home pregnancy wand when something nagged at me. I looked more closely at one of the clippings. Miss Okrafest had achieved her ephemeral rhinestone glory from the Powata town fathers.

And one of them probably worked in the office where Seth Smitherman had obtained his driver's license only a month ago.

Powata, Arkansas.

Millicent was still by the front door, ushering in members of the congregation and steering them in an orderly manner toward the buffet line. From the living room, I heard Mrs. Jim Bob extolling the virtues of the Maggody web site to the Internet illiterati (among whom I counted myself). Dahlia's double stroller was parked in the foyer; I had no doubt she had found a way to jiggle and juggle the twins as she loaded up on corn pudding, pot roast, garlic potatoes, and huckleberry jam.

Huckleberry jam on crusty homemade bread.

I asked Millicent to look after Chip, gazed wistfully toward the dining room as my stomach rumbled a suggestion that one measly little garlic potato might be just what I needed to solve the case, and was stoically heading out the door when Eileen Buchanon caught me.

"Can I talk to you?" she whispered.

"For a second."

She glanced at Millicent, who was edging in our direction, her ears aquiver. "Out on the porch."

"I'm in the middle of a criminal investigation," I said as I allowed myself to be hustled out the door.

"It's about something I saw on the computer," she said. "Or maybe I didn't. Maybe I'm crazy. Maybe I should take a change of clothes and go live in a cave with Diesel."

I wasn't quite sure how to respond. "Why are you telling me this, Eileen? I don't know anything about what you may or may not have seen. The one time I was in the lab, the computers were turned off. Shouldn't you be confiding in Justin?"

"It's too embarrassing."

"What is?"

She sat down on a wicker rocking chair. "I'm reluctant to admit even to myself what I thought I saw. My mother went through menopause at about my age. I don't reckon her hot flashes were quite this . . . hot, though. I can't sleep for more than a few minutes without waking up covered with sweat—all on account of what I saw, if I saw it. I swear, if my mother had been faced with this, she would have packed her bags and lit out for Kansas City instead of making biscuits from scratch every morning until she had a heart attack and died at the age of eighty-seven. She was wearing her apron when they found her."

I might as well have been standing in the middle of a field of corn, surrounded by sheep dressed in tutus. "What are you talking about, Eileen? The Internet is causing you to have hot flashes? I've heard that constantly flickering lights can induce epileptic seizures. Could that have something to do with it? Have you talked to a doctor?"

"Earl," she said. "I saw Earl."

"Okay," I said cautiously. "You thought you saw Earl

on the computer screen. I didn't think he'd been coming to the class."

"Oh, he's vowed never to so much as lay a finger on a keyboard. His idea of technology is the remote control for the television. One evening I tried to tell him about a web site devoted to professional wrestlers, but he got so mad that he stomped out of the house and stayed at the pool hall past midnight. He's like one of those barbarians that believes a camera can steal your soul."

"But you saw him? What exactly was he doing?"

She covered her face with her hands. "I can't bring myself to tell you."

This was a situation requiring a shrink more skilled than yours truly. "I wish I could stay here and try to help you, but I ought to be going. It's going to be common knowledge before long that Gwynnie was murdered. I need to be dealing with that. Ruby Bee knows more about this computer thing. Why don't you talk to her?"

"Earl was buck-naked."

Since I was heading down the steps, it was a toss-up between busting my tailbone or breaking my nose. At the fateful moment, I caught myself and stared back at her. "What did you say?"

"I said he was buck-naked like he just climbed out of the tub. What's more, his privates . . . well, this is the craziest part of all, but they weren't his."

"Whose were they?"

"How should I know? All I can say is they weren't his. I've been married to him nigh onto thirty years. Don't you think by now I should be able to recognize my own husband's privates?"

"Yeah, I guess so," I said, sitting down on the bottom

step, "but you're not sure you even saw . . . them. Lots of women are finding relief with estrogen replacement. Now there's something you can research on the Internet."

"You think I was seeing things, don't you?"

"You yourself suggested the possibility, Eileen. If Earl's never so much as sat down in front of a computer, so how could—"

I stopped as I remembered Jim Bob's apprehension that photographs of him might be circulating on the Internet. If Jim Bob had been displaying his privates, however, they surely would have been his own. I had no idea how Earl might have acquired someone else's.

"What?" she snapped.

"I'll see what I can find out. Right now Sheriff Dorfer's waiting for me to give him a report. Have some supper and try not to worry."

Eileen stood up. "I'd like to think you're not going to start telling folks about Earl's privates, no matter whose they might turn out to be."

"I promise not to say a word, unless, of course, it comes down to the necessity of a lineup over at the county jail."

"I am not about to stand in front of a window and try to recall what I saw, if I saw anything, which I'm beginning to think I didn't. What's more, it wasn't like Earl was in the midst of committing a crime. He had that stupid grin on his face like in his picture for the electric co-op board of directors annual report."

Trying not to envision a dozen middle-aged and elderly men, potbellied and balding, struttin' their stuff on an annual report, I fled to my car and drove back to the Flamingo Motel.

Harve came out of number six, flecks of meringue clinging to the corners of his mouth. "I reckon you were right, Arly," he said, which was as close to an apology as I'd ever get. "The boys are still collecting samples. It could have been somebody else, but from what Estelle said, Gwynnie was about the only person that could have taken the key. There ain't much doubt why she did. There was an empty vodka bottle under the bed and a sprinkling of marijuana in the wastebasket."

"You need to tell McBeen that she was apt to have been pregnant."

"McBeen won't care. He did the preliminary, but that's all. We won't get a comprehensive autopsy from the state lab for three or four days, if we're lucky. Could be as much as a week." He pulled out a handkerchief and wiped his mouth. "Who do you think's responsible?"

I perched on the hood of my car. "Have you done a background search on Gwynnie?"

"The records are sealed on account of her age. Should I be goin' after a court order to open them?"

"No," I said, shaking my head. "As I'm sure McBeen would agree, she had her three strikes and she's out. Anyway, I've got a lead."

"Need backup?"

"Swing through the bar and have another piece of pie before you leave. I'll call you when I have something."

Harve was glaring at me as I drove away.

13

Sweat was not dribbling tentatively down Brother Verber's face—it was coming down in a briny deluge that was nigh on to unmoppable. His nose was redder than the lead reindeer's on Christmas Eve. Was it possible he was nurturing a deeply buried desire for Idalupino Buchanon? Idalupino Buchanon, of all wimmen? The same Idalupino that wore such heavy makeup that her facial features seemed to be in danger of sliding down to her chin, that never shaved her armpits or her legs or her upper lip? But how else could he be sitting there in front of the computer, imagining her ripe bosoms overflowing from a slip of a itsy-bitsy bikini top—and the bottom pulled down to expose auburn ringlets?

Why, he'd barely ever said more than a few words to her while she checked his groceries and offered him a choice of paper or plastic. She was hardly a member of the congregation, being the sort to spend her Sunday mornings nursing a hangover—and not in her own bed.

He wiped saliva off his chin. Here he'd come to the lab to write up a real nice paragraph about his sermon in the morning, and all he could do was think inappropriate thoughts about a woman that was rumored to have sex with her uncle, not to mention cousins across the county.

He scrolled back and read the Bible verse he'd put up the day before to stimulate some soul-searching before the sermon. "Whosoever looketh upon a woman to lust after her hath committed adultery with her already in his heart. And if thy right eye offend thee, pluck it out, and cast it from thee, for it is profitable for thee that one of thy members should perish, and not that thy whole body should be cast into hell."

At the time, he'd figured Matthew had the likes of Jim Bob in mind, since Jim Bob did a lot more than looketh. Not that he was the only one. Brother Verber'd heard the rumors about Justin and Gwynnie. Kevin Buchanon had been thrown out of his home, probably for cause. Earl had been seen at the pool hall late at night, drinking beer and telling off-color jokes. Jeremiah McIlhaney had been spotted in Starley City with a woman with bleached-blond hair; his wife was the only person in Maggody who'd believed for a second that it was his half-sister from Helena.

He clicked the sequence of buttons to exit from the web page and was preparing to leave, when Lottie Estes came into the classroom.

She stared at him, her eyeballs bulging like a bullfrog's. "Brother Verber!"

"Afternoon, Lottie," he said. "It'd be a lovely spring day if we hadn't heard about the terrible trouble on Cotter's Ridge, doncha think? I went by Leona's and spent some time ministering to her in her hour of need. She's holding up well, considering." He edged back as Lottie began to tremble. "That fruit salad you took was mighty tasty. When I was a boy, there was nothing I loved more than climbing a tree out in the orchard and eating juicy, ripe peaches. Each golden bite was a piece of heaven melting in my mouth. I'd be so sticky afterward that I'd have to wash up in the creek, but it was worth it. Sometimes we should study the Bible and ponder its mysteries, but other times we got to let loose and enjoy the purely physical pleasures God has granted us."

"Don't come near me!"

Brother Verber frowned. "What's wrong with you, Lottie?"

"You so much as take one step in my direction and I'll scream so loud they'll here me on the far side of the Missouri line."

"I don't understand why you'd think for a second that I'd so much as lay a finger on you, unless it was to offer my blessing."

"What you do doesn't constitute a blessing, you pervert. I'm gonna leave now, but if you try to follow me, you'll be right sorry."

She backed out of the classroom. He watched from a window as she scurried to her car, made a production of locking the doors, and then drove away in a screech of loose gravel and dust.

It was a puzzlement, he thought as he went outside and hurried to his own car. Sister Barbara had mentioned the possibility of exorcism, and he was beginning to think she might have been on track. Satan had moved into Maggody. One by one, he was tainting minds with evil. It was most decidedly time for a glass or two of sacramental wine, and maybe a frozen pizza.

Due to the vast powers of his opponent, Brother Verber thought a pepperoni supreme might be required.

I drove out to the trailer farthest from the gate at the Pot O' Gold. On cop shows on television, the witness was always cowering inside his apartment, willing to blurt out a confession before the commercial break. Seth Smitherman had apparently not been a fan of such shows. He'd left the door unlocked; I quickly determined he wasn't there. Since I lacked a search warrant, I did not make any effort to uncover evidence of illegal activity. If I'd chanced upon anything, it would have stood up in court about as long as Kevvie Junior or Rose Marie.

I couldn't remember if Seth had specified where he worked. It was a sunny Saturday afternoon, and if he wasn't toiling away for $5.35 an hour (poultry processing was a twenty-four-hour-a-day, seven-day-a-week business), he might well be fishing or drinking beer in Farberville. An APB would have been a stretch. Growing up in Powata was not an indictable offense, and nobody had hinted at a link between him and Gwynnie.

It was a helluva coincidence, though. Seth had done time for grand theft auto; Gwynnie had been busted for joyriding. Chip's father had been killed in a car crash.

For the moment, there wasn't much I could do. I leaned against the hood of my car for several minutes, listening to the whoops of the pint-sized savages as they raged through the Pot O' Gold, shooting each other with their index fingers and sprawling dramatically in the mud. Cops 'n' robbers had probably given way to more sophisticated scenarios involving star troopers and alien life forms, but I was well out of the Saturday-morning cartoon loop.

Then again, we were well into Saturday afternoon and I'd nobly bypassed the garlic potatoes and huckleberry jam at Leona's house. I had not lingered at the crime scene for a cheeseburger or a piece of pie. If I continued to drive around in circles, which as far as I could tell was all I'd been doing for several hours, I was likely to end up depicted in a cheap print on the wall of Leona's study, my halo aflicker and my ribs resembling a washboard.

There was undoubtedly a vacancy at the Vatican for a martyr with fluctuating blood sugar, I thought as I drove to Ruby Bee's. As Harve had avowed, her cheeseburgers were supreme. A grilled-cheese sandwich would not suffice; I felt a craving for red meat.

Medium well, anyway, with tomatoes, lettuce, onion, and mayo. Mustard and ketchup were for Yankees.

"I was wondering when you'd show your face," said Ruby Bee as I came inside the barroom. "Harve and his boys left a few minutes ago, but they wouldn't say diddly-squat about what they found. I just can't believe Gwynnie would take the key and carry on like that in one of my units. All I wanted to do was help her. I paid her decent money to clean out the pantry, even though it could have waited another six months. I told her that she and Chip could stay here for free. I feel so stupid, Arly."

I went behind the bar to hug her. "You shouldn't feel that way. You were kind and generous. She may have had big brown eyes, but everything I've learned about her suggests she was a cold-blooded schemer. She was living with Daniel and Leona to avoid doing time in a juvenile detention center. Leona described it as a summer camp, but from what I've heard, there's no canoeing or volleyball."

"She seemed so sweet."

I blotted her cheeks with a napkin, then retreated to a stool. "Any chance of a cheeseburger and a glass of milk?"

"What's going to happen to Chip?"

"A foster home, most likely," I said. "It's hard to imagine Leona and Daniel taking in a child that age on a long-term basis."

"What about Jessie? Could he adopt Chip?"

"I don't think so."

Ruby Bee sighed. "I'll fix a cheeseburger. I just wish you could fix everything else."

"Me too." I sat in silence as she put a beef patty on the grill and began to slice an onion. "Did Gwynnie ever mention someone named Seth Smith or Smitherman?"

She looked at me. "Eula said that was the boy shooting off the rifle at the Pot O' Gold a while back."

"Did she say anything else?"

"He keeps to himself, unlike that horrible Lazarus, who this very morning, carried his garbage out to the Dumpster dressed in nothing more than his underpants. Eula liked to have fainted, or so she said."

"She watched him every step of the way, I suppose?"

Ruby Bee flipped the burger and put a piece of cheese on it. "There are innocent children living in the trailer park. Someone has to be alert."

"And that would be Eula."

"The only reason she keeps an eye on her neighbors is to protect the rest of us. Lazarus is up to no good. Eula told me that not only Gwynnie but a lot of other girls were going into his trailer at all hours of the day and night."

"Gwynnie?"

"Among others," said Ruby Bee as she slapped together

my cheeseburger and tossed a bag of potato chips in my direction.

"Why? What's he doing?"

"If Eula knew, she'd have said as much. She's not a private eye with all kinds of fancy equipment, and she can't stand at the window all day, due to her varicose veins and tendency toward phlebitis. If you want to know what he's up to, you should ask him yourself instead of expecting Eula to write up a report and lay it on your desk."

I blissed out on the cheeseburger, then said, "He's most definitely high on my list."

"Are you going over there now?"

I slid off the stool. "No, I'm going over there later."

"Where are you going now?"

"I'm going out the door." Ignoring her questions, I left the barroom and climbed into my car. A sunny Saturday afternoon. Some of the high school boys might be poaching squirrels or lurking outside liquor stores in Farberville, trying to find someone over twenty-one to buy them beer, but I had a good idea where to find the girls.

The Dairee Dee-Lishus was doing a brisk business in cherry limeades and greasy french fries. The two picnic tables were populated by the usual suspects: Darla Jean, Heather, the Dahlton twin sisters, Billy Dick McNamara, Baxter Bean, and a couple of neckless wonders who were clearly Buchanons. A pair of pimply dweebs had been permitted to hover nearby, but not, of course, too closely to the football players and homecoming princesses.

They all glazed over like porcelain figurines as I parked and got out of the car. "Pretty day," I said as I went to the counter. The surly Hispanic guy was even less pleased to see me than the kids.

"You want something?" he demanded.

"A limeade, on the rocks," I said, then turned around to smile at my momentarily captive audience. "Did you all hear about Gwynnie Patchwood?"

"Shitty thing," muttered Billy Dick as the rest of them grimaced.

I put down a dollar and picked up my drink. "Yeah, I guess dying at seventeen is shitty, Billy Dick. Real shitty."

"We didn't really know her," Heather volunteered. "I mean, she showed up at church, but her aunt and uncle didn't let her hang around outside after services. She didn't attend our Sunday school class. Brother Verber most likely would have let her go on the senior trip to Branson."

Baxter stopped stuffing fries in his mouth long enough to say, "I thought she was hot, but when I tried to talk to her at the supermarket, she acted like I was dirt."

"You are dirt," said Darla Jean, then looked at me. "My ma made me call her a couple of weeks ago and ask her to go riding around or whatever it is my ma thinks we do on the weekend. Gwynnie made it clear that she was way too 'mature' to hang out with the likes of us. I didn't bother to argue with her, but Baxter's got a bastard son over in Starley City, and just last week Carlotta . . ."

"Darla Jean," Carlotta inserted icily, "we agreed not to discuss this. One more word and I'll start remembering what happened at the mall just before Christmas."

"I was not shoplifting!"

"Walking out of the store in three pairs of jeans and four blouses?"

I held up my hands. "I'm here to talk about Gwynnie. Seventeen, and dead. Her body's on the way to the state lab in Little Rock. Once she's there, she'll be laid flat on a metal table. The first incision will be from her chin to her pubic bone. The medical examiner will crack open her rib cage and remove her organs. Anybody want to make a joke?"

Nobody did.

I pointed at Darla Jean and Heather. "In my car, now. We need to talk."

"Why do you always pick on me?" asked Darla Jean as she stood up. "I already said I don't know anything. Last time you made me go for a ride, Billy Dick here accused me of being a snitch."

"If Billy Dick repeats that accusation, I'll jerk out his tonsils and feed them to the turtles," I said levelly. "That goes for the rest of you. A seventeen-year-old girl was murdered last night. She will not be buying a dress for the prom, or skinny-dipping in Boone Creek when the weather gets warmer. She will not be sitting on a blanket sipping cheap wine on a starry night. She won't be going off to college or finding a job in Farberville or hitchhiking to California or getting married—or turning eighteen. I assume you can figure out exactly what she will be doing two months from now."

Heather and Darla Jean got into the backseat of my car. I gave the Hispanic guy an apologetic smile as I drove away; having customers hijacked was hardly good for business. I drove to the north end of town and parked by the remains of Purtle's Esso.

"I sold ads for the yearbook," I said, twisting around in the seat to look at them. "Thing is, I sold them in the fall. The deadline was December first."

Darla Jean chewed on this for a moment. "Maybe back then it was."

"Yeah," Heather added earnestly. "Everything's computerized these days. We can sell ads right up until the page proofs go to the printer."

"And the yearbook sponsor will confirm this?" I asked. Squirm city.

Darla Jean made an admirable try. "That'd be Mr. Kennismith, but he's just doing it because Miz Bealford quit last month and Mr. Darker dumped it on him. He doesn't know how it works."

"I do."

Heather pushed her hair out of her eyes. "What're you gettin' at?"

I managed a faint smile. "Let's go find a log and sit beside the creek. This may take a while, but at some point you'll have to tell me what's been going on."

"Nothing's been going on," Darla Jean said defiantly, eyeballing Heather. "Nothing at all. We may have missed the deadline for yearbook ads, but that ain't a crime. Maybe we thought he'd pay in cash and we could pocket it. It's not like he was gonna demand a free copy two months from now. Isn't that right, Heather?"

"Out of the car," I said.

"You're kidnapping us," said Heather.

I gazed coldly at them. "Don't make me shoot you and bury your bodies under the bridge."

"You know," Darla Jean whined as she and Heather followed me down to the creek, "just because we're minors doesn't mean we don't have the same rights as everybody else."

Gesturing at a relatively dry log, I said, "Would you prefer that we went by your homes and informed your parents that I was taking you to the sheriff's office for interrogation? They'd have at least half an hour to arrange for lawyers to meet us at the jail in Farberville."

"What's your problem?" Heather demanded as she took a pack of cigarettes out of her purse and handed it to Darla Jean. "Nobody hung out with Gwynnie. She couldn't have found the Dairee Dee-Lishus on a bet. Maybe we saw her around town, but that's all. Shouldn't you be talking to Jessie Traylor?"

"Or Justin Bailey?" added Darla Jean.

I sat down across from them. "Either of you heard anything more than gossip?"

Darla Jean avoided my eyes as she lit a cigarette. "I s'pose not. Can we go now? My ma says I have to finish the ironing if I want to go out tonight. Billy Dick and me are aimin' to go to a movie."

Heather stiffened. "I thought you and him broke up last weekend."

"We did, but then on Tuesday he left a real sweet note in my locker, and on Wednesday we—"

"Okay," I said hastily. "I'm sure everybody in town will be relieved to know the two of you have reconciled."

Darla Jean choked on a lungful of smoke. "We've never done no such thing! My pa'd whip me if he heard something like that. We may have gone out to Boone Creek last night, but we sure didn't reconcile, or whatever you're calling it. We're not even going steady!"

"Easy," I murmured.

"Well, we didn't!"

I bit my lip for a moment. "Let's go back to yearbook ads and Lazarus. What were you really doing there? Hoping to buy drugs?"

Heather stared at me, and if her fingernails had not

been digging into her thighs, I might have bought her reply. "No way! He's so creepy he ought should be living in a swamp. Darla Jean and me just wanted to get a closer look at him."

"What if I said I had a witness who's seen you two going into the trailer on several occasions? Do you know how easy it's going to be for me to get a search warrant?"

This shut them up for a good minute. Heather finally flicked her cigarette into the water and said, "You're planning to search his trailer?"

Darla Jean groaned. "I'm gonna throw up."

I helped her to her feet and aimed her toward the brush behind us. When she finally trudged back to join us, I had great expectations that they would proceed to blurt out their innermost secrets and throw themselves on my mercy.

"I wanna go home," wailed Darla Jean. "I got a belly-ache."

Heather jumped up off the log. "I can't believe you're being so mean, Arly. You might as well be swimming out there with the water moccasins. Darla Jean, do you think another cigarette might settle your stomach?"

"I wanna go home!" She staggered back to the brush and made more disgusting noises. "Help me to the car, Heather. I reckon I'm about to pass out."

"Either of you enrolled in drama this year?" I asked as we scrambled up the slope.

"That is so rude," Heather said with a sniff of adolescent indignation. "Lazarus was not selling drugs. I swear it. Help me get Darla Jean in the car before she pukes all over both of us."

I opened the back door and stepped back as Heather

coldheartedly shoved her friend onto the seat. Darla Jean's face was the same greenish hue as the bubbly scum in the creek, and her cheeks were inflating ominously. Heather found it prudent to sit in the front seat across from me.

"Is she pregnant?" I asked quietly as I started the car.

Heather shook her head. "No, she asked me for a tampon earlier this afternoon. You just got her all upset, accusing us of buying drugs from Lazarus."

"You just swore he's not selling drugs," I pointed out.

Her chin shot out. "As far as I know, he's not selling drugs. If you want to get a Bible, I'll put my hand on it and say as much. I don't know anybody that's bought drugs from him."

"What *is* he doing?"

"You'll have to ask him yourself. Maybe he's snatching up those nasty little brats at the Pot O' Gold and grinding their bones to make his bread."

Darla Jean promptly did a number in the backseat. Heather and I mutely rolled down our windows.

"What do we do now?" I asked.

"Darla Jean'll kill me if anybody catches sight of her like this."

"Shall I take her home?"

"So her parents can kill her?"

I braked for the stoplight, which always turned red when it sensed my approach. "I'll drop you off at the Dairee Dee-Lishus so you can get your car, then I'll take Darla Jean back to my apartment. She can take a shower and borrow some clothes. Afterward, you can drive her home."

Heather looked at me out of the corners of her eyes.

"You're going to do that, even though you still think we're lying to you?"

"Yeah, I am—and, yeah, I do."

"Because we'll be so grateful that we'll tell you the truth?"

"That would be nice, but that's not why I'm doing it, Heather. Consider it a legacy from Gwynnie."

The other teenagers had cleared out from the picnic area. The Hispanic guy would no doubt have knocked me upside the head with a tamale if I'd given him half a chance, but I merely let Heather out of my car and drove to my apartment. It may have lacked a view of skyscrapers and the East River, but it had decent water pressure.

Darla Jean was going to need it.

As for everything else, screw it. The day had gone on too long, caused me too much pain, confused and bewildered me, obliged me to be rude, pricked too many nerves. Once Heather hauled away Darla Jean, I intended to clean up the backseat of the car, open a beer, heat up a can of soup, and stare at the TV set.

At some point, I might even turn it on.

"You know what riles me?" Raz demanded, stomping back and forth in his living room. "They're all saying my 'shine is what killed that girl in the shack. Can you imagine such a thing?"

Marjorie couldn't.

"My 'shine is pure as mother's milk. Ain't nobody ever gone blind from drinking it. You seen how I use only the finest corn mash, and my pa hisself welded ever' seam of the copper cooker. Now if I was makin' rotgut like that ol' boy over in Maducca County, running it through a car radiator and adding wood-grain alcohol, I'd be the first to say so. Ain't no one ever died from drinking my 'shine in forty years. You recollect when that biker at the pool hall bet fifty dollars he could down a whole quart jar and walk out the door? He was mighty wobbly, but he made it. I still feel badly about him driving into a tree, but you cain't go blaming me on account it bein' foggy."

There was no hint of accusation in Marjorie's gaze.

Raz wheeled around. "It's all that sumbitch Diesel's fault. Iff'n he hadn't gone and stole my stash, I never would've been obliged to mention it to Arly. The ridge is plenty big for the two of us, long as he keeps his distance. But then he ups and steals my 'shine! I oughtta track him down like a rabid dawg and put a bullet between his eyes. I reckon I'd git a medal like a war hero."

Marjorie blinked in awe.

"That's right! Why, Jim Bob hisself would pin the medal on my overalls while the high school band played the national anthem. Ever'body would get all misty, excepting maybe Petrol, but who gives a sorry shit about him!"

Marjorie slithered off the couch and lumbered into the kitchen to bury her glistening pink snout in a bowl of kibble. It was hard to say what she was thinkin'.

Raz, on the other hand, was intent on vengeance.

Chapel sat on the sofa with the remote control in her hand. "I can't believe there's no cable," she said. "They have cable in Latvia and Estonia. They get CNN in Nepal."

"You want to go to a movie in Farberville?" asked Justin, admittedly without much enthusiasm. Fishing had involved more than dangling a rod over the water and waiting for some mindless piscine to impale itself on the hook. They'd careened down a practically nonexistent road, and then hiked for most of a mile, weighted down with rods, reels, creels, a couple of coolers, and a picnic basket filled with sandwiches and cookies, struggling through endless patches of poison ivy and briars. He'd twisted his ankle, bumped his head on a branch, and taken a hard fall in the mud beside the river. Mosquitoes had attacked his exposed flesh, and clouds of gnats had surrounded his head, determined to take up residence in his nose and mouth. He'd been picking off seed ticks in the shower when he'd been interrupted.

"You look a little worn," she said. "I bought some wine after I finished up at the library. You want some?"

"Yeah," he said. "You heard about Gwynnie?"

"I heard she was missing. They find her?"

Justin repeated what he'd been told, as well as what he'd learned when he'd gone to the supermarket to buy calamine lotion and sunburn ointment (neither of which thus far had offered any relief). "Her body was discovered in a shack somewhere up on that ridge on the west side of town, but the buzz is that she was killed at the Flamingo Motel."

Chapel filled two plastic glasses with wine and sat down next to him. "Gawd, I feel terrible. The chief of police came by this morning to say Gwynnie had disappeared. I shrugged it off."

He took a swallow of wine. It was not full-bodied or frisky or fruity or smoky, but it went down as well as any wine could that came with a screw cap and cost less than five dollars a gallon. "Arly seems to think I might have been fooling around with Gwynnie."

"It's occurred to me."

"Well, you're both wrong. She was a pathetic little thing. I dealt with her as I would any particularly tiresome student."

"When was she killed?"

"Sometime after the class last night, when I was in Farberville."

Chapel put down her glass. "Will LaRue confirm that you were at his house?"

"He wasn't home," Justin said. "Earlier this afternoon I reread the E-mail he sent, just to make sure he was talking about last night. I realize that at times I get confused about dates, but this wasn't one of them."

"Did you call him today to ask where the hell he was?"

"He didn't answer, but he usually takes his laundry over to his mother's house on Saturday afternoons and hangs around until she feeds him dinner. Eventually, if he stays long enough, she breaks down and gives him the leftovers."

Chapel tried not to sigh. "You'd better print out the E-mail and save it."

"You're acting like you don't believe me either."

"There's more than one buzz at the supermarket," she said coolly as she picked up the remote and turned on the local news. Gwynnie Patchwood's murder was the lead story.

"I heard tell this is fake," Kevin said, watching the screen as the two hairless men bounced off the ropes, waving their arms and belly-bumping each other with sadistic glee. "They git together aforehand and decide which of 'em is gonna do what to the other."

Earl stared at Kevin from the recliner. "Son, there are days I still think I can whup some sense into you, but they're getting further and further between. Are you saying that Rocky Horror and Blondo here aren't really slamming each other's faces on the mat? Did you see Blondo's foot stomp down on Rocky Horror's back just now? How's anybody gonna fake something like that? I know for a fact there are paramedics waiting just in case they have to take someone to the emergency room. Why'd they be doing that if this was faked?"

Kevin winced as Rocky Horror staggered off the rope and took a fist to his throat. "Do the paramedics ever hafta carry somebody out?"

"It's a matter of time," said Earl. "Go get me a beer and see if there's any more onion dip. I can't believe your ma'd go off and leave us like this. We're out of bologna and pimento cheese. I ate the last of the meat loaf for breakfast this morning. What does she reckon we're gonna eat come tomorrow?"

"Do you know anything about women, Pa? What makes them act the way they do?"

Earl belched thoughtfully. "Ain't no man that understands women. Take your ma, for example. I come home from mowing the back pasture, all filthy and sweating like a pig, wanting nothing more than a cold beer and a hot supper, and she asks me what I think. 'About what?' I say. She gets all mad and stomps off to the bedroom. Now how in tarnation am I supposed to know she had her hair fixed a different way? I ain't some faggot hairdresser. If she'd had it shaved off or dyed green, I most likely would have noticed."

Kevin thought this over. "Dahlia's temperamental, but her hair's the same."

"She buy a new dress? That can be dangerous."

"Not in a long while. She just kicked me out. Whenever I try to talk to her, her lips get all puckered and there I am on the porch."

"There's your problem," Earl said. "No man should be trying to talk to a woman. They're a whole different breed, all the time wantin' to know how you feel about things. Buy her a big bottle of cologne at Wal-Mart and tell her you like her hair. Just don't sound like a faggot, okay? Keep in mind God ain't married. Now go get that beer."

<hr>

"You know anything about men?" Dahlia asked her mother-in-law while they took turns dipping into the bowl of popcorn.

"I've been married to one for over thirty years," said Eileen. "Far as I can tell, they're all the same. The only reason they have faces is so we can tell 'em apart. Hardly worth the bother, if you ask me."

"So what should I do?"

"Cross your fingers that someone puts out an owner's manual. Otherwise, we're all stuck with 'em as they are."

<hr>

Brother Verber stayed in the shadows of the Dumpster, trying to decide what to do. He'd waited behind the SuperSaver until Idalupino had come outside and gotten into her car, then followed her at a most discreet distance as she drove to the Pot O' Gold and parked by a trailer scarcely larger than a camper. He was pretty much sure it was hers, since she'd stopped to pluck several items of intimate apparel from the clothesline before going inside. The lights had come on seconds later.

The curtains were drawn, though, and he couldn't catch so much as a glimpse of her—much less any auburn ringlets. Earlier, his plan had made perfectly good sense. If he could confirm what he thought he'd seen, then he'd seen it. If he couldn't, well, then he'd convince himself that he hadn't. The last thing he could do was march up to her door and demand that she pull off her panties so he'd know if he was crazy. Idalupino's hair changed on a weekly basis; she'd been blond, red-haired, brunette, and even raven with a white streak. There was no telling what her true hair color was.

A shadow moved across a small window that might well be a bathroom. There was maybe an inch or so where the blind didn't quite hit the sill. Brother Verber eyed his options. The aluminum chairs were rickety. Her car was parked a sight too far away. The only possibility was a spindly pine, nothing that would ever qualify for tinsel and fragile glass ornaments.

Leaving himself in the hands of the Lord (and his shoes on the patio), Brother Verber began his ascent.

When Mrs. Jim Bob heard the kitchen door open, she shrugged off her bathrobe, slipped her feet into high heels, and unsteadily stood up. Her lungs were paralyzed, and she could literally feel the blood draining from her face. Dropping her bathrobe on the floor next to the sofa, she adjusted the pink negligee to expose as much of her bosom as she could bear.

Despite the urge to dash upstairs and lock herself in her bedroom for a year or two, she forced herself to wobble toward the doorway of the kitchen.

"I've been waiting for you," she cooed as she came around the corner. And stopped as she met Elsie McMay's horrified expression.

Elsie put a plate down on the dinette. "This is from Leona's house," she croaked. "She said she thanks you kindly for the pineapple salad and for coming by. . . ."

"I can explain," said Mrs. Jim Bob, then realized she couldn't.

"Please don't. I should have knocked, but I thought I'd just pop in and leave this for you. I gotta be going."

"Would you like a cup of tea and a slice of lemon pound cake?"

Elsie shook her head so vehemently that her bifocals slid down her nose. "I can see you're busy. I'll have that pound cake another day, if it's all the same."

Mrs. Jim Bob was still standing in the doorway when the kitchen door closed with a resonant click.

14

I gave myself a break in the morning. Sacrificing biscuits and gravy in order to avoid the Methodist version of the Inquisition, I walked over to the SuperSaver and bought a Sunday paper, then flopped on my sofa to read about all the heinous and/or hilarious activities in the world while I drank coffee and nibbled on toast made from bluish-gray bread, which well could have dated from the Civil War. Gwynnie's murder had warranted two paragraphs on a back page; it was hardly a newsworthy story outside the confines of the county. Once the details came out, I suspected we would be fending off tabloid journalists demanding details of the "Moonshine Murder." When that happened, I intended to be elsewhere, be it an opulent Dallas spa or a pup tent alongside Boone Creek.

I'd toss a coin when the time came.

I read everything except the classifieds and the sports section, then reluctantly buffed my badge and forced myself to go across the street to the PD.

The first order of business, I told myself as I started a pot of coffee (which, in all reality, *was* the first order of business, but let's not get technical), was to call the Powata police department and learn what I could about

Gwynnie and Seth. Directory information obliged with a number and went so far as to offer to dial it for a mere ninety-five cents.

I declined and dialed the number all by myself, despite the fact my fingers were crossed that I'd connect with someone over twenty-one and lacking an attitude.

"Powata Police Department," said a charmingly adult female voice. "Officer J. J. Cater at your service."

I explained who I was, and why I was calling. "I need some background information," I continued, my fingers still crossed since I was asking her to violate state laws concerning minors and privacy. "Gwynnie was telling a lot of tales. I need to know if any of them were true."

"I doubt it. The last time she responded without a sneer was when the doctor slapped her behind in the delivery room. She wasn't happy then, and she never was afterward. I'm sorry she's dead, but I'm not turning cold and clammy with shock. For the last five years, I've kept a toothbrush with her name on it in my desk drawer."

"Meaning?"

"Meaning she spent many a night here for shoplifting, driving without a license, possession of drugs, trying to buy beer, crossing paths with some idiot old enough to buy her beer, public obscenity, disturbing the peace, and so forth. I usually offered to release her on her mother's recognizance, but she preferred to sleep on the urine-stained mattress in the cell we set aside for juveniles. We should have put a plaque with her name on it above the door. Most mornings I'd just send her on home. You know how it works in a small town."

"I don't have a cell," I said, trying not to sound envious. Then again, if I had one, all I'd be doing was running a bed and breakfast for Buchanons, and gawd knows they'd all faint dead away at the sight of a bagel with lox and cream cheese. "Her juvvie records are sealed. Can you tell me what's in them?"

Officer Cater chuckled. "You know damn well I can't, Chief Hanks. If I could, all I'd say is that she and some other kids stole the state senator's shiny new Lincoln Continental and went for a ride. It's hard to know who had the drugs and who had the booze, but the driver had too much of one or the other and drove off a bridge. Luckily, my brother-in-law and his cousin happened to be passing by, and they fished the kids out of the water. One of the boys died from a skull fracture when he slammed into the windshield. A fourteen-year-old girl suffered permanent brain damage, effectively ending her dreams of becoming a doctor, lawyer, or Indian chief. The rest of them were eventually hauled to court and slapped on the wrist in varying degrees, depending on their past records and degree of involvement."

I shivered as I imagined Darla Jean, Heather, Billy Dick, and all the other teenagers doing the same thing—and ending up in the same bleak situation.

"Can you tell me about Gwynnie's home life?" I asked.

"Nothing that's uncommon around here," Officer Cater said. "Her father died six or seven years ago. Her mother, who was a real pain in the ass, if you don't mind me saying, did the best she could when she wasn't at church or sermonizing at city council and school-board meetings—which was what she did best. I seem to think she was working at the shirt factory until she, and most of the town, got laid off. We would have come out better if we'd had tornadoes and the county'd been declared a disaster area. Last I heard, she went off to Africa to pester those poor folks. Every time I read about a civil war in some African nation, I wonder if Dolores Patchwood is making them crazy."

"What about Gwynnie's stepfather?"

"That would have been a fairy stepfather. Dolores didn't remarry after her husband died. I'd be surprised if she ate or slept, what with her devotion to eternal salvation, welcome or not. One of the neighbors tried to convince the social services department that Gwynnie and her brother were neglected. Nobody investigated. They were fed and clothed, and frankly, having a fine time without supervision. Gwynnie seemed to have a ready supply of cash. Some nights I'd run her by her house to pick up her homework before I locked her up. Nobody was ever home."

"And I suppose her mother didn't have boyfriends?"

"Just the twelve Apostles. Give me a minute and I can rattle off their names. I did my time at the Baptist church. Let's see . . . you've got your Matthew, Mark, Luke, and—"

"That's okay," I said. "What can you tell me about Seth Smitherman?"

"Interesting you should ask. His family lives three, four miles north of town, farming a hundred acres or so and raising hogs. The children—there's a passel of them—are home-schooled. The Smithermans keep to themselves these days."

"Why's it interesting? Was Seth involved in the accident?"

"He was the driver."

I rocked back so hard I banged into the wall.

Cautiously exploring the backside of my head for blood, I said, "So he was nailed with grand theft auto?"

"State senator's car, and therefore a mighty poor choice. Any other car in town, he'd have been put on probation. 'Oops,' as we in law enforcement say."

I tried to imagine Harve saying "Oops." Not in my lifetime. "Officer Cater, I know you're reluctant to pass along gossip, but I was told that Gwynnie got pregnant by a local boy and was sent off to an unwed mothers' home. Do you know who the father was?"

"I learned to gossip through the bars of my crib, girl. The boy who was killed in the wreck had been seeing Gwynnie on the sly for several months. After his death, his parents wanted nothing to do with her. The scuttlebutt at the cafe was that they weren't about to acknowledge any grandchild with Patchwood blood. Nobody blamed them. The mother-daughter team was known locally as 'Nut 'n' Slut.' Both of them took to haranguing the boy's family until the circuit judge had no choice but to issue a restraining order. When Gwynnie violated it—which she did within a matter of days, if not hours—her probation officer and the county prosecutor decided she needed to be packed off. She was given her choice of the relatives in your neck of the woods or a detention facility."

"Too bad the juvvie records are sealed," I said dryly.

"Her probation officer's my sister and the prosecutor's my first cousin. Hard not to hear things."

"Are there any Patchwoods left in Powata?"

"A couple of ancient ones at the nursing home. Dolores had a few kinfolk in the area, but they seem to have moved on. If you're wanting to get hold of an address for her, I can ask the pastor at her church as soon as services are over."

"Thanks," I said, then gave her my telephone number and expressed my gratitude until she got bored and terminated the call.

I was putting together this not totally surprising image of Gwynnie when the telephone rang. I allowed the machine to deal with it.

"Arly? Are you there?" demanded Ruby Bee. "You are, aren't you? Don't think for a second that I don't know you're sitting in that cane-bottom chair, grinning at this damnfool machine and forcing me, your own flesh and blood, who suffered through seventeen hours of back labor—"

I retrieved the receiver, so to speak. "What's crawling up your leg this morning?"

"I was expecting you for breakfast. You always come over for breakfast on Sundays."

"I happen to be investigating a murder."

"That ain't ever made a noticeable dent in your appetite. If you keep neglecting to eat, you'll be nothing but skin and bones afore too long. Your breasts will deflate and you'll get bags and wrinkles under your eyes. You might as well move out to the old folks' home so you can make Easter decorations out of egg cartons. You'll be sucking jelly beans with Dahlia's granny and fretting on account of Hiawathie Buchanon filching your pudding cup when your head's turned."

"I may have a few more good months left in me," I said mildly. "I'll make a deal with you, okay? Breakfast in exchange for everything you know about what's been going on at the Pot O' Gold. No more evasions. Deal?"

Ruby Bee paused. "I reckon you're right. It's not like Estelle and I committed a felony that'll hold up in front of a jury."

"A felony?"

"Just get yourself over here." She hung up abruptly, her customary way of ending a conversation not to her liking.

I decided to swing by the Hollifleckers' before I indulged in grits and the gritty. Gwynnie had accused so many men, including a number of apparently fictitious ones, of abusing her that I was far from sure what, if anything, Daniel might have been guilty of doing.

Leona's face was paler than the underbelly of a sow when she opened the door and gazed blearily at me. Her bathrobe was loosely sashed, exposing bony shoulders dotted with moles and blood blisters. Her hair would have sent Estelle diving under the porch. "Arly? You'll have to excuse me. I must've dozed off on the sofa."

"Let me fix you some coffee," I said as I edged around her and continued into the kitchen. The church ladies had left everything in immaculate order, from the neatly folded dish towels to the aligned salt and pepper shakers on the dinette. I found a can of coffee and filters, and began to fill the pot with water. "Is Daniel back?" I asked as I heard her shuffle into the kitchen.

"No. I left another message about six o'clock, but they must have been at supper. I was meaning to call later. I guess it slipped my mind. Most everything does these days. Having Gwynnie and Chip living here has been real stressful. Now all this . . . I don't know what to make of it."

"I'm trying to track down Gwynnie's mother. I may

have an address or even a telephone number later today."

"What's the point?" Leona said as she sat down and began to shred a paper napkin. "Dolores isn't going to drop whatever she's doing and fly back just so she can bury her daughter. They weren't what you'd call close."

I turned around. "How's Chip?"

"I called Dahlia earlier, and she came over and picked him up. I can't deal with a two-year-old. All he does is fuss and carry on, and there's no way telling what's wrong with him. Neither of us got more than ten minutes of sleep last night."

At least one person was doing the right thing, I thought, vowing to take Dahlia a package of Twinkies and a grape Nehi. She may not have been playing with a full deck, but the heart suit was intact.

"So you didn't talk to Daniel yesterday," I said. "Have you tried this morning?"

She made her way to the refrigerator and filled a glass with orange juice. Keeping her back to me, she added a hefty splash of vodka from a bottle in a cabinet. "No point in trying. The seminar's over at noon, so he would have checked out of his room first thing. He should be home by the middle of the afternoon."

"How 'bout I call Millicent to come over and keep you company until he gets here?"

"I don't need any company, including yours. If you'll excuse me, I'm going to my office to read the Bible. I'm just not up to going to church this morning, but that doesn't mean I can neglect my soul. You might consider turning to the scriptures, too. There is great comfort to be found."

"I'll leave the coffeepot on," I called as she wandered toward the back of the house.

After a long moment of hesitation, I left and drove to Millicent McIlhaney's house. Odds were that the family would be at church for another hour, but I felt as though disaster was percolating along with the coffee.

Darla Jean looked slightly better than Leona as she answered the door, but not by much.

"What?" she squeaked.

"Is your mother here?"

"I reckon not. It's Sunday morning and the sun rose in the east, so she's at church. Are you aiming to tell her? Shit, Arly, I thought I could trust you after you helped me out yesterday afternoon. Why don't you just haul me over to the sheriff's department and lock me up? I'd rather sit in a cell than face my parents."

"I suppose I could do that."

"Can I least comb my hair and put on some mascara? I don't want to look like a zombie when they take my mug shot. It'll probably end up on the Maggody web site. I keep waiting for report cards and test results from gynecologists to show up. Doesn't something in the constitution guarantee privacy?"

"I don't know. Shall I wait out here and think it over?"

Darla Jean dragged me inside. "The way things are going, some nosy neighbor'd drive by and see you." She pushed me down on a chair in the entry hall. "Sit here, all right?"

She went through the living room, and seconds later I heard the back door slam. Obviously, Darla Jean believed I was onto something, although I had no clue what it might be. As I'd said to Heather the previous day, I was fairly sure they'd been lying to me, and in some way Lazarus was involved. And, as I replayed remarks, Gwynnie Patchwood.

Surprise, surprise.

~~~~~~~~~~~

Brother Verber stood on the porch of the Assembly Hall, shaking hands and offering genial observations about the weather. Some Sunday mornings, he was there for more than half an hour, but this morning the turnout had been so low they might as well have all slept in. Among the AWOLs were Sister Barbara and Jim Bob, Eileen and Earl, Kevin and Dahlia, Lottie, Leona and Daniel, and even Eula, who always could be counted on to set out the hymnals. Miz Ferncliff rode with Eula, so she hadn't come either. Once a month or so Miz Twayblade brought a van of denture-clicking residents from the old folks' home, but she'd made it clear she was an equal-opportunity patron of religion (within the confines of respectability, of course), which meant she had many other denominations to cover with her charges. Little had she known this had been the morning Brother Verber would have come darn close to kissing Petrol's stubbly, sunken cheek.

Or hers, for that matter.

Millicent McIlhaney stopped to compliment him on his sermon, despite the fact they both knew he had rambled on for most of forty minutes and hadn't made a bit (or byte) of sense. "I couldn't help noticing that bump on your nose," she added. "Did you run into a door?"

Jeremiah grinned. "Looks more like you grabbed the wrong end of a weed wacker."

"I have been wrasslin' with Satan," said Brother Verber

darkly. "Be sure and tell Darla Jean we missed her this morning in Sunday school. Her class is making plans for the senior trip to the water theme park up in Branson. I hope we can count on your support for the bake sale at the end of the month, Millicent, and yours, Jeremiah, for the car wash come Saturday. Darla Jean signed you up for the first shift, so we'll expect you at eight. Bring a garden hose and sponges."

Millicent stared at her husband until he mumbled something and went down the steps toward their car. "Have you been over to see Leona this morning?" she asked.

"I was thinking I'd go over directly."

She waited until Bojangles Buchanon shuffled by, bobbling his head like a dashboard statuette and grousing at an unseen companion. "I ain't sure what to make of this, Brother Verber, but I found a memo in Daniel's office that laid out the details of this seminar in Springfield, with the times and where they'd be staying." Her eyes shifted uncomfortably. "I figured Leona wouldn't be in any shape to call him later in the evening, so I called the motel. He never checked in yesterday."

"Do you think he could have been in a wreck on the way up there? Should we call the hospital?"

Millicent wondered if she'd go to hell if she started attending the Methodist church. "If Daniel'd been in a wreck, Leona would have been notified. He was driving his own car and presumably had his wallet with him."

"You think he might have been arrested and thrown in jail? If that was the case, he could have been too embarrassed to call her."

Millicent propelled him back into the vestibule. "No,"

she whispered, "I don't think he was arrested. I don't think he went to this seminar to begin with."

"Then where'd he go?" asked Brother Verber, his eyes wide.

"I don't have any idea where he went. How could I, for pity's sake? All we can do for the time being is pray he shows up this afternoon. If he doesn't, in the morning I'll call over to his office and see if anyone there knows where he might have gone."

Brother Verber may have had welts and scratches over most of his body, as well as a swollen purplish-yellow bruise the size of a cantaloupe on his backside, but the one part of his anatomy that hadn't bounced off Idalupino's patio was his head. "Do you think this has anything to do with Gwynnie?"

Millicent had not allowed herself to consider this. She went into the auditorium and sat down in the last pew. Darla Jean had sworn she and Gwynnie were not friends, but there'd been some hushed conversations on the telephone late at night when Millicent had heard Daniel's name. Not that she'd been eavesdropping, mind you, but the mother of a teenaged girl has the God-given right to linger on the way to the bathroom.

"The Hollifleckers have been members of this congregation for ten years," she said as Brother Verber sat down beside her. "Daniel's always seemed upright as a rail post. He's been a deacon for the last four years, hasn't he? He was on the school board. There's been talk he wants to be elected to the town council."

"I don't reckon this should go any further for the moment," said Brother Verber. "Daniel may have decided to stay at a different motel in Springfield, and is driving home as we speak. Don't go repeating anything about this, Millicent."

"I am not inclined to gossip," she said coldly as she stood up. "I'll go by Leona's and set out leftovers for those who care to come by to offer condolences. I expect you'll be there?"

"Yes," he said with a forced smile. "I have my duty to the members of my flock."

If Lottie Estes had chanced to overhear that remark, there was no telling how she might have reacted.

"Are you aimin' to spend the rest of your life in there?" asked Jim Bob, standing outside his wife's bedroom, his jaw jutted out so far he looked like a belligerent bulldog intent on a mouthful of bloody flesh.

"Maybe," she responded in a thin voice. "I am praying for guidance, or at least I was until you started pounding on the door. Go on about your business. I got nothing to say to you."

Jim Bob ran his hand across his head. "What exactly is it you're thinking I did this time? Last night I came home soon as I locked the supermarket. I may have been expecting warmed-up leftovers and a cup of coffee, same as any hardworkin' husband would. I may have hoped to find my breakfast on the table this morning, but I made do with a piece of pie. I didn't say anything when you didn't gripe at me to get dressed for church, but now it seems to me that you should be downstairs in the kitchen, frying chicken and stringing beans and that kinda thing."

What was really pissing him off was that he hadn't

actually done anything of note lately. For most of a
month Cherri Lucinda had been appeased with grandiose
(and possibly less than sincere) promises of perfume,
chocolates, and roses. Rowena had sounded kinda
relieved, since she never knew for sure when her husband
might park his rig in the yard and come thudding into the
house. Idalupino had told him to kiss her ass, which had
pretty much put that relationship on hold until he could
figure out her problem. Even the Dew Drop Inn had been
obliged to survive without his company at the pool table
in the back room.

Hell, he thought, he might as well have gone over to
the Assembly Hall an hour earlier and passed the fuckin'
collection plate. Instead, he was stuck with a demented
woman that showed no signs of ever coming out of her
bedroom. Peach pie might serve for breakfast, but Sunday
dinner was different. Hadn't she promised to love,
honor—and obey?

"Come out of there!" he bellowed, thumping his fist
with each word. "I expect my wife to put my Sunday dinner on the table. You hear me?"

Her lack of response implied she hadn't, didn't, or
wasn't about to. Jim Bob stomped down the staircase,
stopped in the kitchen to make hisself an onion and mayonnaise sandwich (tasty, but a far cry from fried chicken),
and then called the Voice of the Almighty Lord Assembly
Hall rectory to report this infraction of sacred matrimo-
nial vows. She was gonna be real sorry when Brother
Verber showed up to chew her out, he told himself as he
tapped his foot. He couldn't recollect one single time in
all their years of marriage when he'd been in the right,
instead of having to grovel and get down on his knees to

beg her forgiveness, and then agree to pay for some damn-fool thing or another, be it a Cadillac or upholstery.

This time was different.

Brother Verber failed to cooperate by answering the telephone. Jim Bob fixed another sandwich, wondering all the while how hard it'd be to get her committed to one of those places with padded walls, then hollered that he was leaving and went out to his truck.

If he'd looked in the rearview mirror as he drove away, he might have noticed a wisp of smoke drifting out of her bedroom window. As it was, he was too busy grappling under the seat for a pint bottle of bourbon.

Later, he would tell anyone who'd listen that it was her own damn fault.

———————~~~~~~~~———————

I knocked on the door of Eula's trailer, then leaned against the teetery wrought-iron rail and waited, hoping she hadn't gone to Leona's for a second round of casseroles and commiseration.

"Oh, good," I said as she opened the door. "May I come in?"

"I'm not dressed for company," she said, blocking the doorway. "I haven't had a wink of sleep for two nights now. You don't seem the least bit interested in protecting us from that psychotic killer across the road, but I know for a fact he's intended to murder us since the day he moved in. Miz Whitbread has taken to her bed with a hot-water bottle. Idalupino saw him just last night, leering at her through the window when she got out of the shower. He scuttled away like a lame crawdad before she could grab her pepper spray and get outside to show him a thing or two. This morning she stopped by to ask me to collect her mail for the next few weeks, while she stays with her sister in Crossett."

"Are you talking about Lazarus?"

"No, Arly, I'm talking about Elvis. It seems he followed Estelle back here to Maggody, and is sharing a cave with Diesel up on the ridge. You got any more stupid questions? I skipped church this morning, so I'm listening to the Pentecostal service on the radio. Considering how they carry on, it'd be more entertaining if I could watch 'em on television, but we don't get cable."

"I've noticed," I said weakly. "I just now knocked on Lazarus's door. He's not home."

"I reckon he's not even in the county by now. He strapped a couple of duffel bags on his motorcycle this morning, then squealed out like a bull getting castrated."

"Does anyone have a key to his trailer?"

Eula stepped back to allow me inside. "This ain't a hotel with a desk clerk. I send my rent money to some real estate company in Starley City. If I'm three days late, a smarmy little thing calls to ask real sweetly if I have a problem. When the sewer line backs up or a gas line leaks and I call them, I get the answering machine. The smarmy little thing's too busy to call me back." She waved me toward the sofa. "I don't reckon you, or even Ruby Bee, understand what poverty means. I can afford to buy food, and most months I can pay the bills. I can't make long-distance calls to my daughter in California, though, and I can't send birthday presents to my grandchildren. Lottie takes me into Farberville every now and then so I can buy greeting cards and a book of stamps. I can barely remember their names and faces these days. I've never held the two youngest ones."

"Eula," I said, for the first time actually looking at her, "I didn't realize . . ."

"Don't go feeling sorry for me," she said as she went to the kitchen window. "Bernard died all these long years ago. I'm just biding my time until we can meet up again. I'd like to think Saint Peter issued him a washrag and a bar of soap before he was allowed inside the Pearly Gates. The last thing I want to do is spend eternity with a man who neglected personal hygiene after his retirement."

I was trying to come up with a response, however lame it was apt to be, when she said, "I wonder who's over there now. If it's Bernard, I'm gonna have to rethink things. The Pot O' Gold for all eternity—I ain't so sure."

I nudged her aside and looked across the street at the double-wide trailer that had been occupied by Lazarus until some point earlier in the day, when he'd roared out on his motorcycle. I had no doubt that I could break into the trailer, but the lack of a warrant was a problem.

"Why do you think anyone's there?" I asked.

"Because someone snuck inside."

"Ah," I said, ever so wisely. "Did you get a good look?"

"Wouldn't I have said so if I had? Now if you don't mind, I'd like to make a cup of tea and elevate my leg. I've been in the hospital twice this last year. The last thing I aim to do is give Lazarus the satisfaction of putting me in my grave."

"You said something yesterday about how rude he was when you and he went into Farberville and—"

"Go away and let me be. Miz Whitbread and I always share a can of soup on Sunday; this is her turn, so I suppose we'll have cream of mushroom, along with those cardboard crackers she buys at Wal-Mart."

No fewer than a zillion responses went through my mind, but not one of them was adequate. "I guess I'll go see who's in Lazarus's trailer," I said.

"Then do it," she said as she limped down the hallway, her housecoat flapping. "Miz Whitbread and I can get along just fine without anyone's pity. What's more, I reckon I can protect us if Lazarus comes back."

"Perhaps we should discuss the gun," I called. "It's not nice to shoot your neighbors, Eula."

Eula did not slam the door as Darla Jean had done. She simply closed it.

15

It churns my stomach to admit this, but what I really wanted to do was to settle my butt in my chair, prop my heels on the corner of my desk, and talk to Harve, not because he was a guy so much as because he'd been down most of the back roads of Stump County, in the figurative sense (and possibly in the literal, as well). Ruby Bee and Estelle seemed to think I could solve dilemmas by putting one of my four remaining bullets in the gun and shooting someone, randomly if need be. Brother Verber would advocate the inspiration to be gained from a substantial tithe. Mrs. Jim Bob might be more inclined to think she could rev up her Cadillac and eliminate the problem at fifty miles per hour. Which she could, but it would lead to complications.

It being Sunday afternoon, however, Harve was undoubtedly in a john boat in the middle of a river, stretched out within reach of a cooler of beer, ham sandwiches, and hunks of his wife's chocolate-fudge brownies with caramel icing. He'd have a greasy canvas hat pulled down to shield his eyes, and a slathering of gunky white sunblock on his nose. A vile cigar would be threatening the continued well-being of the nearby fish more so than any hook, line, or sinker.

But Eula had seen someone go inside Lazarus's trailer, and Harve wasn't going to offer up any wisdom in the immediate future.

Reminding myself that I'd survived several courses in self-defense at the police academy (for the most part learning how to shout "Toyota!" and "Mitsubishi!" at the top of my lungs while gesturing in a vaguely menacing fashion), I walked across the road and banged open the door. "Nis-san!" I hissed, stressing the second syllable and hoping it sounded like an obscure samurai death threat.

Seth Smitherman was seated at the dinette. He stumbled to his feet and pretty much crashed into the refrigerator. "What are you doing here?" he gasped.

I uncurled my fists. "What are you doing here?"

He pushed his hair out of his eyes. "Nothing, really. Lazarus said I could use his computer whenever I wanted, and I was just kind of—"

I glanced at the monitor. "Looks like porn to me."

"Justin has everything blocked at the lab. Women don't seem to understand why men like to look at stuff like this. There's no harm in it."

I caught his wrist before he could make the screen go blank. "No harm in it? This is Darla Jean McIlhaney, in the flesh, so to speak! Billy Dick McNamara is hovering over her, brandishing his magic wand. What's going on, Seth? How could these pictures be on the Internet? These are local kids, damn it! They are not runaways sleeping in alleys off Times Square, posing for a few dollars to buy a hot meal."

"I didn't have anything to do with it," Seth said, twisting free of my grip.

"But you knew how to find it."

"Maybe."

"There is no 'maybe,' Seth. You and Lazarus seem to be buddies. Do you know where he is?"

"He left. He told me to look at his computer equipment and make an offer. He's gonna let me know where to send him the money."

"Which would be?"

"He said he'd be in touch. All I'm doing is trying to put a price on it. Computers are out of date the week after you buy them. This printer's not bad, and the scanner is fairly new. The digital camera's real nice. Still, the modem's slow and—"

"Shut up unless you want to wait while I go back to the PD and get my radar gun. I will annihilate you and sell the ashes to a web site featuring cremains."

Seth sank down on the stained sofa. "I'm looking to buy his computer equipment. No crime in that."

"Is there in stealing a car and driving off a bridge?"

"Heard about that, huh?"

"Yeah, Seth. I also heard Gwynnie Patchwood was in the car."

He looked as though he wished he could slither under the sofa. "Okay, but it was more than two years ago. It was all really stupid, especially on my part. I paid for it."

"Why did you come to Maggody?" I asked.

This was, from the look on his face, a question of boundless metaphysical implications. The meaning of life would have been a piece of cake. The nature of reality might have been on the tip of his tongue. Global economics, quantum mechanics, even something as simple as quadratic equations—these issues he could have fielded without working up a sweat.

"I dunno," he said.

"Because of Gwynnie?"

"Not necessarily."

"That's a helluv an answer," I said as I stood up. "I can book you for murder, Seth. You were stalking her. Did you think she was in some way responsible for the incident that landed you in prison? It won't take much to convince the county prosecutor that you came here to get revenge. Gwynnie's dead. Her child will spend the next sixteen years in a series of foster homes."

"Nah, she wasn't responsible. She had a joint, but one of the guys had a bottle of whiskey and some beer that his brother bought for him."

"So why did you come to Maggody?" I repeated. "Don't bother to say it's because of the cheap rent at the Pot O' Gold. There are more trailer parks in this fair state than Buchanons behind bars. There are motels that charge a hundred dollars a month, although I suspect the maid service is spottier than the bedspreads."

"I had to go someplace."

"Your family wouldn't take you back?"

"My pa said he'd beat my backside with a shovel before he'd let me move home."

"I can see that didn't appeal," I said, "but why here, Seth?"

"No reason," he said stubbornly.

I gave him a momentary break. "Does this computer hook up to other computers?" I asked as I sat down at the dinette. "Can you get on the Internet and that kind of thing?"

"Almost all computers are linked to the web."

"Can I look at the Maggody web site?"

Seth nudged me out of the chair and began to click the keyboard. The images of Darla Jean and Billy Dick vanished in a keystroke. "It's kinda clunky because there are a lot of graphics. All this shit about the history—"

I dragged over a chair and sat down next to him. "Just show me."

Muttering to himself, he continued to do whatever he was doing until the web site appeared, complete with a photo of the pockmarked city-limits sign and a list of names across the bottom. "Anything in particular?"

"My name is included," I said, jabbing my finger at the screen. "What's that mean?"

Seth smirked. "Well, let's just see." We sat in silence as a recent photo of yours truly appeared. I was coming out of the PD, scratching my chin and squinting at the sky, oblivious to the camera. He did something to change the screen and my high school yearbook photo came up, along with the list of clubs and activities. Now my hair was lacquered, my lips glossy, my demeanor blasé but with a hint of desperation. I tried to remember if I'd ever actually attended a meeting of the Future Teachers of America or the Spanish Club. Probably not. The banks of Boone Creek'd had their allure back then, too, although, based on my noticeable lack of rapport with the current crop of teenagers, I was beginning to wonder if we'd been in danger of raptors rather than rapture in the good ol' days. I did my best with the kids, but there were times that I could hear Ruby Bee's voice when I opened my mouth. If I'd started sounding like Mrs. Jim Bob, I'd be obliged to steal a state senator's car and drive off a bridge, preferably one spanning the Grand Canyon.

"Who else?" I demanded.

As I sat there, Seth clicked on candid photos of Ruby Bee, Estelle, Jim Bob, Mrs. Jim Bob, Brother Verber, and almost everybody else in Maggody. Raz and Marjorie, both glaring at the camera from the doorway of his barn. Eula, pinning brassieres on her clothesline. Roy Stiver, his mouth agape to catch flies as he slept in a rocking chair beside the door of his store. Dahlia and Kevin pushing the stroller down Finger Lane. Petrol Buchanon, pissing on a bush outside the old folks' home. Peteet, his eyes on the heavens.

"Where did these come from?" I asked.

"The students have a camera that can feed photos directly onto the web site," Seth said. "They can also scan old photos, documents, and whatever, and put them on. Want to see your mother's blue-plate specials for the week?"

"No. What's the map?"

He did more clicking and up came a hand-drawn map of Maggody. "You live here," he said, moving the cursor on the antiques store. "I live just about here," he said as he shifted it to the trailer park.

"And Gwynnie's body was found where?"

"From what I've heard, somewhere on Cotter's Ridge. How should I know?"

"Robin's cabin is the square at the end of the wiggle going up Cotter's Ridge, but she was killed right here," I said, touching the crude outline of the Flamingo Motel. "Friday night, after ten. Where were you?"

"I wasn't anywhere."

"That would be a first, Seth. Care to elaborate on how you managed to deplane the planet?"

He sat back. "I was just around, okay? I got off work, I

came back and showered, I went over to the Dairee Dee-Lishus and picked up a burger, then ate it while I watched television. Lazarus dropped by and asked if I wanted to go to Farberville, but I said no. TV sucks out here; we got more channels in the rec room at the state pen than we get here. I took a walk, spooked a couple of cows and what looked to be a coyote, and went to bed."

"Tell me about Gwynnie back in Powata," I said.

"She was a real mess, but she didn't have a chance of being anything else. Her ma was one of those do-gooders who didn't want to do good; she just wanted to bully everybody else into her version of righteousness. The pool hall used to send out scouts at closing time. Nobody wanted to run into Dolores on the sidewalk."

"What about Gwynnie herself, though?"

"The kids at school were hateful to her on account of her thrift-shop clothes. There were times when it was hard to ignore that she hadn't bathed or washed her hair, but half the time they couldn't pay the water bill. Everybody knew she slept at the jail often as not. I liked her spirit, though. Some evenings I'd go by her house and we'd sit on the back porch, or walk down to the pond. I almost invited her to one of the school dances, but I didn't, because I knew she couldn't afford to buy a new dress. Powata's not all that much different from Maggody. Wasn't there one kid in your class who everyone bullied?"

"I suppose so," I admitted uncomfortably. "But Gwynnie did date a boy from a prominent family, didn't she? Is that why she was with you on the night of the accident?"

"Yeah," he said, "Harris Rossen, though they weren't exactly dating. He didn't have the balls to invite her to the movies or sit with her in the cafeteria or anything like that, but after he'd take home whichever perky blond cheerleader he was going steady with, he'd go looking for Gwynnie. She wasn't all that hard to find, and most always agreeable to a drive out to the lake."

"And the night in question?"

"The basketball team won some stupid district title. Harris had been the high scorer, and he was fired up. Some of us were walking over to his house when we saw the car just begging to be taken for a test drive. Gwynnie and a couple of other girls like her were hanging out in front of the gym." He stopped and looked away. "I'm not making any excuses for what happened. I was drinking too much and driving too fast. I was able to hang on to Gwynnie when the car hit the water. Harris was riding shotgun; he wasn't wearing a seat belt, but none of us were. If there was an instant replay button on my life, I'd rewind it and go home that night. I'd brush my teeth and go to bed. I'd get up the next morning and slop the hogs, then go into town. Shoot hoops at the park. Eat a burrito at the convenience store and try to persuade Alice Ann to go to the junior prom with me. Alice Ann didn't go to the prom with anyone; she went to a nursing home to vegetate. Harris went to the cemetery, and I went to prison. I wonder what might have happened if we hadn't won the game that night."

"What a great idea for a miniseries. Alternative reality. What would have happened if the irresponsible teenagers hadn't stolen the car and swilled so much booze that the driver went off a bridge? Would they all have gone on to medical school and worked as a team to come up with a cure for cancer?"

Seth was silent.

"Did you know Gwynnie was living here with her aunt and uncle?"

"Everybody in Powata knew. It was the hot topic at the Sunshine Cafe and Bait Shoppe."

"And that's why you came here?" I persisted.

"I figured I couldn't get into any trouble in a place like this."

"But you came to a place like this, Seth, and for a reason. After the accident, Gwynnie knocked on the door of the richest family in Powata and tried to convince Harris's parents that they had a paternal obligation to take care of her unborn child. They didn't buy it, did they?"

"They wouldn't acknowledge anything, and they didn't have to, since they pretty much own the county. Most folks are beholding to them, in one way or another. They subsidize most of the crop-sharers, and float loans to farmers like my pa. They paid for the gymnasium at the high school, the new roof at the library, prescription drugs for the homeless at shelters, things like that. They just weren't able to believe their precious golden boy had impregnated a Patchwood."

"Did he? What if you and she did more than hold hands at the pond? Did you come here looking for Gwynnie—or for Chip? Did all that jailhouse religion convince you to take responsibility for your son? Did you think you could get enough evidence to prove that Gwynnie was a less fit parent than you?"

He shook his head with unconvincing defiance. "I came here on account of cheap rent. My trailer costs eighty-two dollars a month, with utilities. I can save a couple of hundred dollars a week for six months, then head for California, or maybe Arizona. Maybe I'll find a job in a casino in Las Vegas or one of those places. Maybe I'll be a forest ranger in Yosemite and warn people not to feed the bears. Maybe I'll end up in a cabin in Alaska, hoping the bears don't feed on me."

Unlike Seth's aspirations, the conversation was going nowhere. "Okay, then," I said, "tell me how these photographs of the local teenagers ended up on the Internet. Was Lazarus responsible?" I paused for a moment. "Why did he choose Maggody? This isn't a dream destination on *Wheel of Fortune.*"

"I don't know."

Obscure neurons were firing. "Had you ever met him before you came here, Seth?"

"Not that I recall," he said, turning even pastier than Ruby Bee's pie shells.

"In Powata, for example?"

Squirming like a cornered cockroach, Seth eyed all possible exits. "I suppose he could have been there, but . . ."

"Should I call the Powata Police Department and inquire about Dolores Patchwood's maiden name—and the whereabouts of her unsavory relatives?"

"So maybe Lazarus was Gwynnie's uncle. It's no big deal."

"Was he making these disgusting videos back then? Did he follow Gwynnie just so she could provide more actors, or in this situation, victims?"

"How should I know? I'm just buying his computer."

"As a favor?"

"A favor for what?" he said. "He may have bought me a half-pint of whiskey once in a while, but that's about all."

"Unless he agreed not to mention that he'd seen you with Chip out behind the supermarket. I can understand why you'd want to hold your son, if only for a minute, and it's clear you didn't harm or frighten him."

"Chip's a sturdy little guy, isn't he?" Seth's face glowed with the pride I'd been seeing on Kevin Buchanon's the last several months.

"Okay," I said with a sigh, "put those photos back on the screen. I want to see the background."

Grumbling to himself, he clicked various things until the photo of Darla Jean and Billy Dick appeared. Behind them, cheap paneling and a window with a limp green curtain. "Don't move," I said, then went down the hall and looked inside the bedroom. Cheap paneling and a window with a limp green curtain. Heather had been adamant that Lazarus had never *sold* them drugs; perhaps the more old-fashioned barter system had been in effect. I looked around for anything that might give me a clue to his whereabouts. As if I were going to find a map marked with an X or an itinerary for a series of connecting flights to Brazil.

I decided a pattern was emerging as I heard the front door close. If I could develop the same reaction from vermin, I thought as I poked at discarded clothes and fast-food wrappers, I could become an incredibly wealthy exterminator. I would have no need of a flute; my presence would be all that was required to set off a frenzy at the exit.

Eventually, I went back into the living room and determined that Seth had indeed left the building. Darla Jean had left her house. Lazarus had left town in what might turn out to be a permanent change of lifestyle.

I sat down in front of the computer and stared at the photo of Darla Jean and Billy Dick. Both of them were smiling, but their expressions were so unnaturally taut that they might have resulted from jabs with a cattle prod.

Gwynnie had come to Maggody. Lazarus had appeared shortly thereafter. He had no means of support. Picking produce out of the Dumpsters behind the supermarket might reduce the monthly expenses, but the same real estate company that cashed Eula's check was hardly apt to be thrilled with a payment in discolored oranges.

"Ergo," I said aloud, although I wasn't real sure what it meant, "he was peddling teen porn and Gwynnie was helping him with recruitment." Or Seth was, or Darla Jean, who may have had heretofore unacknowledged entrepreneurial skills, or even Jim Bob, though he most likely wasn't quite that sleazy. Or Justin or Raz or Idalupino or Marjorie or LaBelle, for that matter.

After a long minute of glaring, I put my hand on the rounded plastic object I assumed was known in the lingo as a mouse. A blinky little thing on the screen moved. I shifted my hand; the thing shifted accordingly. Cool, I thought, although my nascent skill was hardly worthy of an offer of an executive position from Bill Gates.

I fooled around for a few seconds, then abandoned the mouse and did a more thorough search of Lazarus's trailer. He'd left behind a few oddments of clothing, but mostly cleared out his stuff. The tube of toothpaste in the bathroom was flat. The milk in the refrigerator had the consistency of cottage cheese; the cottage cheese itself was a lovely shade of pearly gray. The plates in the sink were dotted with fuzzy turquoise balls, which in another galaxy (far, far away) might have been someone's cherished pets.

It was ridiculous, I thought as I went outside. Colonel Mustard in the billiard room or Miss Scarlett in the conservatory were concepts I could handle. I'd dealt with greed and envy and tangled emotions and revenge. The computer on the dinette, as well as the tidy rows of computers in the portable trailer by the high school—all of them were nothing more than keyboards, encased circuits, and blue screens.

Justin Bailey had much to answer for, but he could wait until I'd appeased my mother, who'd been expecting me for the last three hours.

And maybe I was hungry.

"I have called the PD seventeen times!" she shrieked as I ambled across the dance floor. "I told Estelle here that this was the day you'd been run down by a truck and were bleeding to death in a ditch on some county road. If Harve Dorfer had been at his office, I would have carried on until he agreed to send out a posse and scrape up what was left of you before the turkey vultures swooped in."

"That's right," added Estelle. "I even offered to go to the mortuary and do what I could with your hair and makeup, despite what pecking might have taken place. I don't reckon there would have been much left of your eyes to work with." She'd clearly spent some time on her own; the serpentine blue eyeshadow and heavy-handed eyeliner gave her a ghoulish look, which would have fit in nicely in a mortuary ambience.

Bring up the organ music.

"Stop it," I said as I sat on a stool. "I had some other things to do first—okay? If I am ever beset by turkey vultures, you'll be the first to know."

Ruby Bee scowled. "Not if you're in a ditch."

"The state game and fish department requires them to carry cell phones," I said. "I'll gasp out your number with my dying breath. What's the lunch special?"

"It's three o'clock in the afternoon," she shot back. "Do you think I fixed a plate and kept it in the oven just in case you bothered to show up, Miss Not Much Better Late Than Never?"

"I am eternally optimistic."

She banged into the kitchen and came back with a plate heaped with ham, candied sweet potatoes, collard greens, pickled beets, and a square of corn bread. "Don't go thinking this'll happen every time you go waltzing around for half the day, then come in and demand to be fed."

Estelle sighed. "It's a darn shame what you put your mother through on what's becoming a distressingly regular basis."

I took a bite of ham. "I could move back to Manhattan and work for the Mob. Pay's good, or so I hear, and I've always wanted a godfather. Don Juan has a nice ring, but I might have to settle for don we-now-our-gay-apparel. Egad, would I have to become a lesbian? Would Marjorie start to look more fetching than Raz?"

"You're not as funny as you think," said Ruby Bee as she set down a glass of milk. "Did you talk to Leona this morning?"

"She's not doing well. Chip's over at Dahlia's house for the time being, but it's not even much of a short-term solution. I'll wait until Daniel gets back before I call social services."

"If he gets back," muttered Estelle, her nose buried in a glass of sherry.

I glanced at her, my fork halfway to my mouth. "Why'd you say that?"

"Millicent McIlhaney came over here looking for you. She says Daniel never went to the conference in Springfield."

"Where'd he go?"

"Millicent has no way of knowing that. She came across the number of the motel in Springfield and called it on account of Leona being . . . preoccupied."

I banged down my fork, inadvertently sending a slice of beet in Estelle's direction. "He was here when Gwynnie was killed, and long gone when her body was found yesterday morning." I muttered a decidedly uncouth word under my breath. "And he didn't go to Springfield to learn how to maximize the chicken-plucking line."

"Lazarus is long gone, too," said Ruby Bee. She held up her hand. "Don't get your nose out of joint. Eula told me how he tore out on his motorcycle this morning. Did you find anything incriminating when you searched his trailer?"

"Do you also know when I last sneezed?" I asked as I resumed my assault on the ham and sweet potatoes.

They backed off, although we all knew it was temporary at best. After I'd cleaned my plate (my mother was in close proxim-ity, after all), I wiped my chin and said, "Let's talk about the computer lab. Eileen seems to think she saw something odd while she was reading her E-mail. Did she tell either of you?"

Ruby Bee's jaw dropped. "Eileen saw something odd? I thought I was losing my mind when I saw . . . well, it wasn't pretty, if you get my drift. It wasn't but a blink, and then it was gone. If Justin had been there, I might have tried to tell him about it, but later I decided I was just too darn old to be surfing the web like a teenager in one of those beach-blanket movies."

"What did you think you saw?" I asked, wondering if she was about to comment on Earl's privates.

"I don't want to talk about it."

"I saw something, too," said Estelle, "or I reckoned at the time I might have. I couldn't hardly sleep that night, and the next morning I studied all the labels on my cosmetics in case one of them contained some peculiar chemical. Don't ask, 'cause I ain't gonna even think about it."

"Eileen saw a picture of Earl," I said cautiously.

Ruby Bee took my plate and went into the kitchen. Estelle found a need to disappear into the restroom. Neither seemed in any hurry to return.

It would have been really, really interesting if either of them could repeat Eileen's claim, but I wasn't going to hang around. Something damned odd was taking place in the portable building beside the high school gym. The one person who had claimed to have mastery over this small domain was going to have to answer for it.

Five minutes later I parked beside the Baileys' trailer. Rather than storm the door, however, I sat and thought about what I'd learned. Gwynnie Patchwood may have had some justification for her behavior, but she'd lied to any and all who might have had something she wanted. And what she'd wanted most of all was to avoid a future of cramped apartments in bad neighborhoods and a reliance on the bureaucracy to send her a piddling check each month. Jessie Traylor had not been good enough. Seth Smitherman did not seem likely to end up with a string of car dealerships—or even a string of pearls. Lazarus was a purveyor of pornography and based his daily diet on the discarded produce behind the SuperSaver. Daniel may or may not have provided pocket money in exchange for sexual favors, but she must have suspected what drove Leona to the close encounters with vodka. It was hard to imagine Gwynnie was quite as dedicated to the concept of obtaining her GED and taking courses at the community college.

No, she needed a father for Chip and a husband with the potential for financial success. Relationships might smolder on the Internet, but they could be set ablaze closer to home, too.

I was still sitting in my car when Justin came out of the trailer.

"What do you want?" he asked. "If you're looking for Chapel, she went into Farberville to spend the afternoon and evening with friends. She won't be back until nine. I've already told you everything I know about Gwynnie Patchwood."

"Get in the car," I said.

"Why?"

"Because, Justin, you promised this town that you could control the images on the Internet. I hate to say it, but I'm not convinced you've done a bang-up job thus far. We're going over to the lab."

"Can I put on some shoes?"

"No need," I said with the warmth of Genghis Khan on a bad hair day. "Just get in the car. If it looks as if we'll be there all night, I'll run you back so you can leave a note for your wife. I'm sure you'd never do anything to cause her any unnecessary pain."

"What's that supposed to mean?" he asked as he sat down in the passenger's seat. "You don't know anything about my relationship with Chapel. She wasn't happy about moving here, but she's adjusting. She understands that once I get my graduate degree in five or six years, things will be better."

I backed up and headed for the gate. "And you see Chapel standing next to you when you have your portrait taken with a new Porsche?"

"Why wouldn't I?"

I kept my lips tight as I drove to the high school gym. "Watch out for broken glass," I said politely. "I'd hate to have to drive you to the emergency room for a tetanus shot."

"Thanks a lot," he said as he grimaced over every last bit of gravel. It was clear he could never dance alongside Boone Creek, even with a bottle of wine under his belt. Maggody boys had a tradition of stamping out bonfires with their bare feet.

Two of said critters were inside the trailer, both hunkered down in front of a computer. It took me a second to recognize them from the second-class picnic table in front of the Dairee Dee-Lishus. It took them a split second longer to erase the images on the monitors in front of them. Poor reflexes on their part.

"Hey, Mr. Bailey," one of them said. "What are you and her doing here?"

I crossed my arms. "Maybe finding out what you've been doing here. Want to give us a hint?"

"I was thinking about buying a used truck," one of them said. "I wanted to compare prices."

"Yeah," the other said, his voice squeaking. "That's all

we were doing. We'll just go on so's not to bother you. I'll be over at lunch time tomorrow, Mr. Bailey. You can show me more about setting up a database for the football team."

I stepped back and allowed them to flee like the terrified bunnies they were. "Were those a couple of the boys you mentioned as being adept at this?"

Justin nodded. "Yeah, Byron's been fooling around on computers since kindergarten. I'm surprised he's not at home on his own system."

"He might have been worried his parents could walk in at any minute. Did you see what they were doing?"

"I know I said I could block porn," Justin said as he pulled off his glasses and cleaned them on his shirt, "but I also said some kids would find a way to get around my filters. Byron and Widget seem to have discovered one."

"No kidding. Can you read everybody's old E-mail?"

"Whose do you want to see?" he asked as he sat down in front of the computer recently abandoned by the boys.

"Eileen Buchanon's. She said she saw a ghost."

He began to click furiously. "Lottie Estes tried to tell me the same thing, but I thought she'd been having a spinster's version of a wet dream." The cursor danced between columns and columns within columns, but he seemed so confident of what he was doing that he continued to converse. "Most people think once they've deleted something, it's gone for good. In reality, it lingers like a suppressed memory. Don't ever write anything on a computer that might bring down the feds on you. It can be tracked back to the very machine."

"What about secret passwords?"

"NASA and the Pentagon use secret passwords, but the

hackers get in anyway. It's easier for me, since I'm the systems administrator. Okay, here's Eileen's E-mail. Most of it seems to have gone to other people in the lab such as Kevin and Dahlia. She must have met someone in a chat room last week; these E-mails are from someone who goes by the screen name 'TDrinker.' Nothing too exciting there. She sent an E-mail with a cookie recipe to someone called 'Granny234.' "

"What about this ghost?"

Justin chewed on his lip, his fingers never slowing down. "If she saw it, it's in here, attached to an E-mail she sent or received. It won't take up more than a microbyte. Okay, maybe this."

The screen flickered.

Justin and I stared at each other.

"Who was that?" he asked.

"Earl Buchanon, purportedly with hijacked privates."

16

When Earl went out into the front yard to change the oil in the pickup, he couldn't help but notice the smoke drifting out of the house across Finger Lane. It wasn't billowing or anything alarming like that, and there weren't flames licking out of adjoining windows. Just wispy smoke, like flutters of tissue paper.

He scratched his head. Jim Bob was usually sent out to the porch to puff on a cigar, and that didn't happen all too often. What's more, the porch was vacant and the smoke was definitely coming from an upstairs window. For a moment, he wondered if Mrs. Jim Bob had taken to sneaking stogies.

"Kevin!" he bellowed. "Git your ass out here!"

Kevin came stumbling out the door and nearly made it down the steps without tripping over his feet. "What, Pa?" he asked as he got up and brushed grass clippings off his shirt, having mowed the lawn as an act of contrition for whatever his love goddess thought he'd done wrong.

Earl gestured at the opposite house. "What do you make of that?"

"It's right handsome. I'd sure hate to mow that yard, though, unless I had one of those rider-mowers with an umbrella and a cup holder. It must take most of four hours."

"I am speaking of the smoke."

Kevin hung his head. "Sorry, Pa, I thought you was asking about Jim Bob's house. The one and only time I smoked a cigar, I turned pea green and came close to puking my guts out. With Ma gone like she is, I reckon you can do what you like out here, but it'd be risky inside. Ma has the nose of a bloodhound, and she said if you ever—"

Earl held back a growl. "I am speaking of the smoke coming out of a bedroom on the second floor, son. It don't look like there's a fire, but I might should call the volunteer fire department in Hasty, just to be on the safe side."

"I don't see anything."

Earl turned around and stared across the road. He knew damn well what he'd seen a minute ago, but now Kevin was giving him a funny look. "Not right now, mebbe."

"Then right now not be the time to call the volunteer fire department," said Kevin, making more sense than usual. "Most of 'em are probably out fishing or watching baseball on TV. I don't think they'd take kindly to rushing over here for no good reason."

Earl went to the edge of the road. "Mrs. Jim Bob's Cadillac is there, but Jim Bob's truck is gone."

"Jim Bob goes to the supermarket on Sundays to work on the payroll, except during football season. We're all grateful to get paid by Friday till after the Super Bowl. Luckily, he ain't much on baseball. He sez they wear girly pants."

Yanking off his cap, Earl continued to stare at the red-

brick house. "You know something, Kevin? I wish your
ma was here. She'd know what to do."

Kevin wasn't sure what his ma would do if his pa
dragged her outside and started carrying on about smoke
that only he could see, 'specially these days, when she fancied herself to be a tugboat. It was all too mysterious to
think about. "You want to come watch the Cubs game?"
he asked his pa. "We got lots of pretzels, and I kin put a
frozen pizza in the oven if you want."

"Just go get the hose out of the shed," snapped Earl.
"Get a bucket while you're at it."

"Whatever you say," Kevin said, wondering if he'd
hafta start looking at nursing homes afore too long. His
parents were in their mid-forties, which seemed a might
young for senility to strike, but their behavior was gittin'
downright odd. And hadn't his own granny kept a rowdy
flock of sheep in the parlor for the last eleven years of her
life? It occurred to him that the room in which he was
watching the ball game was taking on an eye-watering
stench, mostly on account of the accumulation of beer
cans and bean burritos he'd bought for lunch from the
Dairee Dee-Lishus.

He didn't want to be there if and when his ma came
home.

--------~~~~~~~~~--------

I finally regained my composure. "It's not like I can identify Earl's own privates," I said. "What's going on, Justin?"

"Someone's been having a fine time—and most likely
the culprits are Byron and Widget. Let's look at other E-
mail." Again the clickety-clackety. "This is Mrs. Jim Bob's
mailbox. She's received digests from a coalition advocat-

ing antiabortion violence and one that parallels flag-burn-
ing with Nazism. She was E-mailing what seems to be a
cousin in Omaha, and . . ."

"What was that?" we said in unison.

After a minute of silence, I realized it was getting dark
outside and got up to close all the gingham curtains. "You
saw it, too," I said as I sat down.

"I don't know all that much about Earl's privates, but I
doubt Jim Bob was ever photographed in a negligee," he
said weakly. "Red's not his color."

"Good for you, Justin. You may have made your first
joke."

"You want to hear the one about the programmer with
the floppy disk?"

"No, I want you to tell me how this ephemeral image
of Jim Bob was created. Did it originate from this lab?"

"I'll find out."

Screens filled with gibberish came and went almost as
quickly as the images had. If a nonexistent sprinkler system had gone off, Justin would not have faltered. A bomb
in the parking lot would have caused no more than a
moment's hesitation. I was afraid that so much as opening
my mouth might cause flames to erupt from not only the
computer, but also his ears and nostrils.

Systems administrators were kinda scary.

"Okay," he announced, resting his hands on the edge
of the desk, "all of it came from this very machine. Byron,
I'd think. He was clipping faces off the Maggody web site
and pasting them on . . ."

"Naked bodies from other sites?" I suggested.

"And then sending them in split-second E-mail. I
need to apologize to Lottie Estes, and everybody else in

this town. I'm not as good as I thought I was. Byron's fifteen, but he outwitted me. He downloaded a program called—"

"This kid and his cohort terrorized the adults?"

"It looks like they clipped faces from one source, then pasted them onto other . . . well, poses. I'm sure they thought they were being funny."

"Will they think a hundred hours of community service is funny? Will they think those orange vests are funny while they pick up litter from here to Missouri?"

"A couple of kids," Justin said lamely. "Smart ones, I admit."

I put aside the avowed retribution for the moment and rubbed my face. "Let's look at Gwynnie's E-mail."

"She wasn't getting these images," he said after a few seconds.

"What was she getting?"

"One was to someone named Broz; it's kinda cryptic."

"Then let's read it."

Justin reluctantly sat back. "All it says is that he's heading off. He wishes her well. Here's a generic one from Brother Verber with a Bible verse and an invitation to participate in the spring talent show. She sent one to Ruby Bee to confirm what time she'd be at the bar and grill to clean out the pantry."

I saw him wince. "Why don't you go back to that last one? I didn't have a chance to read it."

"It doesn't make any sense."

"Go back, Justin, or go away while I call in experts from the state FBI. If you can get it, so can they."

If he'd possessed any cognitive skills outside his field, he would have laughed and turned off the computer, the

FBI most likely not having been at my beck and call—or my beck and anything. "It doesn't make any sense," he repeated.

I leaned forward. "Gwynnie sent an E-mail saying she was pregnant. Who's it to?"

"An E-mail address in Germany. There's a 'de' in the address that identifies the origin. Byron's most likely behind this, too."

"Show me the next message," I said coldly.

Justin was looking less and less confident as the next message appeared. "It's from the same address in Germany," he said. "Must have been a person she ran across in a chat room."

"How would someone in Germany know about the Flamingo Motel?" I asked as I peered at the screen. "How would someone in Germany expect to meet Gwynnie and Chip in the last unit on the right, and then take them into Farberville to a safe house until he could divorce his wife and marry her? And, look, Justin, this person in Hamburg or Guttenburg has the same first name as you. The World Wide Web is just amazing, isn't it? The global community is shrinking every minute."

"I didn't send her this!"

"When did she receive it?"

He ran his finger across the top of the screen. "Friday night, about eight o'clock. I swear I didn't send her this. We were both here. Why would I send E-mail like this when all I had to do was talk to her?"

"You couldn't have this conversation with Ruby Bee and Lottie hanging on your every word, could you? If you didn't send it, then who did?"

"Anybody. It's an anonymous server. A subpoena

might jar the provider into identifying the account holder, but it could take months. Byron probably has dozens of accounts like this. It takes a matter of minutes to set one up."

I stood up and moved away from him. "A pimply fifteen-year-old would hardly interest her. Semen samples from the sheets at the motel are on their way to the state forensic lab, and you can expect a deputy on your doorstep in the morning to take your fingerprints to compare to those found at the scene. You must have heard by now that she was murdered at the Flamingo Motel on Friday night in the very same room where she got pregnant. Later, her body was moved to a shack on the ridge."

He stood up, but to my relief moved to the other end of the trailer. At worst, all he could do was pull pens out of the plastic holder in his pocket and hurl them at me like inky little spears. "It's possible I had sex with her," he said, "but I wasn't responsible for her pregnancy. I took precautions."

"Semen stains on the sheets, Justin."

"She said she was on the pill."

"How might this have worked? You told your wife you were going to Farberville, but instead went to the Flamingo Motel and poured enough alcohol into Gwynnie to silence her permanently. You then put her body in the trunk and took Chip into Farberville. Later, you left Gwynnie in the shack."

"What shack?"

"The map's on the web site, Justin. While you were fishing yesterday morning, whoever was maintaining this 'safe house' panicked and dropped Chip at the hospital."

"I don't even know what a 'safe house' is! I never saw

the E-mail and I had no idea she was pregnant. I didn't meet her at the motel. I didn't kill her."

"But you admit you slept with her?"

"Of course he did," Chapel said as she came into the portable classroom and carefully locked the door behind her.

Inky little spears were one thing, bullets another.

—————

Daniel smiled sadly at Miss Benightly, who was having trouble with the snaps on her brassiere. She was so blond, so svelte, so filled with enthusiasm for the less intellectual pursuits of life. He'd sworn to see her only twice a year, but what with Leona's increasingly pervasive problems, he was tempted to rethink his vow. A sin was a sin, no matter how often it was committed.

"I may be up this way next month," he said as he watched her wiggle—something she did with great charm. "Perhaps you might put me on your calendar."

"Whatever you want, honey," Miss Benightly muttered. "Aw shit, I think I broke a nail! If I did, it's gonna cost you extra."

—————

"This is by far the stupidest thing in my entire life I've ever been talked into doing," whispered Estelle as she and Ruby Bee made their way along the increasingly familiar road in the Pot O' Gold. Most of the lights on utility poles had been used for target practice, and potholes were darn hard to see in the dark.

"Eula saw Seth leave Lazarus's trailer, and he looked pained, according to her. Arly's already searched there, but I don't reckon she's thought to search Seth's trailer."

"We don't know anything about him, including whether he's at home with a loaded rifle across his lap."

Ruby Bee hung on to Estelle's arm, as much to prevent a defection as to keep her footing. "All we're gonna do is get close and take a quick peek in the window. If he's not there, we'll—"

"I'd like to think I know the drill by now," Estelle said with a snort. "I hear there's a cable channel called 'A & E.' Maybe they'll start a new one called 'B & E,' featuring us. Each week we can break into a different trailer."

"Nobody said we were gonna break into it. All we're gonna do is peek in the window. I don't reckon there's any harm in that."

"What good's supposed to come of it? Just because Eula saw him earlier doesn't mean anything. Maybe he remembered it's his ma's birthday. Maybe he was feeling the aftermath of a chili dog from the Dairee Dee-Lishus."

"Keep your voice down," commanded Ruby Bee. "There was something wicked going on in Lazarus's trailer, and this boy named Seth was involved. I wouldn't be surprised if he was the one who killed Gwynnie and kidnapped Chip."

"And why would he do something like that?"

Ruby Bee tightened her grip. "If you don't hush up, Idalupino's likely to come barreling out of her trailer with a can of pepper spray."

Estelle yelped as she stepped into a good three inches of slimy water. "For your information, Idalupino's gone to Crosset on account of all the perverts lurking around here. Anyone with a brain half the size of a peanut would steer clear, but here we are, begging to get ourselves murdered. Pictures from our funerals will be showing up on the Maggody web site."

"Here's the trailer," Ruby Bee said, "and the lights are off. You go around that side and I'll stand on my tiptoes on the patio. If you see anything, hoot like an owl and I'll find you."

"I don't know how to hoot like an owl any more than I know how to swoop down out of the sky and snatch up a field mouse."

"Just do something."

"It ain't gonna be hootin', " said Estelle, then began to edge around the trailer. She'd taken no more than half a dozen tentative steps when an explosive sound of gunfire erupted in the darkness behind her. A pinging sound against the siding suggested a bullet had been aimed in their direction. A second shot shattered the window above Ruby Bee's head.

They had no choice but to duck under the trailer. The muck was no better or worse than either expected. It was getting old, though.

—————wwwwwww—————

"Where did you get that?" Justin asked Chapel. "A year ago you organized a demonstration on campus to ban handguns. You and Armenia passed out flyers at the farmers market only last fall. Shouldn't you put it down before somebody gets hurt?"

Chapel's smile was chilling. "Somebody already got hurt, Justin."

"Gwynnie, for instance?" I suggested, always helpful.

She aimed the gun at me. "Do you know anything about Gwynnie? As a feminist, I suppose I should have set aside my class prejudices and tried to help her reaffirm her identity as a worthwhile woman. She was one little bitch, though. Real women don't betray each other, but she was intent on snaring Justin, no matter what damage resulted. Then again, we all have our goals, don't we?"

"And what's yours?" I sat down, not so much out of bravado as necessity, my knees having turned into something resembling Mrs. Jim Bob's molded pineapple salad.

"I thought we could stick it out here for a year," she said. "I was even thinking I might write an article or two about my experiences in whichever ring of hell this is. Assuming we survived, Justin would have a graduate post and we'd be able to escape into an intellectual community, where the most fiercely debated topic was not the need for a palace coup in the Missionary Society. We'd have children and a modest house with a driveway cluttered with tricycles and anatomically correct dolls. Once the children were of an age, I'd organize a community day care center, and eventually a cooperative preschool. Perhaps we'd get a grant and be able to open a private academy."

"And Gwynnie was in the way," I said. "How did you find out she was pregnant?"

Chapel laughed, but her eyes were filling with tears. "Gwynnie thought she was sending her little love notes to Justin, and receiving them from him."

"She never said anything," he protested.

"I doubt she ever said much of anything at the Flamingo Motel!" snapped Chapel, sounding the tiniest bit unhinged. "You and she were too busy for conversations, weren't you? She only determined that she was pregnant on Friday morning. She was assured via E-mail that you were pretending to go to Farberville so that you could meet her at ten. 'Don't bring anything,' the message read. 'If you get caught sneaking out, you can say you were going for a walk.' It was lame, but she wasn't likely to win any international prizes in physics, was she?" The laughter was too shrill for a woman holding a handgun. Way, way too shrill.

"What about Chip?" I asked ever so calmly. "Were you planning to include him in the community day care and cooperative preschool?"

She wrinkled her nose. "I knew Justin wouldn't tolerate having a baby for a year or two. A toddler might be different. They're quieter and more interactive."

"You didn't think he'd wonder where this toddler came from?"

"I hadn't quite worked that out, but once he found out Gwynnie was pregnant . . ."

"He'd feel obliged to do the right thing? Divorce you and marry her to provide for the baby, even if it meant delaying his graduate degree?"

Justin moved into the middle of the trailer. "Excuse me? Shouldn't I be included in this conversation?"

"I suppose so," Chapel said sourly. "It's all your damn fault, anyway. If you'd screwed around in high school like other post-pubescent boys, you wouldn't have started panting when some marginally attractive young woman winked at you. You know something, Justin—you're still a virtual virgin."

We all froze as the door opened, proving you'll never achieve a high level of security with what amounted to a flimsy storm door.

Jessie Traylor took a step or two, then saw the gun in

Chapel's hand. "Lab closed, Mr. Bailey?" he said in a voice that might have qualified him for the Vienna Boys Choir.

"For the time being," I said as I tackled Chapel, who sprawled onto her backside. I retrieved the gun, then sat up and frowned at her. "Which of you was driving the four-wheel that night? When I cruised by, all I saw parked out front of your trailer was a battered compact. Trust me when I say it takes a serious vehicle to get that far up Cotter's Ridge."

Chapel sat up and glared. "When Justin came home and fell asleep, I drove back to the motel and tossed Gwynnie's body in the back of the car. The next morning, I drove to the shack and left her."

I took a deep breath. "So which one of you had sex with her that night—and left semen stains on the sheets?"

Justin moved away from me, which was for the best, since I was not disinclined to shoot him. "Maybe I was at the motel," he said. "The E-mail was crazy, but if she really was pregnant, and I was responsible . . ."

"Then you'd have to kill her," I said flatly, "which you did. You didn't bring a quart of vodka on a whim, or fail to notice that you were pouring the booze down her throat after she passed out. You're too much of a geek to cover your tracks. You're damn lucky your wife came through."

Jessie Traylor would have handed over a month's salary to be anywhere else, but nobody was beaming him up. "He killed her just because she was pregnant? Chip's a fantastic little boy. I would have taken them in and raised Gwynnie's baby as my own. I may not have a college education, Mr. Bailey, but I ain't a cold-blooded killer."

I waved the handgun so that both of the Baileys understood they had no options. "No, Jessie, you may earn minimum wage and get your kicks at the pool hall on a Saturday night, but you're not and will never be a cold-blooded killer. Folks like Justin and Chapel assume they're superior, that they shouldn't have to suffer any conse-quences when their inferiors disrupt their carefully pre-pared plans. At this point, I'm not real sure which one of them killed Gwynnie—and I don't care, since I can nail them both with conspiracy." I stared at Chapel. "Were you really going to shoot a sister in the cause?"

"Yeah. There's something about your scrawny ass that pissed me off the first day I met you."

I was offended, but I did not, for the record, retaliate against Chapel in any way, form, or fashion. It is possible, however, that a number of ~~cockroaches~~ did not live to see the sunrise the next morning.

Life does or does not go on, depending.

———————∿∿∿∿∿∿∿———————

Earl bit the bullet, in a manner of speaking, and called over to the house formerly inhabited by Kevin and Dahlia. "Lemme speak to Eileen," he said when the latter answered. "It's real serious."

"Is something wrong with Kevin? Is he sick?"

"Just get Eileen, okay?" He picked at a scab on his arm until she came on the line. "This ain't about me," he said hurriedly. "There's something strange going on at Jim Bob's house. I called over at the supermarket, but nobody's seen him all day. Kevin here says I shouldn't call the fire department, but I ain't sure. Where there's smoke, there's fire, or so everybody claims."

"What are you talking about, Earl?"

"A while back I noticed smoke coming out of a window over there. It stopped for a time, but it's started up again. I figure Mrs. Jim Bob is in there."

"Did you go over?" she asked.

"The doors are locked. I shouted, but she didn't poke her head out the window. You think I ought to break down a door and barge upstairs?"

"How much smoke is there?"

"Not much, mostly little puffs. What if the second story's liable to burst into flames any second? I was thinking she might listen to you and get out of the house."

Eileen sighed. "Fetch the garden hose from the garage, just in case. I'll be there in five minutes." She hung up and took her car keys out of her purse. The twins and Chip were asleep, as well as Dahlia, who'd spent most of the morning throwing up in the bathroom and deserved whatever rest she could get.

Earl was standing by the mailbox when she drove up. "See what I was saying?" he demanded, pointing at the window in question. "It looks to be getting worse. I went back over and begged her to come out. Now I ain't so sure she's even in there."

"Wait here." She drove between the brick pillars and up the hill to the house and stood under the window. "Mrs. Jim Bob?" she yelled. "If you don't answer, we have no choice but to call the volunteer fire department in Hasty. They'll come tearing over here and park their pickup trucks all over your yard. I'd hate to see anything happen to these azaleas, but—"

Mrs. Jim Bob appeared at the window. Her eyes were red, most likely from the smoke, but she didn't appear to be on the verge of passing out. "Everything's fine."

"It doesn't look fine. What's burning?"

"It's under control," Mrs. Jim Bob said firmly.

"Then if I come upstairs, you'll let me in?"

"I know you're acting out of Christian charity, Eileen, but this is not the moment. Maybe I'll see you Wednesday at the potluck."

Her head popped out of view. Eileen drove back to her house. "It's all right," she said. "I don't know what all she's doing, but it's none of our concern. Don't call Hasty unless the roof goes up."

Earl scuffled his feet in the driveway. "I appreciate you coming like this. I wasn't sure what to do. What if you and me go into Farberville and see a movie?"

"Where's Kevin?"

"I sent him to get the hose. It's like to be wrapped around him like one of those South American snakes. Guess I'd better fetch him before the breath's squeezed out of him."

She got out of the car. "No, you go put on some clean clothes and comb your hair if you want to be seen in public with me. I need to have a word with him."

She found him in the garage. The hose was not attacking him, but somehow he'd managed to loop it over both arms and his neck. "Listen up," she said, ignoring his bleats, "Dahlia has two things that are making her miserable, unless I count you. For one, she's exhausted on account of not having a single decent night's sleep for five months. From now on, Kevvie and Rose Marie will have to make do with bottles after bedtime—and you're going to be in charge."

"Okay, Ma," he said as he tried unsuccessfully to squirm free of the hose. "What's the other thing?"

"She doesn't realize she's pregnant."

"She's what?" he yelped as he lost the battle with the hose and fell back into a wheelbarrow. Once he'd struggled to his feet, he cleared his throat and said, "But she's still breast-feeding. The nurse at the clinic told us that she couldn't get pregnant until she stopped."

"Stop by the SuperSaver on your way and buy a home pregnancy test. Buy some rocky road ice cream while you're at it. You're going to need it."

Eula stood in the middle of the road, the gun wobbling. "Now that the moon's full, you think you can sneak back here and murder us, doncha?" she shrieked. "I saw you sneaking by, you filthy animal! If you so much as stick your nose out from under that trailer, I'll shoot you! We got no tolerance for this kind of behavior at the Pot O' Gold. I'm not a good shot, but I got a pocket full of bullets and as much time as you do!"

"This ain't going well," Estelle commented as she tried to find a more comfortable position.

Ruby Bee wasn't doing much better. "She can't stand there all night. I don't want to think what she'd look like if she didn't get her beauty sleep."

"This is not the time for jokes, Mrs. Milton Berle."

"It ain't like we can play pinochle."

Mrs. Jim Bob counted the socks laid out on her bedspread. She'd started with seventeen, each one black. No two had matched. They were of different lengths and styles, and in an amazing array of subtle variations of black, which heretofore she'd always considered a consistent color. Over the years, she herself had methodically thrown away seventeen socks because they didn't have a match and Jim Bob had been a real stickler.

Seventeen socks, retired prematurely because he'd been leaving them in the bottom drawer of his dresser. How one but not the other was assigned to such a fate might possibly go beyond human understanding. She'd certainly never ask him.

But these socks had faced nothing more than a meaningless existence in a smelly drawer until she'd decided to liberate them, one by one, in the metal wastebasket. The negligee had gone first, of course, and she was down to the last six socks.

After she was done, she figured she might take a second look at all of his underwear.

—————————vvvvvvvvvv—————————

It was after midnight when I left the sheriff's department. Harve had shown up with a sunburn and a frown, but he'd lightened up when I assured him I would not attend any press conferences. Child endangerment, even if the child had never actually been endangered, always played well with the media.

Harve had pulled me aside and asked what I was planning to do in regard to said child. I'd shrugged, but I had a feeling Seth Smitherman would be over at the social services department bright and early in the morning, trying to establish paternity and take custody. Testing was likely to back him up, and no one else would be contesting it.

When I got back to Maggody, I swung by the

Hollifleckers' house. Daniel's car was parked in the drive-way. The upstairs was dark, but a light was on in the back of the house. I supposed Leona was too seasoned to play with matches.

As I parked beside the exterior staircase to my apart-ment, I heard what might have been gunfire. Wondering if Raz was on the ridge doing his best to hunt down Diesel and demand reimbursement, I made my way to the landing.

If Raz had looked up, he would have seen there was ample moonshine for all of us.

There's More to Maggody Than Meets the Eye

Come visit the town of Maggody and its hilarious inhabitants on the Web.

www.Maggody.com

Raz Buchanon, Estelle Oppers, and Ruby Bee are waiting to show you around!

POCKET BOOKS

2383

Also available from

JOAN
HESS

MISERY LOVES
MAGGODY

An Arly Hanks Mystery

"Raucous and rollicking fun!"
—*Tampa Tribune-Times*

POCKET BOOKS
A VIACOM COMPANY

3078

Visit
❖ Pocket Books ❖
online at

---

www.SimonSays.com

Keep up on the latest new
releases from your favorite
authors, as well as author
appearances, news, chats,
special offers and more.

SIMON & SCHUSTER
A VIACOM COMPANY
www.SimonSays.com

Pocket
Books

2381-01